BEST CANADIAN STORIES 2018

BEST CANADIAN STORIES 2018

RUSSELL SMITH

EDITOR

BIBLIOASIS

WINDSOR, ONTARIO

FIRST EDITION

ISBN 978-1-77196-251-3 (Hardcover)
ISBN 978-1-77196-249-0 (Trade Paper)
ISBN 978-1-77196-250-6 (eBook)
ISSN 0703-9476

Edited by Russell Smith
Copy-edited by James Grainger
Typeset by Ellie Hastings
Cover Design by Chris Anderchek

Published with the generous assistance of the Canada Council for the Arts, which last year invested $153 million to bring the arts to Canadians throughout the country, and the financial support of the Government of Canada. Biblioasis also acknowledges the support of the Ontario Arts Council (OAC), an agency of the Government of Ontario, which last year funded 1,709 individual artists and 1,078 organizations in 204 communities across Ontario, for a total of $52.1 million, and the contribution of the Government of Ontario through the Ontario Book Publishing Tax Credit and the Ontario Media Development Corporation.

PRINTED AND BOUND IN CANADA

CONTENTS

INTRODUCTION

RUSSELL SMITH

IN DECEMBER 2017 the *New Yorker* published a short story, clearly marked "fiction," called "Cat Person," by Kristen Roupenian. It was a clever and elegant little story, reminiscent in theme at least of Alice Munro. It's in the third person. A young woman has a disappointing sexual encounter with an older man. She then tries to avoid the man, who is first crushed and then nasty. It ends with a string of texts from him that begin with pleading and end with insult. The last text—and the last line of the story—is "Whore."

It's a good story because it's honest: both characters are venal and desperate in one way or another, just as most of us are. The girl's motivation is convincingly complicated and needy. But it is about more than those two individuals: it also describes a moment in a culture, a contemporary moment; it documents liberated sexuality and its discontents on a university campus; it exemplifies precarious labour; it illustrates power dynamics and a kind of generalized loneliness in an age of digitally-assisted sexual opportunity; and finally it situates all this in a real and textured college town and a Honda Civic with candy wrappers in the cup holders. This is what art does best: it situates the political in the body and the landscape. In this it rises above argument.

The piece came out, of course, at the height of #metoo in the United Sates and Canada. It appeared at a time of multiple essays and confessional accounts of bad dates, in thousands of blogs and print magazines. Because of this simultaneity, it circulated very quickly online, and then a strange thing happened. People on the Internet started arguing with it. First they were angry with the man in the story and sympathetic to the woman, then there was a backlash and conservatives wrote that she was embarrassingly narcissistic and that this was typical of contemporary misandry... It became rapidly clear that many people who read this story around the world did not know that it was a piece of fiction. Because of the way they had received it—as a link in a tweet or an email, as part of the news/opinion flow—they had missed its label. It was being judged as another confessional essay, and in that genre the author's moral failings are quite simply a flaw.

My friend A. is an intersectionalist activist who campaigns for gay and trans rights. She does not read fiction because she imagines it will be too earnest for her. She told me that when her gay and trans friends recommend fiction to her it is sci-fi with strong female characters of colour in it. She said that sounds like church. Anyway, A. was sent a link to "Cat Person" and read it because she thought, like so many, that it was a true story, meant as some kind of feminist argument. She was a little startled by its confessions of narcissism, but strangely, she enjoyed it. She asked me if I had read it. I told her excitedly it was a piece of fiction.

See, I said, what I mean about fiction? You might like it.

Huh, she answered. It was true that she never imagined fiction reading like that. At least, she said, it wasn't *literary* fiction. God save us from that.

I explained with some alarm that it was in fact literary fiction; that this was exactly and typically what we meant by this phrase. In fact, I might have added, I wonder how excited the fans of "Cat Person" are going to be when they discover Alice Munro, who has been writing variations of that same story since about 1965. She won the Nobel Prize, which is, you know, pretty literary.

Huh, said A. She is still not convinced, I think. I think she is still pretty sure that literary fiction must be a multi-generational family saga.

We all read, now, dozens of news stories, personal stories, arguments and anecdotes every day on our screens, and whether they be Facebook updates or essays, they all claim to be true stories. Fiction has always been good at seeming like a true story too. Often it is. These things are hard to separate.

Autobiographical fiction has always been written. Whole university courses teach "creative non-fiction" that encourage reporters to explore the novelist's bag of tricks. "Autofiction," a variant of memoir that takes the form of a novel and does not promise exact truth as a memoir would, has further confused our definitions.

In light of these borrowings, many enlightened people claim that further taxonomy would be useless and unproductive. It absolutely doesn't matter if a piece is true or not; it should be judged by the same esthetic or moral standards.

I think that the "Cat Person" fallout shows us the limitations of such willful blindness. When an entire intellectual culture is immersed in the didactic, it loses its ability to see that which is not didactic. Art has a role that polemic does not. There is a value to being removed from one's ideological position for a moment of escape into the nearly-real.

Canada this past year has seen a number of scandals at universities where creative writing is taught, involving several cases of teachers accused of sexually harassing students. This led to a number of attacks on something called "Canlit," a thing never defined but always held to be corrupt, racist, colonialist and violent to women. It turned out that what most essays meant by Canlit was the university system (both creative writing programs and academic study of literature as produced by English departments). Canadian literature itself—that is, the corpus—was not mentioned so much.

When literature itself—as opposed to Twitter feeds or panel discussions—was criticized (and this was extremely rare), it was not hard to find evidence of dangerous sexism in it. Especially in the fiction of Margaret Atwood, who took the wrong side in an internecine political battle regarding the human-resources regulations surrounding a faculty firing.

I remember reading one long blog post, written by a university instructor of geography who had taken a loud role in the controversy, analyzing characterization in Atwood's 1988 novel *Cat's Eye*. This essay triumphantly pointed out that the women in the story were unkind to each other.

This novel, you will recall, is a bleak and melancholic book. In it, girls and women are indeed very unkind to each other. A couple of young women at an art college have sex with a forlorn male professor. He behaves badly but he is also manipulated. He is in part a pawn in the battle between the girls. The geography instructor pointed out that Atwood's professor was not sufficiently condemned, and the women were too complicit in his crimes to be believable. This demonstrated Atwood had never sufficiently understood or taken seriously the violence inflicted on women by their art teachers. Here was Atwood blaming the victims just as the patriarchy does. This was reflective generally of Atwood's views about women, which were fundamentally unprogressive.

The point was admittedly to prove that Atwood was a bad feminist rather than a bad writer, but I doubt this difference was comprehensible to this critic.

I single out this marginal bit of writing because it is actually not so marginal—it is entirely typical of contemporary intellectual approaches to fiction. This post was widely praised by many intellectuals, including by some actual fiction writers who should have known better. It displayed an absolute lack of understanding of what fiction attempts to do and even a lack of interest in *trying* to understand what fiction might accomplish. This approach is the one that sees "Cat Person" as a conservative critique of young women or as a misandrist humiliation of men.

Just today I read a short story by Zadie Smith, a satirical piece about a university environment. The narrator is reprimanded by her friend for enjoying an old movie about bad people. The narrator confesses, "I instinctively sympathize with the guilty. That's my guilty secret."

She can say that—this is a piece of fiction.

If fiction does anything at all, it enables us to sympathize with the guilty.

My predecessor in editing this series, John Metcalf, once described listening to a group of English teachers attempting to explain a Hemingway short story as being like "watching a group of frowning chimps trying to extract a peanut from a medicine bottle." This scene was from fifty years ago. I thought of exactly that line when reading the geography instructor trying to penetrate Atwood's gimlet-eyed novel. Nothing has changed.

Indeed, the way we communicate now has if anything deepened this misunderstanding of ways in which fiction can excite. The "Cat Person" incident demonstrated that, in a textual universe largely constituted of claim and counter-claim, a made-up story that represents human failings as complicated and possibly even alluring is hard for people to assimilate. People don't really get what fiction is for.

What is it for then?

I can't answer that exactly but I can give you the following stories.

They are disparate in style and setting, but they are all about flawed and guilty people, and they are all blindingly honest about these imperfections. They are equally honest about the petty, the triumphant and the disastrous. They are not trying to convince you of the superiority or inferiority of one gender or another. You are reading them to imagine yourself in a real situation. There is nothing, I think, in any of these situations that one can disagree with. One cannot disagree with a situation.

Here is an example of this terrible unflinchingness: in Deirdre Simon Dore's story "Your Own Lucky Stars," a boy's foster mother rereads, while cleaning up his room, witty letters she wrote to him while he was in an institution. Her realization of what effect her letters had on the troubled boy comes just as the reader's does, and just as the shocking truth of what has happened to the boy is revealed. This is a moment of pure collective guilt—and, miraculously, sympathy for the haunted protagonist. Here is the pain of guilt in all its complexity. It is a situation, not an argument. It all happens in silence, in an attic.

Because of internet publishing, there were more stories available for me to read this year than there have been to my predecessors. I read all the online litmags as well as the print ones, and I solicited unpublished stories from writing communities. I have attempted to group here some representatives of a few different formal trends from these sources.

Many small magazines, particularly online ones, which I find tend to appeal to younger writers, have been publishing very short pieces that straddle the line between poetry and prose. This preferred length may well reflect habits of communication that come from writing for social media and websites. The form demands economy and focus. There are two beautiful examples of it here: Tom Thor Buchanan's "A Dozen Stomachs" (the first story, I think, to appear in this anthology written from the point of view of a human stomach) and Reg Johanson's "a titan bearing many a legitimate grievance," a prose poem whose disjointed and associative style miraculously sums up a life of error and love.

The influence of technology on our writing must be acknowledged, which is why Lynn Coady's "Someone Is Recording" is so timely. It consists in its entirety of one side of an email exchange. The larger story, clearly exploding in real space outside these emails, can be surmised.

To further accept the technological creep into literature, I include here an extraordinary experiment: a story by Stephen Marche ("Twinkle, Twinkle") that was written with the assistance of a story-generating algorithm. This is almost certainly the first AI story included in *Best Canadian Stories*. I have included with the story the author's notes on its creation (and his resistance to the machinery), as I think its genesis is actually what the story is about. This is both story and meta-story.

In recent years there has been much discussion of the rising status of genre fiction, especially since so many Canadian novelists have branched into thrillers and paranormal stories. However, fantasy and speculative fiction were hardly at all represented in short fiction in our journals last year. Canadian fiction still tends to focus on the domestic and the relational, and it is just as hard as it ever was to make this field of activity exciting.

Enter Alicia Elliott, whose story "Tracks" takes a family situation—a tense funeral—and teasingly—like a vice slowly gripping—reveals the guilty secret that animates it, turns this domestic tension into a dark and beautiful drama. Here again a protagonist's shame make her no less compelling a human—and the thrill of this story's turn is that it hints at an eroticism that exists outside the page.

The family is also the setting of Brad Hartle's unease-stirring drama "For What You Are About To Do," in which a well-intentioned father, sandwiched between a criminal son and criminal father of his own, must somehow assuage his stress. This is a highly topical story. My favourite lines in it: "Mom's front window is broken and jagged. The boy gets to his feet and bolts for his car. As the recognition of what he's done comes to me, so does the urge to hurt him."

Kathy Page's delicate and heartbreaking "Inches" is one of only two stories here set in a previous decade, but it so finely prefigures the sexual revolution to come it is in a sense about the contemporary. Again, here the sadness of an individual family is the product of a vast societal transition; Page's skill is in how she locates this so minutely in the personal.

Has the Canadian short story evolved? I was excited to find so many stories, like this, about the larger mechanisms of society: about our contemporary workplaces and how they function (as important, I think, as how we function in them). In Michael Lapointe's creepily convincing "Candidate," a political consultant's life story underpins—and in a sense explains—new forms of populist extremism.

In Amy Jones's mysterious "Gravity," a bland call centre becomes the site of an awkward young man's unexplained slips into an alternate reality.

And in Bill Gaston's gripping "Kiint," there is no way we can understand what is really going on until we understand exactly how a fish farm in British Columbia operates. This too is a story about large political forces, but seen from inside a highly idiosyncratic individual body.

There are three stories here about educational workplaces: the Lynn Coady I have mentioned, Shashi Bhat's "Food for Nought," in which a schoolteacher makes a mistake that makes her doubt her calling, and Liz Harmer's "Never Prosper," a brilliant dance around the minds of brilliant people, complete with philosophy jokes. Honestly I have always wondered why we have had so much published fiction about the unemployed and illiterate in this highly educated nation. Surely most Canadians have spent at least half their lives in classrooms? I am actually surprised we don't have a named genre for fiction that deals with graduate students pretending to be fishermen. I would rather publish stories that honestly show what a large section of the readership of this kind of book actually does for a living.

A much more rare but still very Canadian kind of job—that of hockey enforcer—comes in for some heart-wrenching existential analysis by David Huebert in "Six Six Two Fifty," in which a violent loser of a protagonist is as articulate as any philosophy prof. This man knows that, "There are few things as lovely as the sight of blood pooling on white ice. No red has ever seemed more red—like a rose blooming out of a snowbank."

And this ultimately is where we always return, regardless of subject or setting: to the extraordinary power of the surprising sentence.

Alex Pugsley's reminiscence of middle-class intrigue among the prominent families of Halifax in the 1970s, is spoken in an almost Proustian voice, whose nineteenth-century inflections enable him to pinpoint the exact commotions in inarticulate childhood. A story whose first paragraph contains a spoiler like "But the final ruination of the family was set in motion years before, on the day I met Cyrus Mair, when his father's body was found floating in Halifax harbour, on this side of McNab's Island, the first in a series of bizarre events that would conclude with a house fire on the snowiest night in a century"—well, you know this story will be told with a certain confidence.

This is the confidence with which Lisa Moore recounts the dark events of "Vision"—a small town pervasively shaded with menace, a fish plant that burns down, a threatening stranger, all seen through the shade of a failed marriage—this confidence almost indescribable except through quoting her carefully fragmented perceptions—images like light broken by a prism. "A marriage is this: Put the glasses with the glasses, put the cups with the cups. Every morning you do this and I come down. The cups and the glasses." Later, on driving: "The wiper with the rubber flange torn away from the metal arm so that the strip of rubber wiggles over the glass like a maddened eel. The metal arm scratching an arc in the glass." The rhythm of those sentences is itself the scratching of an arc in glass.

These sentences alone serve as explanations for why we read this genre.

FOOD FOR NOUGHT

SHASHI BHAT

THIS STUDENT of mine has turned in an eating disorder poem. She's not the first. There's one nearly every semester—thin, with loopy handwriting. I admit there is something poetic about self-starvation, and though Jessica's poem included a tired metaphor about a broken ballerina, she also surprised me by describing hipbones as shark fins jutting from ocean water. A month or so ago she turned in an impressive sestina about mirrors. It's clear this poem's about her, which makes it hard to give feedback. "Try to experiment more with enjambment," I write. "Too many similes?" I query. I consider writing "This poem makes me want to be sick."

Grade 10 English is the period after lunch, but because I spent my lunch hour at the QEII visiting my father, who has just had a heart attack, I'm eating the sandwich I brought with me at my desk. It's kind of a sad sandwich—potato curry on Dempster's multigrain, but one slice of the bread is the loaf end, because that was all I had left. I have it in one hand while eating, hoping I have enough time to finish chewing and marking before class starts, when Jessica comes in early, presumably because we are workshopping her poem today. It's the third or fourth poem they've written for me; I'm never sure whether to count the haiku or not. "Hey there," I say stupidly, through potatoes. She adjusts her lean body neatly into her front-row seat, and for the next seven to ten minutes, she watches me eat my lunch, which, I realize, too late, is composed entirely of carbohydrates.

While examining him after his stent surgery, the doctor had said to my dad, "Oh, you're Indian. You've been eating too much butter chicken!"

"I told him real Indians don't eat such things, and our South Indian diet is very different than what you see in restaurants here. In fact is the utmost healthy cuisine," my dad said to me. He eats nothing but rice and vegetables. He doesn't eat butter, salt, cream, or fried foods. I've never seen him eat a dessert, though he once claimed to have a weakness for maraschino cherries. He's been a lacto-vegetarian his entire seventy-two years, except for one single bite of a hot dog he took at my tenth birthday party. Lying in his hospital bed, he still regretted that hot dog: "All of you were eating them," he said, "you and those friends of yours, eating hot dogs with such relish"—he laughed at his intentional pun—"and I thought, this is a real North American item I must try..." I told him not to blame that hot dog for his current situation, and that my doctor friend said Indian men have notoriously small arteries. I was sorry I said it, because my mother, who I had forgotten was in the room with us, started to cry. She was wearing the same colour blue as the plastic chair she was sitting on, and it looked as though she'd grown four metal limbs.

The rest of the students arrive. Some days my class looks particularly hostile—there's the frowning one and the one who always crosses his arms and the one who rolls her eyes when I use *Pretty Little Liars* as a hip pop-culture reference. I wonder how aware they are of their facial expressions. The best semesters are the ones when I have nodders, students who nod whenever I say anything even half true. "Poetry is still relevant," I say, and they start to nod. In my Psych 101 class in undergrad, the professor told us if you are in a conversation but don't know what to say next, you should start nodding, and the person will be motivated to keep talking. Nodding can influence the nodder's own thoughts, too, so even if I believed that poetry was entirely irrelevant—which I don't but I'm just saying— if I nodded vigorously enough, I could convince myself otherwise.

So we start class and I talk about last night's episode of *Pretty Little Liars* and how that show has way too many suspicious hunks. I say something trite about body image and the media, as an easy segue to talking about Jessica's poem. "Sooo, what did we like about this poem?" Two other girls seem to be texting each other. I see one type on her phone and the other start suppressing laughter, and then she types and the first girl smirks. If only they weren't laughing, I could pretend they were texting about what a great teacher I am.

"I like that this poem is relatable," says one student who I'd been calling Mike the first month of the semester because that's the name on my attendance sheet, but then he told me he prefers being called Matt, except I can never remember in the moment which it is. So now when I say his name I make the M sound and sort of muffle the part after that.

"This poem flows really well," says another student. I like her, despite her use of poorly defined verbs. She wears unassuming hoodies and showed up mid-semester with a nose ring. I think we would be friends if she weren't my student.

"Well, what's up with this rhyme scheme?" says my devil's-advocate student, and then I hear, "I don't know if anorexia is really worth writing about," from my controversial student. The class erupts into a fantastic debate about whether some topics are more worthy of literary rendering.

"Just look at *Seinfeld*," says our one nodder, "It's a show about nothing!"

"But that's not literature!" another student practically shouts. I'm not even participating in the discussion, just sitting back and picturing this scene as a scene from one of my favourite movies, *Dead Poet's Society* or *Mr. Holland's Opus* or *Dangerous Minds* or *Sister Act 2*. Excellent movies about excellent teachers, where all they have to do is deliver some quotable quote—"Play the sunset," or "Once a marine always a marine," or "I'm not really a nun"—for their classes to pass the standardized exam or win the national choir competition. Twenty minutes pass and I conclude the discussion by gently discouraging one student's suggestion that the poem be made into the shape of an hourglass.

I give a brief lecture and then assign an in-class writing exercise. Five minutes before class ends, I look up to see if they're still writing. Jessica is not writing, but has her arms stretched out in front of her, her pencil clenched in both hands. With their flexed tendons, her arms look like the braided wires that hold up a suspension bridge. Her head bends down almost to touch her paper. It might be a yoga pose. Her hair, falling over her arms, is of such an indefinite brown that when it goes grey, probably no one will notice.

Two weeks later I'm grading poems at my parents' house in the North End. My dad has returned from the hospital and taken a leave of absence from his job as a real-estate agent. He spends his time discovering innovations from a decade ago. "I just opened a Twitter account," he tells me. He has it open on his laptop screen while another window streams *Slumdog Millionaire*. Lately he's been really into Indians who've succeeded in Hollywood. "Indians have come such a long way," he says, and starts googling pictures of the actors. One features the ragamuffin children from the movie wearing tuxedos to the 2008 Oscars; another has them lined up at the Mumbai visa office. He turns the screen to show my mom.

"That was us!" he says.

"Speak for yourself," says my mother, chopping a large pile of vegetables. We're in the kitchen. My dad and I are at the table, and my mom seems to be cooking dinner with foods I've never seen in our house—kale and flaxseed and avocadoes—I can't imagine how she's going to combine it all. She pulls out an egg carton from the fridge. I am certain my parents have never eaten eggs before, a thought that's confirmed when my mother cracks the egg by tapping on it with a spoon. She breaks it over a bowl and attempts to separate the white by using the spoon to scoop out the yolk.

"The nutritionist suggested egg-white omelettes," my dad says.

"And salmon," says my mother, shaking her head.

"And she said to stop eating white rice," my dad adds. "Can you believe it? I've been eating white rice two meals a day since I was a small boy."

My father launches into a story about growing up in a village house. It sounds like the home of a cartoon gopher: clay walls, red dirt floors, root vegetables piled in a corner on a scrap of burlap. My father's sister still lives there, her back perpetually bent at a ninety-degree angle, a result of the house's low ceilings and doorways, and of carrying heavy things for long distances. My father claims they took ten-kilometre walks with bags of rice hoisted up on the tops of their heads. This image clashes with the one I have of him yanking bags of rice from the trunk of his SUV.

"But one day," my dad continues, "there was no rice in the house." They went ten days without rice, eating curries made from gourds as they waited for their arecanuts to be harvested and sold so they could afford to go to the store. "For an Indian, rice is everything," he says, closing his eyes. I remember the time he made mushroom risotto from an Uncle Ben's packet, stirring, tasting it with a look of surprise, then stirring again, patiently, as though he could coax it into tasting better.

I don't know how to respond. You can't trade stories with people who've lived a long time, because yours will come out meaningless. You can't trade stories with people who've been hungry.

I root through my pile of poems, find Jessica's, and read it aloud.

"I don't know what to do with this," I say. "We discussed it in class, but it's like there's something missing from the discussion. Everyone loudly tiptoes around the fact that she's writing about herself. Of course it'd be worse if they did acknowledge it…"

"Don't you think you should inform someone? Her parents? Or the counselling office?" asks my mother.

The guidance office in our school consists of a gym teacher in a skirt suit. It's clear: a girl in my classroom is gradually destroying her body. But then, aren't the smokers out by the bus stop doing the same?

"The first time somebody turned in a poem like this, I handed it back with a little note saying she could talk to me if there was a problem or I could make her an appointment with the counsellor. The student never came to me, but one of my student evaluations that year said I should 'mind my own goddamned business,'" I reply to my mother, who has somehow burned the omelette and is scraping the pan off into the sink and rinsing it, gagging at the smell.

Perhaps it's mass hysteria—all the other students start writing about their bodies, too. We read one poem about budding breasts that actually uses the word "budding." There's one about skin picking that I recommend the author submit to the school arts magazine. There are only two boys in my class, and one of them writes about the pressure to take steroids and the other writes about being short. Jessica proposes a class project: "Let's build a plaster woman," she says, and explains that we should each contribute a body part, even the boys (to symbolize a non-binary view of gender). Then we will fasten the parts together with wire.

"We could write lines from our poems on it," suggests the impassive student, and the nodding student begins to nod, and soon everybody is nodding, and I agree, since really you can do anything in an English class as long as you assign a writing response afterward.

The next day they bring in rolls of plaster of Paris bandages and economy-size tubs of Vaseline. We fill empty yogurt containers with water from the bathrooms and space them out on the desks. One student plays music from her tablet, a mournful playlist full of violin solos. It's not what I thought my students listened to, and I wonder how well I know them, despite their thinly veiled autobiographical writing. The humble notes of a bassoon form a backdrop to nineteen people covering themselves in plaster by dipping crumbly sheets into cold water and molding them on to greased upper arms and calves and necks and noses. It looks like a plastic-surgery recovery room. One girl carefully covers her chin, the waffle weave bandages spreading upwards like wings.

Two girls each volunteer a breast, and one more says she'll do her upper thighs. They build a privacy curtain by draping jackets over chairs and backpacks in a huge pile. One of the boys heads over there, where he's left his backpack—"Gotta check my phone," he says, and I point him back to the other side of the room.

"Can we use your stomach? You have such a flat stomach," somebody says to the likeable student, and Jessica looks angry. The likeable student declines, wrapping her arms protectively around herself.

"I was going to do my hand," I say to her. "Why don't you do yours instead?"

She offers her hand up to them—"Why would we want your hand?" somebody asks. Jessica says she'll do her stomach, and instead of going behind the privacy screen, she lifts up her shirt and knots it high above her midriff. Three girls begin rubbing Vaseline on her and wrapping plaster around her in the shape of a corset.

I excuse myself from the classroom, promising to return quickly, though honestly, I want to get away from all the bodies. At the guidance office I find the school's one counsellor, who is wearing sweatpants today. "Hey Joyce," I say, "congrats on the Senior Girls' win last week."

"It was all them," she says, swivelling her chair to face me. "They're a hardworking bunch of kids. Really put in the effort to improve." Volleyball trophies decorate her office shelves. "Can I help you with something?" she asks.

"Well, I have a quick question...say one of your girls was showing signs of...a personal problem. An eating disorder. Would you confront her about it, or...?"

"That can get serious," Joyce says. "We had a player at an away game once who vomited so violently it ruptured her esophagus. We had to take her to the ER in Moncton. You better give me the student's name."

On the weekend, I go with my parents to the gym because my dad has signed us all up for a discount family membership he found on Craigslist. We walk purposefully into the lobby, where we are suddenly unsure of what to do with ourselves, never having been inside a gym before. My mom signs up for a spin class and later, disappointed, tells us that "spinning" is only another word for indoor cycling. My dad experiments with weight machines before a gym attendant hurries over and tells him to stop.

I escape to an elliptical machine. I am thinking about what an odd contraption the elliptical is, and how it doesn't translate to real life the way a treadmill or bicycle does—I imagine separating this machine from its base and using it for travel—and then I worry that if I don't concentrate, I might fall off and become tangled in the equipment's swiveling parts, when I think I see Jessica immediately ahead of me, climbing on to a treadmill. She walks for a while and then starts running. There's an episode of *Full House* where D.J. starts dieting and over-exercising. In one scene she walks off the treadmill and immediately passes out. One of the show's numerous father figures has a concerned talk with her. D.J. never skips a meal again.

I notice that on the treadmill next to Jessica is another one of my students, the nose-ring wearer, the one I like best. I hadn't realized they were friends outside of class. I wonder if Joyce has called her to the office or telephoned her parents. Does she know it was me who reported her? There's a giant mirror on the gym wall, and I imagine the girls spotting my reflection and glaring at me in unison. I leave the elliptical under the pretense of buying a bottle of water. I imagine going to school on Monday and finding an empty, boycotted classroom. I imagine a workshop mutiny, where everybody disagrees with every single thing I say—all nineteen of them sitting in their desks, frowning and crossing their arms and keeping their heads perfectly still, two of them texting each other to say that I am not a good teacher after all.

The school lobby forms a T-shape with its intersecting hallways. At the top part of the T, inside a display case about nine feet long, is the plaster woman, wired together and suspended with rope. It looks like a body cast without a body, displaying its hollow eggshell insides. They've installed it in a sideways swimming position, with one arm stretching forward and one backward, bent realistically at the joints. Her outside is painted in streaky maroon and powder blue—the class couldn't agree on a colour. She shimmers garishly under two coats of varnish. Instead of clothing, she wears glitter that spells out lines from the class's poems in confrontational block letters and alluring italics. I lean close to read them and they are all about acceptance and hope and loving your body—lines from poems so sentimental that the students themselves, when forced to read their work aloud to the class, blush and stammer, admit to having written them the morning they were due.

I turn left with the intention of heading to my classroom. It's early, so the hallway is empty except for one caretaker and one chair outside the guidance office, where Jessica is sitting. She sees me and says, "I don't have an eating disorder."

"It's okay," I begin, but she interrupts.

"No. I don't. *Nur* is bulimic."

Nur is the name of the likeable student, the one who uses the word "flow" in workshop. When confronted with this class project, she did not eagerly sacrifice her body to the cold strips of wet plaster. She unveiled her hand from under the long sleeve of her shirt, which billowed like a poncho when she sat near the air vent.

Around the corner in the hallway behind me, Nur's hand, narrow and bony and now replicated in plaster, is fixed to somebody else's forearm, behind glass. Her hand's so small it holds only a single letter, the "o" in the word "steroid," likely not even a word she'd find meaningful to her situation. The "o" could easily be mistaken for a sparkly hair elastic.

"I'm sorry," I begin apologizing. She's wiping her eyes. I try to think of the most reassuring words I can say. "I'll let them know it was my mistake," I tell her.

"It doesn't matter," she says. "Her parents checked her into the hospital."

"They'll be able to help her there," I tell her, hoping this is true.

"Her liver is all messed up," she says. "And now she hates me because I had to tell my mom and then she called Nur's parents. You know, you could have just said something to me instead of going and telling the school. Now my parents think *I* have a problem."

At my parents' house, my father sits in front of his computer, eating unsalted almonds from his palm. "Monounsaturated," he tells me proudly. He pushes his weight back against his chair and crunches an almond. "Look here, Nina," he motions for me to lean in to the screen. It's playing a video of somebody's echocardiogram, and I wonder: at what point of starvation does your heart start to weaken? Does it matter how small your arteries are when you are only a teenager? I guess it's more about chemicals—mineral deficiencies, electrolyte imbalances, things English teachers don't know about.

I'll later hear from Joyce that Nur left the hospital using a walker, and that a month later she checked back in again. She'll lose muscle and bone mass. Jessica will organize a fundraiser to help Nur's family cover her hospital expenses. Nur's organs will fail one at a time. Jessica will enroll in the nursing program at Dalhousie. By then I'll have left teaching for good, without telling anyone the reason: that I don't want this kind of responsibility; that it feels like a job for somebody both more and less human than I am.

The plaster woman will hang in the school hallway for years.

A DOZEN STOMACHS

TOM THOR BUCHANAN

1.

A STOMACH is an organ in a moving body. It is pale pink in colour and shaped like a crooked knuckle. It is able to sit, lay down, stand again, balance on one leg. It has a large range of motion, opposable thumbs, the ability to distinguish the specific from the general. It retains memories that may influence its behaviour in the future, either consciously or not. It has a suitable amount of biography. It jostles against other organs, it moves through crowds. It demarks a boundary between the external and the internal, is a mediator through which certain forms of matter become comprehensible. It possesses its own complex interior ecology, something akin to a system of weather. It makes decisions about what to accept and what to reject.

2.

A stomach is riding the Yonge-University line at 6:32 p.m. It's sitting on a bench. It makes a fold, it makes a shape. Its skin stretches and contracts in ways that make it feel disfigured in some way. It transfers at Bloor and experiences a crew-change delay at Christie station. It gets off at Lansdowne and walks north, past Wallace Street and the Salvation Army. At Dupont there are sparks being emitted from the streetcar wires. The stomach shifts beneath its shirt, rubs against the cheap metal of the clasp on its belt. It's a cold night, the air is sharp. The darkness is a charitable blue colour.

3.

A stomach is sitting in an eggshell-blue office chair. It's filling out some forms on a clipboard. The woman who has given the stomach these questions has left the room to afford it some privacy. It's answering a series of questions about the way it feels. To each question it must answer either "strongly agree, somewhat agree, somewhat disagree, or strongly disagree." The stomach has trouble pinning its feelings to these positions, it feels like trying to strike a fly with your bare hand. It strongly disagrees that the world is out to get it. It strongly agrees that it often feels that others are scrutinizing it in an unrealistic way. It somewhat agrees that it has made mistakes leading to its current situation. It strongly disagrees that it is potentially a danger to others. It somewhat agrees that it is potentially a danger to itself.

4.

A stomach is stealing food from its roommate. The stomach doesn't buy any groceries because the stomach isn't eating right now. It has decided not to eat. Its side of the refrigerator is empty except for a few old pickle jars. Hunger has become constant and unnoticeable, like wallpaper. Until it becomes unbearable. The food it's stealing is particular. The stomach's roommate is a beekeeper. In a big cabinet in their kitchen, the roommate keeps a dozen jars of different kinds of honey. The stomach takes them all and arranges them on the counter in front of it. Each one tastes different. The stomach dips a spoon into one and tastes sage. It dips the spoon in another and tastes lavender. It tastes basswood, alfalfa, tulip poplar. The honey doesn't taste like food. It tastes like process and labour and great distances. The issue of the many creatures that made it. It tastes perfect: sweet, alien, brief. The stomach very quickly eats about $200 worth of its roommate's honey. It puts the jars back in the cabinet and washes the spoon.

5.

A stomach is sitting at a conference table in a room. Other than the stomach there are four people at the table with it. Each one of them is wearing a lanyard around their necks with their name and a small photo of them. Hands are in laps. One woman is explaining to the stomach that they are concerned about the stomach's attitude. The stomach is not progressing in the program in the way they had hoped. It doesn't seem to be taking part in group activities and has an attitude that has been perceived as confrontational. Its food diaries have not been properly filled out. The people around the table do not think this program is necessarily a good fit for the stomach. They want the stomach to understand that if one person is struggling it can affect the other participants' progress as well. There are certain decisions they have to make for the good of the program. They hope the stomach understands. They are willing to make some other recommendations.

6.

A stomach is on a bench with a friend in Queen's Park. It's a fall day in the late afternoon, and everything is turning rich, steeped colours. There is a statue of a man on a horse that the stomach can see behind its friend's head. Both of them are wearing thin coats. They are drinking some warm beer that the friend brought with him. The stomach is explaining to its friend, trying to explain something about the way it is living. It's trying to describe a feeling of uncertainty, a mode of life. It's trying to explain how it feels tired but is having difficulty. It tells its friend to imagine the feeling of having not slept and trying to remember a phone number. Unable able to remember why you're standing in the middle of your kitchen holding something in your hand. That's not quite it, the stomach says, but it's part of it. Embarrassment is also a part of it, it says. The stomach feels embarrassed even now, talking to its friend. It feels it is revealing something about its sense of self-importance. It doesn't like the feeling of taking up space on the bench, in the park, in the city to talk about all this. As well as its friend time, slowly ticking away, only so many hours left of daylight. The stomach's friend will have to go home eventually, back to his family. The stomach's language is a mess. It doesn't know what it's trying to say. Everything feels wrong instantly. Sentiments have chilled, wrong angles. Time to say the right thing is running out.

7.

A stomach writes something and calls it "Hunger," finding

that easier than saying "I'm hungry." Things feel more bearable when they are put elsewhere, it reasons. The stomach sits for hours in the university library, using its expired student ID, surrounded by books, barely able to stay awake. It reads a paragraph and it feels like the words are knocking sluggishly against it, like a boat tied to a dock. Sometimes later it'll remember something it read but can't remember reading it.

Sometimes, when it is really hungry, the type of hunger that is both an awake pain in the gut and behind the eyes, but also a kind of slow torpor in the blood, purpling fingernails, the stomach believes that a unique feral intensity arrives to it, an ability to concentrate and see things with, if not clarity, extreme magnification. The kind of magnification that lets you see all the tendons along someone's throat and jaw as they chew, popping like cables on a collapsing bridge. It'll think this after calling in sick to work for the fourth day in a row. It'll spend all day watching noise on its computer. The stomach is thinking of a hospital, a circle of chairs, a colour wheel, a woman with a lanyard around her neck. Group activities and the sorting of plastic fruit into tidy, colorful piles. Lukewarm food in foil on a tray. A standing scale with a sliding weight. A body filled to the brim, beyond its ability to bear. A journal, a worksheet, a photocopied affirmation with a spelling error: something perfect to reject.

8.

A stomach reads that cows do not actually have four stomachs. In fact, a cow's stomach possesses a complicated architecture, divided into four chambers which are further divided into a series of sacs, walls, and canals. Food passes through these chambers like a tour group guided through a museum. It is not only digested but also fermented, sucked free of moisture, and regurgitated to be chewed and swallowed again. Because cows chew almost constantly throughout their lives their teeth are always growing, to avoid being worn down to stubs. Their mouths also produce enormous amounts of saliva, in some cases over 100 litres a day.

The interior lining of a cow's stomach is called tripe and can be eaten. Looking at tripe in a supermarket, you can see the individual character of each chamber. Tripe originating in the first part of a cow's stomach, or rumen, is flat and smooth, while tripe from the reticulum is lacy and honey combed. Tripe from the third chamber, the omasum, looks like fine layers of gauze, and is sometimes called "bible-leaf tripe."

Because of its distinct taste and appearance, eating tripe can be described as "intense," and feel almost intimate. After all, these are substances drawn the deepest part of a living being. The stomach imagines being eaten. It imagines being turned inside out and spread flat, like a map.

Historically tripe, like offal, has been disparaged as a "peasant food," something that eaten out of necessity in circumstances where food is scarce and no edible part of an animal's body can afford to be wasted. The history of food is full of admonitions against waste, which is portrayed as a kind of ultimate transgression. Children are told to finish their food on account of the starvation of others half a world away, as though we all sit at the same dinner table. The constant nature of hunger makes the issue of waste a large one. The stomach can recall pouring vinegar onto his dinner to make it inedible or throwing food in the garbage when no one was watching. It has bought bags full of groceries only to let them go black, to rot in its refrigerator. It has wasted almost all the food it has ever seen. Including what it has eaten.

9.

A stomach learns that in the 19th century, adolescent "fasting girls" became famous for their alleged ability to abstain from food for weeks, even years at a time. It reads about Wiley Brooks, the founder of the Breatharian Institute of America, who claimed to survive solely on sunlight and fresh air. In 1983 he was observed leaving a Santa Cruz 7-Eleven with a Slurpee, hot dog, and box of Twinkies. Brooks would later revise his philosophy to recommend that fellow Breatharians periodically break their fasting with a special list of spiritually nourishing foods, which included Diet Coke and McDonald's cheeseburgers. The stomach devotes time to researching the Minnesota Starvation Experiment, fasts undertaken by artists like Adrian Piper and Chris Burden, and popular fads like the "Warrior" diet, which posits that the body gains access to hidden reserves of emergency energy when it engages in strenuous exercise while being partially starved. The stomach makes notes on what it reads, arranges them into lists. The lists feel soothing while it is making them but inert and futile later on.

10.

A stomach is a magnet moved around on a diagnostic grid. It seems as though there is a place for it on the grid no matter how it is living. If it sometimes eats and then feels the need to vomit what its eaten it is moved along a vertical and horizontal axis to a point on the grid. If it restricts what it eats until certain bodily processes begin to fail, if swallowing is no longer possible, it is moved to another point on the grid. The sum of the possible combinations of coordinates on the grid make the stomach feel as though there is no derangement of particularity of lived experience which the makers of the grid have not accounted for.

The stomach enjoys the pressure of the flattening effect, the subtle frisson it feels moving across the grid's cool lines. But it also fears its potential expulsion from the grid on account that it may experience a state which it does not believe the grid has a corresponding coordinate. The stomach feels that it will experience a state which the grid does not consider accountable. It is afraid of being accused of constituting a surplus or an unarticulated position, one for which the grid has no response and as a result will almost certainly deny responsibility for. Which would mean its ejection from the field of recognizability and into a new position that has been deemed unchartable. A magnet swinging wildly, with nothing familiar for it to desire.

11.

The stomach sits at a cafeteria table in the wing of a hospital with a half dozen other people. At this table there are a number of rules that are non-negotiable. The doors to the bathroom have been locked. Diners are not permitted to stand up before their meal is finished. Conversation is permitted, but the topic must be pre-approved. Approved topics include: vacation destinations, popular television and film, and the weather. Unpermitted topics include: food, eating, bodies, physical sensations. A woman with a notebook walks around, inspecting everyone's meal. She asks the stomach to tell her what it's brought to eat. The stomach recites for her: tofu for protein, whole-wheat noodles for carbohydrates, vinaigrette with mustard and olive oil for fats and salt. It holds up its Tupperware. The woman tells the stomach that she doesn't think there are enough calories on its plate. Each meal eaten at the table is bound to a goal, to caloric intake, to dispelling aversion, to restarting digestion. She asks if the stomach would like to add some of the chicken they have in the fridge. When the stomach tells her that it doesn't eat meat, the women reminds it that voluntary dietary restrictions are heavily discouraged while in program. But they also have more tofu. And veggie patties. The stomach looks down at its stupid, grotesque salad. It does not appear edible. The stomach cannot stand the thought that it will enter its body. It knows that if it does not eat this it will not be permitted to leave the table, but it also knows that if it eats this it will begin to cry, or to scream. It cannot stand the frankness of these reactions. It cannot stand the room it's in. It cannot stand the interaction with the woman. It looks at her, a look of benign concern on her face, but an aura of health around her that tells the stomach she is speaking to it from a different place. It cannot stand this day, or the prospect of the next.

12.

The stomach is acutely aware of being a physical organ in a cloud of subjectivities. It stands there, dumb as a mule. All around it are the things being emitted by other bodies, shoveling the air aside to make room. Friends make statements and those statements are inscribed in the permanent body of the world. Language, emotion, desire all appear and sink into the texture of what is passed between organisms.

At times it wishes that it could slough off all this matter, all this biology. It feels the factual as a flesh. It wants to drop out of the metabolism. Peel away fat like waves from a shore. But it is confronted with the fact that it is still just a living sac, a knot of dirty, identity-riddled muscle. Only so much can be repealed before it meets itself bone-deep, a border than cannot be further reduced. Pores remain. Membranes remain. There is no escaping it. DNA like dirt, getting everywhere.

13.

A stomach is dreaming. In the dream the continents of Earth are drawing together again, after so many years. The oceans churn and change direction. Cities crumple like tinfoil. Mountain ranges so famous they're on license plates disappear with a sound like teeth being broken. The continents are racing towards each other, there's no time to understand. In the dream everyone is terrified. They are afraid of sudden death. As the continents draw together they are overjoyed to see one another. It has been such a long time. They embrace. That is to say, the continents hug. Great Britain and the Carolinas are vaporized. Sub-Saharan Africa creaks as it is rearranged into a parabola. The continents dance around in a circle, joining hands. The climate changes, the poles are loosened. The sun drags across the surface of Earth in wild patterns. There is a death toll. It's a number, but it's easier just to say: everyone.

SOMEONE IS RECORDING

LYNN COADY

H I ERICA,
I don't know if you were expecting to hear from me or not after you posted your piece—but here I am. It does feel a bit strange to be getting in touch after all this time and under these particular circumstances. I often thought of dropping you a line in the years after I left Ottawa. I wanted to so many times. But honestly, I assumed you wouldn't be thrilled to hear from me and it was best to let sleeping dogs lie. Now that I've read your essay, I can't help but think that, despite your very clear irritation with me, you were, in your way, reaching out. If that's so, I'm glad you did.

And I'm glad you're giving us this opportunity to hash out what happened. I'll admit to being a little blindsided that you chose to do it in quite this way, and in this particular venue. My wife tells me thepinkghetto.soy is sort of a DIY, Millennial-centric version of Gwyneth Paltrow's website—*Goo*?—with a sprinkling of personal essays. But I suppose a Millennial audience is the only one that matters these days, at least when it comes to those all-important "clicks." Anyway, I'm very happy to know you're still writing—it brought me back to the days when we used to comment on each other's work. And to be honest I'm grateful to you for taking the initiative to re-establish contact in such a decisive and—let's face it—attention-getting way. I understand how important it must've been for you to write that piece. I do wish you had contacted me before taking it online—honestly, my delight in hearing from you again would've overrode any defensiveness or hostility if that's how you were expecting me to respond. But the important thing is it's out in the open now, and we can finally talk about it. It's bothered me over the years, especially after how we left things. And you know what? I'd be lying if I said I haven't missed talking to you. We had some great conversations back then.

Let me start by saying I was young and dumb. I'll cop to that a hundred percent. And insensitive, and kind of pompous and up my own ass, absolutely—a white, male Ph. D candidate in full plumage. Yup. The only thing I really take issue with in the piece is what you call our "power dynamic." Erica, what power? I was a TA. Hollister barely knew my name; it's not like I somehow maneuvered him into hiring me so I could be the one overseeing your grades. Not to mention that our relationship had run its course long before you signed up for the class. And I was fine with that, despite what you assert in your essay. (Relationship is maybe too polite a word for it, but we were definitely involved, I think you'll agree. I think you'll also recall who made the first move. I certainly do. And it's a very nice memory, by the way.)

That's that my only quibble. Otherwise I just want to say bravo. It could not have been easy to put something so personal out there—although one of the things I always admired about you was your fearlessness when it came to "just letting it all hang out" in both your writing and your life. As you know, I tend to be a little more circumspect in my own work, more about ideas than feelings, but maybe that's why your stuff is striking a chord with the kids on thepinkghetto.soy while mine remains a favourite of today's hottest academic journals, ha ha. So, yes, the essay threw me at first. But ultimately it was good to think about those days again and consider another perspective, even if I don't agree with that perspective one hundred percent. It shook me up, but we all need shaking up from time to time.

Anyway, it was great to read your work again—your way with a wry turn of phrase is as devastating as ever—and I'd love to hear more about what you're up to. The bios on thepinkghetto are pretty scant, but exciting to hear you've been making a go of things in New York. Gatineau girl makes good! On my end, I finally landed a tenure track post at a liberal arts college down here in the wilds of Illinois. I have a daughter now who is—if you can believe it (I can't)—ten years old as of last April. She's called MacKenzie—Kenz for short—and is currently obsessed with, of all things, mushrooms. If you'll indulge a doting dad, I can't resist attaching a photo. This was taken by Kenz's mom at the Grand Canyon earlier this year.

Please let me know how you're doing. And thank you, Erica. It's been genuinely illuminating to read your piece, to see things through your eyes and think about those days again. Thank you for giving me the opportunity, and the opening, to be in touch and to renew, I hope, our friendship.

All the very best,

Gary

—

Dear Erica,

I just turned 43, so if memory serves, that makes you around 38? Which strikes me as a little old (sorry) to be hanging out in obscure corners of the Internet, posting your personal correspondence alongside teens girls sharing their diary excerpts and selfies and (this is the first thing I saw when I called up the site, FYI) compilation videos of blindfolded people spraying shaving foam into their mouths after being told it was whipped cream. When I didn't hear back from you, I thought—Fair enough. I reached out, you turned away—that's your prerogative. We don't have to correspond. You've said your piece—said it to all the world, or at least to your snark-addicted young chums on thepink-ghetto.soy—whereas I restricted myself to keeping my feelings about your essay between us. That was my intent anyway. Until you posted them.

It's clear you're not interested in hearing my side of things, and you're welcome to post whatever you like, but I think it was a little offside to cherry pick the excerpts of my letter that you did and then embellish them with your own disparaging commentary. I'm sorry if I sounded at all con-descending previously ("douchey" in your words—okay, I'll own it), but I think you've spent enough time around humanities profs to know douchey is something a hazard of the trade. So ok, now I look douchey in front of your delighted teenybopper fanbase, but is that a fair way to win an argument? Is that "what the kids are into?" Maybe you're no longer interested in what's fair. Is it possible, Erica, this brief spate of online attention has gone to your head a lit-tle? Because this is not the woman I remember you to be.

I remember you as a passionate debater, obsessed with clarity and drilling down relentlessly in every argument to get to the truth. This thing you posted wasn't worthy of that person. Look: I know I was a bastard at times back then. But you have to admit your part in all this too. There's the matter of your hero-worship of Hollister, which I have to say your essay glossed over. You sneeringly call him "the great male author," as if that's not how you actually saw him back then. You were desperate to impress him. (I even warned you about that, about coming off as too abject. Remember?) But when you didn't, you blamed me.

And, fair enough, I was a jerk about it. I was defensive and I'll admit, it was hard to maintain my objectivity after all your accusations. But let's not pretend all this wasn't a two-way street.

I want you to know I shared your latest post with my wife, Andrea. I let her read the first one too, as she and I don't keep secrets from one another. We stayed up late after Kenz had been tucked into bed, talking about everything that happened, and with Andrea's help I was able to put my hurt feelings aside and really come to grips with the role I played back then, and why, after all these years, you are still so angry about it. And so dead set, it seems, on making a fool of me online. Andrea asked me if, in my previous email to you, I ever said that I was sorry. I was sure that I had, but reading it over again I realize that, while apologetic in tone, the email doesn't contain a genuine apology. So I apologize for that and—Erica? I apologize for everything. I'm truly sorry I hurt you. I understand if that's not enough. I won't write to you again.

With only good wishes,

Gary

—

You know, Erica, everything you said in that interview on YouTube, you could have said to my face. Is it that you think I won't hear the things you have to say? Is that why you don't bother? Because I'm telling you, I will. I have been. Can we actually talk? You can Skype me—my handle is *IsntitByronic*—or call my cell, the number of which has been at the bottom of every email I've sent you so far.

We need to work this out between us. I've had to lock my Facebook account thanks to your fan base, who think it's hilarious to post memes they've fashioned from the sections of my emails you made public. The images accompanying *this is not the woman I remember you to be* were in particularly bad taste. My students contact me on there, or they used to. I also had a Twitter account I hardly ever looked at and yesterday a colleague hinted that I should. I saw I had over 100 mentions, all linking to your interview. I read a handful—I can't imagine how empty a person's life must be to spend all their time trawling the Internet looking for strangers to mock and scold. Then I just shut the account down. These are your people, not mine. But maybe it's time we take the dirty laundry inside, what do you say?

You should know I've had one or two people contact me wanting to hear my side of the story. I don't know who these individuals are—honestly the fact that they even care about something that happened 15 years ago in Ottawa of all places strikes me as ludicrous. And splashing my private life across the Internet isn't my way of doing things. But if the harassment continues I'm not sure what option will be left to me.

Or we could just drop all this nonsense and talk like two old friends. The friends I thought we used to be.

Please just call me. Give me a chance to show that I hear you, Erica.

Gary

—

From: Burnam & Pace Law Group
To: Erica Shaffner:
RE: Cease and desist from online harassment

Dear Ms. Shaffner:

This CEASE AND DESIST ORDER is to inform you that your continued actions against our client Gary Weiland, including but not limited to:

1) Publishing false and defamatory assertions in various online venues including but not limited to thepinkghetto.soy

2) Inciting harassment of Mr. Weiland by publishing mocking and disparaging posts on Twitter, YouTube, Facebook, Facebook Live, Snapchat, Instagram, Reddit, WhatsApp Tumblr, LinkedIn and Flickr (where you posted images of Mr. Weiland that had been altered in various unflattering ways, including but not limited to: dressed as a mime, fashioned to resemble the cartoon-duck character Baby Huey, and with face superimposed on renderings of both Catherine the Great and her horse).

3) Giving online interviews wherein you characterize Mr. Weiland with disparaging and nonsensical language which we can only conclude is geared toward inciting the public's hostile interest in him, including the epithets: "assbucket," "shitsplat," "chickentits," and "knob."

We insist you cease these activities immediately. You are to stop discussing Mr. Weiland online and in public and we require that you forward written confirmation to us affirming that you will do so (please see attached template). Severe legal consequences will ensue if you fail to comply with this demand. Your activities against Mr. Weiland constitute harassment and incitement to harass and have had an increasingly deleterious impact on our client's quality of life. Mr. Weiland is prepared to pursue criminal and/or civil legal remedies should these activities against him continue.

This letter is the first and only warning you will receive.
Sincerely,
Amanda Cowan, Esq.

—

Hi Erica, me again. Whew, this whole thing has sort of blown up, hasn't it? I'm sure you were as dumbstruck as I was to see the segment on MSNBC last night, however brief it was. It's amazing what passes as news these days, but I guess that's the age we live in now. I know you never intended for it to go this far. I'm not totally lacking in a sense of humour (you'll remember, I'm sure, that brief but intense limerick writing phase I went through back in Ottawa) and as difficult as this process has sometimes been for me, I do see the joke. The other day I even caught Andrea chuckling at your Instagram feed. It took me a minute, but pretty soon I was chuckling right along with her. So believe me, I get it. The culture is going through some kind of catharsis right now I guess, and catharsis isn't always a logical or intellectual process—sometimes it just involves venting. Society needs its whipping boys and when I consider how easy I've had it up to this point as white, male etc., I realize there are worse things than being made the butt of a joke—even a joke that's gone viral.

So I'm trying to be sanguine about all this. But I realize sending a letter from my lawyer was not a particularly sanguine move, and I'm sorry about that. Amanda isn't even really my lawyer—I mean, she is a lawyer, but she's Andrea's sister (they're twins). She advised me the letter might not be a good idea (let that be a lesson to me: believe women!) but

I was feeling a little at my wits end last week, so I asked her to put her own spin on some boilerplate language and stick on her firm's letterhead. It struck me, reading it over afterwards, that maybe she'd had a little too much fun with it, but then I thought that was probably okay—really the letter was meant to be nothing but a friendly warning and I hoped you would take it in that spirit.

As I said, things were stressful last week. There've been a few crank calls and I had some students walk out of my class. There was even an impromptu sit-in outside the Chair's office so, you know. It felt like maybe not everyone was getting the joke.

Anyway, now that we've had our designated fifteen minutes of fame, I'm looking forward to getting back to my life, as I'm sure you are too. This has been a real learning process for me, and I promise you I've taken a good hard look at myself since your essay was published. As difficult as it's been at times, I'd like to think the experience has made me a better man, husband and father. On that note, Kenz is in the next room, calling for me to tell her a story before bed, so I'd better sign off. She's been a real ray of sunshine throughout all this—I like to think we've done a pretty good job of shielding her from it so far.

I wish you all the best, Erica. Eager to see what you'll do next with your new high profile. It's so impressive how your sensibility seems to have sparked with this new generation—perhaps you've been ahead of your time all these years! Is a book in the works? (I was such a fan of your poetry back in our Ottawa days—would love to see you get back to that.)

Gary

—

Erica, I don't know if you're checking email, but listen I had no idea who this Rand-o guy was when I agreed to the interview and I am truly, truly horrified by what's happened. Rand-o's been in touch on and off for a while now and he came across as sympathetic and thoughtful in his emails. I guess I was just feeling frustrated after your appearance on *Good Morning America* as I honestly assumed you would have gotten all this out of your system by now. Plus, I was floored that any respectable news organization would hold up our personal internet dust-up as something "emblematic" of the "cultural moment"—that had me doing an actual spit-take (which Kenz found hilarious). So, yes, I acted rashly when it came to Rand-o. I didn't do my due diligence.

Certainly, all I had to do was type his name into Google (as Andrea has constantly been reminding me) but who would have dreamt this guy had such a massive following? I was astounded by what they said on the news—three hundred thousand plus followers on Twitter? Conferences, a book deal? He was a charmer, absolutely, but when we Skyped I thought—Oh Christ, he's just some kid in his basement, right down to the vintage movie posters on the wall behind him (guy has a major fixation on *Ghostbusters*). Not to mention the toys—actual toys—on the shelves. I'd felt so ridiculous for having agreed to the interview—he looked barely out of braces. Anyway, I hope your mom is ok. Andrea tells me this swatting thing is a pretty common tactic of the "Randovians," but I promise you I had no idea. I read she was taken to the hospital after the incident but released a few hours later, which hopefully means she wasn't injured? And I dearly hope the damage to the house was minimal.

I know you need to keep a low profile right now, but I'd encourage you to get in touch once the dust settles. I think our only option at this point is to present a united front. We should release a joint statement saying that you forgive me for my part in all this and I forgive you for yours and that we've reconciled our differences. It's the only way this ends.

Gary

—

Really? You're just going to issue random communiqués from your underground internet bunker from here on in? How long do you think you can keep this up? Some of us, here above ground, have lives we'd like to get back to. I'm off work for the remainder of the semester thanks to all this. Students have started boycotting my classes en masse. The administration would dearly love to get rid of me at this point, especially after my impromptu speech in the quad—maybe you caught it on Facebook Live? (I had no idea someone was recording me, by the way—but then again someone's always recording these days, aren't they?) I was actually pretty impressed it got so many views. *Good Morning America* didn't exactly come calling in the aftermath, but a few other people did, and I am weighing my options.

All right, stay underground if that's what you want, Erica. And pop your head up like a feral gopher to bare your teeth at me online whenever the spirit moves you. Just know that you can come out anytime. You can end this. We can end this together—all we have to do is tell the world that I am sorry and you forgive me. And that I forgive you, too, for making such an outlandish stink about all this. (Sorry but I think that needs to be said as well, since it's become a major issue in certain circles—as I'm sure you have noticed.

If we genuinely want to de-escalate, those circles will have to be appeased).

So why the hell don't we?

Gary

PS—I don't suppose you've noted all the renewed interest in Hollister? A former classmate sent me a link—apparently some publisher is reissuing *Psalms of Kanata*. So congrats! It would seem the "great male author" is ascendant once more, all thanks to your efforts.

—

Okay so if I'm interpreting your latest post correctly, the sticking point seems to be that you don't believe I've actually been sincere in anything I've said thus far about what happened FIFTEEN FUCKING YEARS AGO back in Ottawa. And that I've "glossed over" what you call my "actual wrongdoing." Oh my god. This is amazing to me. As thoughtful, careful and abject as I've been in the absurd amount of emails I sent to you—emails you haven't even dignified with a response—and for all my self-flagellation and prostration at the altar of your fathomless feminine rage, nothing I've said has been good enough. Cool, cool. Good to know. Guess I can get up off my knees now.

It's been good to have this time off work and really think about this crusade of yours and the toxic pathology behind it. Andrea and I discussed it at length but she got weary of the subject after a while, which I can't blame her for—unfortunately, unlike her, I don't have the luxury of tuning all this out. It's helped a lot to talk about it online—there are a stunning number people out there who are quite happy to chat with me about it deep into the night. There are wingnuts, sure, like some of Rand-o's boys, but there are a great many more generous, compassionate individuals on the internet than I originally gave it credit for. I've explained to them that even though I'm not teaching right now, I'm still getting paid, but they can't seem shake the idea that I've been kicked out of my job (that's why 4chan posted your boss's phone number and your work address if I'm not mistaken? Which I did not encourage btw). Anyway, they insisted on raising money. The level of support has been really staggering, not to mention clarifying. To know I have so many people on my side in this. You're just one person, Erica. One person who interpreted my actions a certain way, many years ago. I remember things differently. And I have as many people on my side in this as you do on yours. Maybe more, I'm starting to realize.

So I've decided not to look a gift horse in the mouth. I have lots of time on my hands right now, especially with Andrea and Kenz taking a break down in Florida with Andrea's parents, so I'm thinking it might be time to put together a book, maybe using the last couple of speeches I gave as a jumping off point. (Don't know if you caught the most recent one—over 200k views!) As you may recall from our Ottawa days, I've always wanted to try my hand at something book-length. A crossover book—every academic's dream, as Hollister used to say. Poor old Hollister—he always used to wax a little melancholic about his reputation whenever we got together for drinks back in the day. Too bad he didn't live to bask in the attention he's getting now. Then again, I'm not sure he'd know how to handle it. In a way, I'm grateful for my crash course in all things internet these past few months. It's been painful at times, but it was a wakeup call. I really do feel more equipped than ever to embrace a wider audience. I guess I just never had the material before now.

YOUR OWN
LUCKY STARS

DEIRDRE SIMON DORE

BACK BEFORE the troubles started, the boy was a nice diversion for Hank and me to have around the farm. Every summer we took him off his mother's hands, Marj her name was. Hank's younger sister. It started with a week, then more as the years went by, seeing as we had none of our own and at 40 I realized it might never happen and made the mistake of confiding in Marj that having a cat wasn't really doing it for me anymore. That was when she came up with the idea of sharing the boy. More fun than a cat, she laughed, way more fun than a cat. She pretended she was doing us a favour and for awhile she was, though Hank never let Marj forget who was favouring who. I admit I was trepidatious at first.

Me and Hank had been childless so long that we had gotten into certain habits: Hank liked to walk around with just a T-shirt on, I didn't bother with a bra, we ate in front of the TV, watching the shows we wanted, farted at will. The idea of having to watch cartoons made us cranky. But over the years, with TV privileges fully established,

Hank got him outside for chores: collecting eggs, cleaning out the coop, compost, feeding the slop to the pigs, just about anything we asked, while Hank watched baseball and I cooked and set the table for three. Like we were playing the family game. Sometimes I let him dry the good china, but I would not trust him with the weeding, doubt he knew a weed from a bean. Not that he was city bred. Rural to the marrow of his bones. But wild rural, garbage dumps and pissed up pubs and abandoned mine shaft kind of places. Not nice with flowers and gardens and chickens like our place. We got him rabbits, six of them to take care of, in cages that Hank had built. It was the only chore the boy really enjoyed doing.

As the boy neared eleven, the attitudes and atmosphere shifted. He was becoming a thorn in our relationship, not that we had much of one, and we started dreading those two weeks every summer that sometimes stretched to three and even four. For one thing Hank liked to make a lot of noise when we screwed and seeing as the boy was in the room directly below us—well. I kept shushing Hank but Hank wouldn't shush. So I said, 'No screwing while the boy is here.' Which I admit was a nice reprieve, for me at least. Also the boy ate like a starving hippo till Hank put a lock on the pantry. And things went missing. A pocketknife, the cat. Which made Hank narrow his eyes at me in a way that meant trouble. Things like that. But the boy was silently respectful and never seemed anxious to go home and I don't blame him, I had seen his bedroom once, four bunk beds in the basement with all the bedclothes jumbled up on the floor mixed in with the dirty clothes and half-chewed dog bones on the bare mattress. Hank's sister had five others and he was the middle one. Born funny with his intestines lying like grey dumplings on the outside of his body. So there was a lot of surgeries before she even took him home and I read somewhere that this separation probably interfered with the maternal bonding process. It makes you wonder who does these experiments that end in these hypotheses that everyone seems to believe. She was going through a second divorce plus recovering from surgery herself. I caught her showing her new tits to Hank and letting him feel one. I asked him later, 'What did your sister's tit feel like?' He said, 'Just a tit—but an expensive one.' He's got a sense of humour, Hank does. And when the boy was gone, we got another cat.

One afternoon, during the last summer we had him, it was a hot day and he had just come in from the rabbits as I was putting together a rhubarb pie, he came to stand next to me to watch as I demonstrated how to make pastry with two knives scissoring through the cold chunks of butter. He was grabbing bits of dough to eat and I was slapping his hand away, laughing, when Hank walked in behind us. I could feel Hank's eyes on my back but I kept on cutting butter into the flour then handed the two knives to the boy so he could try.

'Maybe that's why your ass is so big' Hank said. 'Ten pounds of butter every night.' And he come right up behind me then and grabbed ahold of my ass with two hands and squeezed, elbowing at the boy at the same time and winking. I flushed red and hissed 'stop it,' my weight was an ongoing issue for me and I didn't like being reminded, but the boy, the boy instead of laughing or leering or getting all embarrassed like Hank expected, he turned to face Hank so fast that he knocked the bowl off the counter. He still had the two knives in his hand and the way he was staring at Hank and breathing hard made me wonder what was going on.

Hank smiled, let go of my ass and backed up, saying Whoa. Relax. He said, 'I like a big ass, boy. One day you'll know. Besides it's none of your goddammed business.' I dropped to the floor to scoop up the mess and carefully pulled the two butter knives out of the boy's hands.

That night at dinner Hank said to the boy without looking at him or bothering to stop chewing, 'Hey. Take your hat off at the table.' The boy looked so cute sitting there, big red freckles and big red ears, little black porkpie hat pulled down over his hair which was hanging in his eyes. He had small eyes the boy did, but bright blue as the sea. He took his hat off and mumbled sorry. I took it from him and put it on the sideboard behind the table.

Hank looked at him. 'Question for ya.' I quietly sat back down and we waited while Hank chewed. 'Was it you burned your mama's shed down?'

We had noticed the charred remains last time we were there but when we asked Marj what had happened she had shrugged. Insurance will cover it, was all she would say, by which we realized not to ask too many probing questions.

Hank piled half the rhubarb pie onto his plate. 'Well? he said, 'was it you?'

The boy blinked at Hank. 'Me? Why would I do something like that?' he said.

Now it's always been my opinion that if someone answers, 'Why would I do something like that?' to a question—that there's more to the story.

That night Hank told me he was done with the boy and never wanted him on the place again. I said, Why Hank? He's your nephew. Why wouldn't you want him? What happened? Is it the shed, Hank? Is it the cat? But he wouldn't answer, he said, You call Marj and tell her we're bringing him back, he's her kid, she can deal with him.

We drove the hour to Marj's in silence and when we got to the yard the boy scrambled out of the car and bolted. There was a cage in the yard, a human cage. It had been dropped there a year before. A set piece from a slasher film shot somewhere in Alberta that one of Marj's exes had snagged, thinking it was outrageously cool but could not think of a damn thing that it was good for and so had dumped it in her yard in front of the workshop, behind the tractor with the broken hydraulics. There it sat making the boy's stepfather furious, he with enough of his own junk to choke a horse, let alone everyone else's.

Once after he had been kicked off the school bus and the rest of the family was either at school or plowing the timothy field or off drinking with Tommy B. the boy was made to babysit and so he lured his younger half-siblings into the human cage and in they went because they trusted him. And there the little ones sat penned the whole afternoon in the cage while the boy ransacked the house for candy and moonshine, watched TV and drank all those tiny bottles of Baileys that his mother had been collecting. His baby sister peed her pink dress and they were horribly sunburned, their throats raw from crying and so thirsty by the time he set them free, all sobbed out by then. Seeing that cage again and remembering that story, I thought to myself, Hank's right. We have no business.

To be polite we hung around for a bit, Hank had a beer and Marj whined. She had an appointment with a modelling agency in the morning and was counting on us, I was counting on you Hankwell, she pouted and bent down a little, showing off her expensive cleavage. I noticed Hank didn't look away. Upstairs I could hear shouting or some noise coming from another room. Then it stopped and Marj's boyfriend—an old logger with a big belt—came in and the boy ran out the back door. At that point, Hank decided it was time to go.

I went out to the truck to get the boy's duffel bag and looking up saw the boy. He stood in a little swamp just behind the house up to his ankles in muck and was screaming at the top of his lungs NOOOO NOOOO NOOOO. I asked Marj what his problem was, she shrugged and said, 'The usual I guess' and walked away. She only had one other kid living with her at that time, the rest having gone to their respective fathers and the other child was in her bedroom memorizing passages from her Bible. Nor was Marj's boyfriend acting too concerned. So nobody wanted to talk about it and that was fine with me. People must respect people's privacy, and boys screaming Nooo—in my limited estimation—had everything to do with cleaning their rooms and nothing to do with anything important. I think I may have even admired him at the time, for being able to let it all out so completely, I couldn't remember the last time I had screamed like that, or even if I ever had, his whole skinny body was vibrating and rigid in rage and I thought of all the oxygen and carbon dioxide that he was inhaling and expelling and how good it must have felt to get it—whatever it was—off his chest. Later, after what happened, I wondered.

Logan, I suppose it would not have been a massively huge deal if the little boy you sold that hit to (hits? tabs? pills? needle?) had fully recovered from that seizure but so far it looks grim and there is almost a sure chance of brain damage but you're a child yourself, don't care who you're screwing or how much you can drink, 12 is not adult.

I had climbed up to the attic to a low sloped roof closet and sat on the floor with a flashlight and a bottle of Hank's whiskey. I had on my lap the thick manila envelope that had come in the mail. I opened it. My handwriting on all of them. Stored in no particular order, in fact out of order, page two's folded into the wrong page one's. A year's worth of letters. Ripped, then scotch-taped back together. Doodled on. A giant mosquito with huge breasts. I took a sip. I breathed in once and out. At random I read.

I gather the children are given different coloured pants depending on the level of trust or responsibility they have reached. A Structured Point Behavior System. And food is a very big deal. Controlled supervision, probation. Custody, open or secure (you), remand (means: being in custody awaiting court hearing or sentencing) New words, new concepts.

Crumpled, sticky with pop.

Instead of this letter I should send you a funny postcard I found showing two old gold panners in Quesnel with their bums on display.

And Christ, there was the postcard. I turned the page.

Sorry but I don't want to talk about your new official label as drug dealer for the eighth grade. Grass, crack, acid anything the elementary school children want. Well. Well well well. What could an old auntie even say about that. I won't even mention what Hank has to say.

I squinted to keep from seeing too clearly. Grateful that Hank was not home to grill me or crow.

Do you have any privacy where you are? Or is it just an open toilet in your cell sort of thing? I gather that having visual access to the children's 'rooms' is key for control and safety.

Eggs needed collecting. Breakfast dishes in the sink. Hank would be wanting his lunch.

… now I'm not even sure … was it crack cocaine? Or crystal meth? Or are those things different or are they the same? My ignorance must seem funny to you, I await your enlightening.

Scrawled across, HAHAHAHA

BUT more importantly I got your essays! Wonderful! But the one called The Uses of Napallm—("napallm is so awsom the things that it can do for exampel the jel that makes it stick iand how it creates carben monxodide wich makes it hard to breth and peple pass out. and if u want to win a war u have to do things that ki8ll the enimy evn if its horibul.") Logan when you get to a word that you don't know how to spell, do you just sort of grab a bunch of letters from the alphabet and throw them at that space in the sentence and see what sticks?

When had I become so pompous?

And the other essay called Shit.

He had drawn a rude sketch on the page, Then X'ed it out.

I wrote a story too in eighth grade. It was called Of Human Courage. All I remember now is the sacred cow (it took place in India) that the running-away-girl bumped into feeling both reckless and afraid.

Reckless and afraid! What was wrong with me?

The title of course I took from Of Human Bondage, that story about the sad brave boy with a clubfoot, but I changed the word Bondage to Courage. Really corny.

Had I really bragged about that story?

I have a spot on my nose, the doctors are treating it and Hank doesn't even know but …

On that one, written across in black felt, *SHUT THE FUCK UP.*

I have waited to mention this but when you visited us last summer, well before your incarceration (incarceration: confinement in a particular place) after you left, things went missing. Hmmmm? A pearl handled pocket knife, with two small blades ring any bells? One that my father gave me not that I expect you to put stock in sentimental value. Also money. Can you say fifty dollar bill with a straight face? Ha ha. Hardy har har. ROFLMAO. More fool I. And a nearly full jar of Nutella that had been sitting in the cupboard for 2 years and I know we didn't eat and yes I do have a bad memory but I'm CERTAIN I would remember eating a nearly full jar of Nutella. I don't expect you to return anything (oh wouldn't that be a miracle of gargantuan proportions) but I do think it's important you be aware that I am aware that we are all aware that things went missing after you left. Nuf said. (ALSO Mitzy started limping rather badly at the same time you were visiting and became withdrawn, not her usual joyful self and I am NOT accusing you of anything but if you happen to have any idea of why or what happened I'd be grateful to know.) When you get out of there and IF you ever stay with us again, I'm afraid there will be rules.

I heard Hank come in the front door. I heard the door close. I heard the refrigerator open. I heard the pop of a beer can. And then noise from the TV. I read on.

I am sorry that your facebook friends call you a loser. They are not real friends but still—12 year olds lamenting their old reckless ways, it's almost surreal.

One summer we had all watched a baseball game together. Logan and I had cheered for one team, and Hank the other. We were so happy, SO happy when our team won and Hank had muttered oh fuck you both and we had high-fived each other as he left the room. The highlight of my summer. Did he hate these letters as much I hated them now?

The "incident" that happened to your cellmate with the dental floss (how is that even possible??)—The thing is that there are two classes of suicide—the completers and the attempters, the second category—attempters—is more a demonstration of angst or anguish or attention-seeking or what have you, the first—completers—is what it is, unless it's a mistake made by someone who meant to be in the second category but was a little over zealous or just plain dumb about it. And I bet he doesn't like being tied to his bed. Would you?

Logan had triple underlined attempters.

I read in the paper last week that two boys had escaped from your institution. One of them, after two nights out in the streets, sneaking from empty garages to dumpsters to gas station bathrooms, was finally found in the library (why the library?) filthy, hungry, sorry, crouched behind the stacks and the police came at him with tasers drawn.

I heard Hank coming up the stairs.

They say a taser can be quite deadly on a youth.

'Yup' in his childish penmanship.

Hank opened the half door to my little hideaway. He stared down at me. He looked at the whiskey.

What are you doing in here? he said.

Nothing.

I held a piece of paper up. It was decorated beautifully in skulls.

I'm reading the letters.

What letters?

The ones I wrote him. Before he— when he was still … Do you want to see?

Hank narrowed his eyes at me for a minute. No, he said, I don't. And walked out. I heard him punching numbers into the phone downstairs.

A doe and fawn are outside my window right now, the window that overlooks the river and it is snowing and their backs are covered in fine white blankets of snow and they are eating windfall apples and every few moments they lift their heads to scan for trouble, it's a beautiful sight, their wariness. I'm sorry I haven't written more. I mean, I have, but so many of my letters seem to end up in my desk drawer and never get posted.

All these useless apologies. Nothing but sorry sorry sorry. And one paragraph circled in yellow magic marker—

p.s. Another point, and I never knew this either. A person doesn't need to get their feet off the ground to hang, in other words you don't even need to dangle, it can happen kneeling or squatting, with body weight & gravity pulling you forward. In 3 minutes you're brain dead, in 6-7 you're dead dead. You might want to mention that to any other 'attempters' you know.

Didn't anyone screen these letters? How could they have let them through?

…your mother wants me to tell you that she will write too, soon as she gets a chance. (She might still be mad about the car?)

I stopped reading. I wanted to stop. The shame I felt was like a sick animal in my gut, chewing at my belly. At the bottom of the stack—

Class: The assignment today is to write a descriptive essay, describing in detail one of your favourite relations. Try to get inside the character a little bit and use language that brings that person to life so that if I were to walk down the street I might recognize him or her.

Stapled to it—

My Antie Dodie

She has brownish hair wich is grey on top and the botom is blondish and its semmy long and not totally stupid like some old peple who cut there hair to look like a poodle dog and then die it purpel wich we call purpel heads and she weres it in a braid which is becorse she dosnt care what peple think how she looks.and never gose anywere. She is not fat but meduim with big hooters and hands that r always rubbing togehter and shortich finger nails. She hs I dont know what coler eyes maybe blue and never wers makeup and has a moale on her on the side of her nose wich after awile you dont think about. I think inside she has one liver and 2lungs and a stumik and 1 heart not that u can see it but i giutted a deer once and i bet that peple have the same insides prety much, everyting shiny and wet and warm and brown except the guts wich r grey. If you saw her that's what she wuld look like. Always moving arownd and making sandwhitches.tlking to hesself or sowing stuff. she always weres a blue ski coat all the time half the time she weres gumboots and other half she weres crocks and cares about walking the dog and feeding the chickens and pigs more than reugular peple. She has a reely nice dog tcalled Mitszy that Uncel Hank hit with hs trakter and i fed the dog my sandwish till she felt beter.

Mitzy. So it was Hank and not Logan. My god.

Dear Logjam (remember that old nickname?), I let your rabbits go. One of the rabbits in his tiny cage, had stopped eating. Even though I cleaned his cage and cleaned his water bowl and put out fresh grass and green dandelion leaves and carrots, he wouldn't touch a thing, waiting for you is my guess. So I let him go. And the moment he was free he started doing back flips, jumping up in the air and turning somersaults. So I let the others go free as well, all 6 of them and they all disappeared. Keep a look out, maybe they're on their way to you. Haha. Enjoying their freedom, if there even is such a thing.

Freedom. I had doubted freedom while surrounded by wild green space, alive and variable.

It's the variation that creates a sense of freedom: the changes in scenery, here a hill, there a river, a hole, a dip, an expanse of field, a flurry of birds, deer bones, horse shit, a downed tree, a clump of winter kinniknick pawed up. Because it changes, you get a sense of freedom. Or illusions of freedom. The thing is, even paradise, if immutable would feel like prison.

And Logan had written in the margin: *Para-para-paradise, Para-para-paradise, Para-para-paralize*

Dear Mrs. Schorn,

I'm glad we had a chance to talk on the phone, however briefly, and we are truly sorry for how things have turned out. Naturally there will be an inquiry and you are welcome to contribute whatever relevant information you might have and you, as his guardian will be allowed access to the report once it is completed and if further steps are required you will be advised as to the procedure. In the meantime I'm packaging up Logan's effects and the originals of Logan's letters and essays and artifacts which he had stored in an empty cereal box in his room. There was no further correspondence other than these few letters addressed from you. He may have lost those or perhaps they didn't exist. Also a package and a letter from you that came today. Please let me know if we can be of any further assistance.

They say the children in Juvie Jail, or the Monster Factory or whatever you call it feel safer inside than they do on the outside. Is that true? It sounds like a lot of bullshit to me. When I think of cages I think of hamsters or guard dogs or Patty Hearst, who the hippies loved at first, made a sort of hero, then either despaired for or cheered on as they watched her engineer her own fall from grace, depending on where you landed in terms of values. For me she was always just pretty Patty Hearst who was lucky enough to get a second chance. Well, you can thank your own lucky stars Logan there will be a second chance for you too when you get out.

That last letter, clean as snow, unread, till now. Would it have mattered or changed a thing? Hank was on the stairs again. His footsteps were fast, and loud like he had business on his mind. The mole on my nose itched. I drank again. I felt reckless and afraid. I whispered, *No*, as loud as I could muster. *Noooo.* But I could barely hear myself, even my breath sounded louder, the heart beating in my chest was louder, even the sweat on my hands was louder. I shouted it. Who heard?

TRACKS

ALICIA ELLIOTT

FOR THE twelfth time in two days I watch as Laura shreds her vocal chords screaming and still she'll take no drugs. Her eyes are hooded with exhaustion, her hair a wet mass on her sticky forehead. It was a twenty-two hour delivery, most of which she spent foodless and hunched over a birthing stool in the biggest suite at Tsi Non:we Ionnakeratstha Ona:grahsta'. She wanted a natural delivery, she'd said. If she could feel the conception she sure as shit was going to feel the birth. That was Laura. Ever crude and to the point.

"Are you sure you don't want to go to the hosp—"

"How many times do I have to tell you? No no no no no no. No. Heck, Roy!"

The camera shrinks away. It focuses on me spitting encouragement through the pulsing crush of Laura's grip. I glimpse up at the camera—at Roy—and give a pained smile. Back then I didn't know for sure that I couldn't conceive but I had my suspicions.

I fast forward to the end, when Sherry is finally in her arms. Laura looks tired as hell, but when the camera comes for a close-up, she swats it away with impressive quickness.

"You're not allowed to catch my wrinkles on camera just because I gave birth to your kid."

There's a time lapse. When the camera starts again Laura's made up like some eager starlet. But she's not looking at the camera from beneath pristine eyelashes or blowing kisses the way she would when she was young. She's looking down at Sherry. Every touch and gesture is full of yearning, for both the present and the future. Tracing Sherry's veins with her fingers like she's following a map. Like in those small bursts of blue, peeking from beneath crystalline skin, Laura saw their lives: love and anger, tenderness and humour, pain and envy. Like Laura saw their worlds—separate but interlocking, like the two halves of a Venn diagram.

No one watching then could have seen anything but a mother and a daughter, each absolutely smitten, adoring and sizing one another up. I'm not sure I see anything different now but I continually find myself trying. Nothing ever really comes out of the blue. There must be shifting eyes somewhere in the grainy footage, a hesitation, a smile held a moment too long.

"Em." Tom is standing in the doorway in a too-big black suit. He's holding my black pumps and watching me, a question on his face. I wish he would just ask it.

"Is it time?"

He nods. I stop the video, get up and grab my shoes.

There is a persistent musty smell in the viewing room. It's hidden well beneath strangers' perfumes and plug-in deodorizers but it's there. I imagine it's the smell of formaldehyde or death, though I've never really smelled either. I've haven't been to a funeral since Uncle Rob's and that doesn't really count. I was so young; for all I remember I wasn't there at all. Laura said she remembered everything, from the music ("Fucking Garth Brooks") to the "huge ass mole" on the priest's chin. I didn't consider it at the time but it was strange a priest was there. Mom said when she and Uncle Rob were at the Mush Hole together, he was constantly in trouble, back-talking the priests and refusing to speak English and biting the unlucky teacher tasked with cutting his long, black Indian hair to a more "civilized" length. They beat him so he hated them; he hated them so they beat him. And yet at the end of his life a priest was praying over his Mohawk soul.

Twenty years after that funeral I'm at this one. Three generations—almost an entire family—gone, all put to rest courtesy of Styres Funeral Home. Laura planned her funeral shortly after she and Roy were married. It should have set off alarm bells but it didn't. At least her preparations have helped Roy. All he's had to do is nod, mute.

The room is orderly enough. Chairs arranged with absurd precision. I have the feeling that were I to take a ruler and measure the distance between each one, I'd come up with the same number every time. There must be some sort of science to grief, some manual funeral home directors adhere to, detailing the most manageable chair arrangement or flower placement for friends and family of the deceased. Everything is too calculated: the beige wallpaper, the overstuffed couches, the pre-packaged condolences.

Aunt Chelsea is at the podium, mascara that took her thirty minutes of applying and re-applying to perfect now sliding, sap-like, down her cheek. Otherwise she is composed, wearing the stiff proud pout of a once-great general facing a war tribunal. Her voice is level and dry.

"Laura was such a smart girl. Rob loved her so much. When we lost him she was four. It was … difficult. But she was strong."

"Smart." "Strong." Adjectives any parent could slap on the dead child they didn't care to know. I look around for evidence of skepticism. Not even a raised eyebrow. No one is thinking about Aunt Chelsea and Laura's relationship, which was tempestuous at best. In the face of death ugly truths are redacted.

As long as I can remember every conversation between them had notes of danger—as though any minute they'd collapse into fists and fire. I don't remember Laura ever mentioning Aunt Chelsea with anything resembling love. Even when she was six and should have still been under her mother's spell, she ignored her almost constantly, called her "Chelsea" with satisfaction.

I remember in grade nine when she was asked to prom by Mark Hanson, a white twenty-year-old senior with a car and nipple rings. She was one of the only ninth graders going—probably one of the only kids from the rez going, too—a fact she loved to remind us, dangling it in front of our faces like a succulent piece of fruit. Laura couldn't do anything without thoroughly pissing off her mother, though, so she decided to wear Aunt Chelsea's low-cut red cocktail dress—the expensive one she bought herself in Toronto to celebrate graduating nursing school. The way Laura told it, she sauntered home drunk at 3 a.m. wearing Mark's leather jacket and swinging her panties around her finger. She greeted her mother with a smile, slurring, "Guess who's a woman now?" before throwing up on the kitchen floor.

"You should've seen her face, Em," she'd said, laughing. "I've never heard her scream so loud. And all for that ugly dress! Never mind her piss-drunk daughter shooting vomit like a fucking sprinkler."

But a month after prom, when it became obvious that Mark Hanson's "gravity's as good as birth control" claim was bullshit, Aunt Chelsea didn't yell or tell her she had it coming, even if she thought it. She calmly described Laura's options, then asked what she wanted to do. When abortion was chosen, Aunt Chelsea didn't flinch or grimace in that self-satisfied way she usually did when Laura chose anything. She diligently set about doing all the work: finding a clinic, booking the appointment in Toronto, borrowing a car to drive us there. All Laura did the week before the procedure was talk about Mark. He hadn't even looked in her direction since prom.

"I'm gonna keep the fetus so I can send it to him. Like in a little jar. Oh! I should put a fake birth certificate in the bag, init? You know, like, 'Mark Hanson Jr. was aborted on this day, child to a naïve girl and a small-dicked asshole.'"

"You haven't been naïve since kindergarten."

"Maybe I should send it to his mom. She'd already be pissed enough an Indian snagged her son, but wouldn't it be great if she was one of those crazy pro-lifers? Like with the signs and bombs and stuff? She might actually kill Mark. Save me the trouble."

But when the day came she didn't even mention Mark. She didn't say anything at all. Afterwards she cried against her mother's chest for almost an hour. It was strange to watch them in that embrace, as though they were any mother and daughter at any moment in history, timeless.

Laura never really mentioned the abortion to me after it happened and out of respect for her, I never mentioned it either. I only heard her reference it once in an offhand kind of way the day Sherry was born. I didn't hear it when she said it, I must have been talking to Roy or Aunt Chelsea. I don't think anyone heard. It was something I noticed when I watched the video. The camera is on her bedside table. It only catches the pale curtain's flutter, but I imagine her gazing down at Sherry, maybe touching her nose with a manicured nail. Then you hear it.

"I get to keep you."

The first time I noticed it I rewound the tape to make sure that's actually what she said. By the first replay there was no question in my mind but I still checked and re-checked. Each time I heard it I felt sick. Even all those years later, on what was supposed to be one of the happiest days of her life, tragedy was playing in the background, casting sinister lights. She put on a good show but she couldn't forget. She couldn't escape. Until she did.

Maybe Laura was trying to atone for her sins. Sacrifice the child she chose for the child she didn't. Maybe that was a clue. A dot I should have connected. As though hearing those words the first time could stop the train that was, months later, barreling forward.

Aunt Chelsea's voice has gotten thicker, the tears faster. She wobbles on her heels. Mom gets up and quietly approaches.

"It's okay, Chels." She tries to lead her away by the hand. Aunt Chelsea only clutches the podium tighter as she continues to melt into the wood. Her cries are guttural, inhuman. She knows she wasn't a good mother—the type who'd stay up all night and watch movies with Laura, or ask what she wanted to do with her life and really listen. She wasn't the type of mother a daughter would come to when terrified by her own thoughts.

Had Laura seen this, she would have offered a bemused cliché. "Better late than never." As if time is infinite and lives don't end. What good is remorse now? It might as well be never.

I lean towards Tom. "I need a cigarette." He moves to get up and I stop him quick with a shake of my head. He settles back into his chair frowning. Any time I'm alone for more than ten minutes he calls to me, or peeks his head in, or comes along with a cup of coffee or a bowl of corn soup. It's suffocating.

I stand in the doorway and inhale deeply. Freshly-shorn grass and charred hotdogs from a fundraising barbecue across the street. Evidence that other lives continue, unchanged. A slow nausea creeps up, stops short at my esophagus.

The only other person outside is a woman wearing a simple black dress. About my age. White, blonde. She's whispering into her phone with her back turned. As the screen door clicks shut she turns around sharply and thrusts her phone into her purse, her eyebrows squeezed in agitation.

"Sorry." I pull out a cigarette and try to light it. My hands are shaky and imprecise.

The woman looks wary for a moment, then all creases smooth.

"It's okay. I was looking for a reason to hang up anyway."

I raise an eyebrow and she rolls her eyes.

"Ex-boyfriend," she offers.

I nod, focusing on my still unlit cigarette. Once, twice, three times, four and still no flame. The woman reaches into her purse, pulls out a red lighter and flicks its head ablaze without hesitation. In a moment the end of my cigarette's aglow.

"Thanks," I say as I inhale.

"No problem."

I can feel her eyes darting back to me as she digs through her purse. I wonder what she sees. Looking in the mirror hasn't really occurred to me lately. I could have grown crow's feet overnight. My lips could have decided once and for all they were done pretending, leaving me frowning forever. I've seen other people like that. Old Mohawk women with faces like scored leather. They couldn't have always been that way. They must have been happy once, even beautiful, before some event came down on them with such unrelenting force that smiling became suddenly unworthy of the effort.

Laura, of course, will remain young, beautiful, tragic.

"You couldn't handle it in there, either, huh?" the woman asks.

"Nope."

She lights her own cigarette and takes a drag. Her nails are a familiar shade of pink. Showy and grossly inappropriate for a funeral.

"Viva la Vulva?"

The woman looks down at her hands and laughs. "It always sounds so much worse when said out loud like that."

"I'm not really a nail polish kind of girl." I hesitate for a moment, then puff out, "But Laura liked that one."

"Is that right? I take it you and Laura were close?"

I let the silence ring for a moment, observing her. She's too put together, too eager. I shrug. "Not really."

The woman turns in towards me. Her eyes are shrewd, calculating like a jungle cat's, her face angular and lean. Her voice drops to a whisper.

"Listen, I have a favour to ask. My name's April Hopkins and I'm a reporter for *The Star*. I know you said you didn't know Laura very well, but I could really use a few quotes. If I could just ask you a couple questions–"

"How'd you find out about this?"

She gives a thin smile. "Just a hunch."

That's bullshit. Nothing was publicized. The funeral's in downtown Ohsweken, a full hundred kilometres from where Roy and Laura lived. None of Laura's flaky friends—of which she had many—were notified. Aunt Chelsea's sticking pretty faithfully to this mourning mother routine. And Roy would never have talked to this reporter. He hasn't talked to anyone, really. I'd hoped he'd talk to me but he will when he's ready.

So then who was the sell out?

"I know it's probably really hard for you in light of the circumstances. But this can be your chance to set the record straight. Show people the real Laura."

Before I can even respond she pulls out a notepad and starts rifling through the pages.

"I'm going to be honest with you. A lot of people I've talked to are saying a lot of really awful things. Kayley Blatchford has gone on the record calling her a sadist. Something about getting in a lot of fights in college, really messing her knuckles up. Made it sound like a form of self-mutilation."

"Well then she obviously doesn't know the meaning of the word 'sadist,' does she? Laura got those scars in grade eight playing too much bloody knuckles."

"Really?" She fishes through her purse for a notebook and starts scribbling immediately. "Now you see why I need more opinions. It's hard to find balance with a story like this. People want a monster, so they create a monster. Especially with the whole race thing." She says it in such a careless, blasé way, the way people do when they don't have to consider the whole race thing in their everyday lives. She's right, though. I've seen it. Figures from Laura's past rematerializing in print and on tape, spinning a common tale of a troubled girl. I knew that people would talk; they did enough when she was alive. But for some reason every time another person came forward I felt attacked. Like I was the one being picked apart and analyzed.

Laura would have loved this. I can imagine her laughing, egging rumours on with some exaggerated truth or outright lie. Always building her own myth, disregarding how it affected those around her. In fact, this may have always been how she wanted her final act to end: with exclamation points and question marks.

That doesn't explain Sherry, though. Laura was different when she had her. She prided herself on being a good mom. Took up baby massage and breastfed, wearing her new role like a badge.

I want to say something that shows this. Even something as simple as, "Laura was a fantastic mother. She loved her daughter." But I can't. Maybe the reporters and pundits are right. Maybe our family is "predisposed to violence." Maybe our people are "naturally self-destructive."

The reporter leans in closer. "Will you help me help Laura? Please?"

People begin pouring out the door. April gives only a cursory glance to the other mourners. Her focus is me. I haven't had much experience with reporters but I can tell this woman's very good at her job. She's going to get her balanced quote—if that's what she even wants—with or without me.

I see Mom basically carrying Aunt Chelsea. Tom walks closely behind them, hands up, as though spotting.

I turn and grab at Tom's arm. "Is it over? Where are they?"

He glances between me and April, then back towards the door. "He won't let them leave yet."

"What?" Tom shrugs and backs away, leaving me once again with the reporter with the camera lens eyes.

"Sorry, did he just say—"

I look April straight in the face and, harshly, bluntly, as though my words were a hammer striking a nail, say "Fuck you."

There are two matching caskets: one large, one small, both closed. There is one picture: a portrait of Laura and Sherry four months after the birth. They look so much alike. Their eyes are a matching shade of amber, sparkling with secrets; their hair is smooth and straight and black. Laura refused to wear matching outfits, so their dresses clash fantastically. Both look beautiful and somehow amused, Sherry already sporting the ironic smirk it took Laura years to perfect. I want to move forward and touch the caskets but my muscles stick. I want to say something meaningful but nothing comes.

"What did you tell her?" Angry, accusatory. So unlike any voice I've heard I'm almost convinced I've imagined it. Then I turn and see Roy standing in the corner, his face a mass of puffy pink.

This is the first time I've seen him since the night it happened. As soon as I heard I went over. He was crumpled in a heap in the corner of Sherry's nursery, her just-used sheets ripped from her mattress and held tight against his nose. "I can still smell her." He repeated it over and over. I pulled a chair from another room and sat. It seemed wrong to sit in the rocking chair.

"What did you say to her, Em?"

I stay very still. "Who?"

"April from *The Star.*" My muscles release, slightly.

"Nothing."

He exhales. "I should've known she'd show up. She's been following me for days trying to convince me I owe everyone a quote."

So that was how April conducted her investigative journalism: stalking. No one actually told her anything. Everyone was loyal.

"You should call the cops. Get a restraining order or something."

"No point. They'd send someone else. I just have to ride it out."

I can understand why Roy hasn't talked in days. These conversations are painful, not cathartic. We're trying to talk like we normally would but it's a poor imitation. We can't even say their names. And yet by not talking about it we're still talking about it. Laura: forever the centre of attention. How she always managed to creep into conversations, sliding in to fill silences even when she wasn't there, will always be a mystery to me. She was the gel in so many relationships. There must be an entire matrix of people connected by their mutual wonder over what she was doing and why.

Her whole relationship with Roy was the centrepiece of college gossip. Once those two got together it was on the tips of everyone's tongues for months. Before Roy, all of Laura's flings were interchangeable. Big sturdy barrels of men with stamina and little else. The closest she ever came to loving a boy was drunkenly tattooing a high school boyfriend's name on her shoulder after graduation. *Ted* inside a heart pierced by a crooked arrow. She never bothered to cover it after they broke up.

Roy was something else altogether. He was the quiet, studious roommate of some moron she was dating in college. I think his name was Bryan. The night Laura met Roy, Bryan drank three pitchers of beer by himself. On their way back to his apartment he collapsed. For some reason, Laura didn't walk away as she normally would. Instead, she dragged his two-hundred-and-thirty-pound frame to the door, swearing and grunting the whole time. As she rifled through his pockets for keys, Roy opened the door: wiry, pale, freckled. Between the two of them, they managed to get Bryan inside. Then Roy offered to make Laura a French press of coffee. And that's when she said she knew.

"Not once did he look down my shirt. And I was wearing my black tank top—you know, the one with the sequins? Cleavage everywhere, and here he is, asking me my opinions on Akira Kurosawa. Like he actually thought a rez girl like me would know anything about Akira Fucking Kurosawa."

She laughed and shook her head. She seemed amazed that there was a man alive who would want to spend four hours talking to her without the promise of sex. That there was a man alive who could see her as a person.

I'm not sure he did, though. Roy marrying Laura was like the bullied nerd finally bagging the head cheerleader. For all his reverence for her, I think Roy both recognized and relished this. It was almost grotesque the way they showed one another off: he with his gorgeous, glowing Pocahottie, she with her white, sure-to-earn-six-figures sugar daddy.

When they announced their engagement six months later it was met with hard cynicism. Typical Laura, everyone back home thought, riding a whim to get attention. I thought so, too, until their wedding day. We were in the back room waiting for our cue to leave, she immaculate in her white gown. After making some joke about screwing half the guests she got quiet. She turned to me, her face pursed.

"Em. What if he finally realizes he's marrying *me* and just leaves?"

She was so vulnerable. I knew their marriage was more than an impulse. It was a dive into the dark and she was terrified.

And yet she left him, willingly, taking everything with her.

I reach over, feel the crisp linen of Roy's sleeve—

"Don't." He brushes my hand off. It was stupid of me to think he could handle these kinds of interactions. I can't even imagine how he could get dressed, much less put up with condolences from strangers. I try to get him to look into my face but he won't. The minutes fall like weights.

"These past few days all I could think about was talking to you. I had a list of questions. A whole goddamn speech. But now that you're in front of me …"

"Maybe this isn't the right time for this," I say. Roy rubs his hands over his face. I feel a numbness creeping up my knees. I shouldn't have worn such high heels.

"I don't want you there. It doesn't seem right."

For a moment the room seems to tilt.

"What do you mean? You don't want me where?"

He blinks and blinks.

"You don't want me where, Roy?"

"The burial. The reception after. I didn't really want you here, but you're her cousin. Her best friend. People would ask questions."

"But … nothing happened."

Roy looks inflamed. Sharp words are waiting to be said, I can tell. I hope he says them. I hope they draw blood. There's been enough pretending for the sake of saving face. We did what we were supposed to. All the tip-toeing, the planning … all of it was for nothing. I never got to taste second-hand red wine on his tongue or feel his slender fingers between my thighs. I never will. I shouldn't feel resentment—not now, of all times—and yet here it is, crippling and noxious.

He looks directly at me and his face is set. "Please. Don't. Come." Each syllable imbued with such meaning there's no need for him to say anything more.

Every five to ten minutes the high-pitched shriek sounds. The wheels are stopped by force. Violent, desperate, like the last moment of struggle before surrender. The subway train smashes to a halt: doors open, people rush, bells chime, doors close. The station left barren.

With traffic it took me two and a half hours to drive here, ten minutes to find parking. St. George. One of the busiest subway stations in Toronto. Isolating even at capacity. It's a depressing shade of green—one I imagine I'd find peeling from the walls of a crack house bathroom on the Trail.

I lean out, well past the platform's yellow line. When I turn back eyes are on me, some wide and worried, some dull and uncaring. People watch and watch but do never do anything.

It happened here, at the centre of two lines. A crossroad, of sorts. Was that intentional? I know I need to stop. There's no meaning in these walls or their placement on a map. Only she knows why she chose this place, if it was even a choice at all.

No two accounts are the same, but all agree she wheeled Sherry off the elevator in that obscenely expensive stroller she loved so much. Either she didn't say anything or she cooed to Sherry as she moved to the end of the platform. The train going Northbound wailed its way into the station. Sherry started to cry. Laura picked her up and clutched her to her chest, kissing her or trying to shush her or looking maudlin. The air started to shift, another whistling could be heard. The TV screen said the next train Southbound would be arriving in less than a minute. Some people thought she was just peeking down the tunnel to see the train, the way people do. Others said she looked distraught. At the last minute she shifted Sherry onto her hip as she took off her purse and thrust it into the seat of the stroller. Or she wasn't wearing a purse. Then she turned her back towards the oncoming train, hugged Sherry tight, and stepped sideways off the platform.

I didn't notice. I was too busy parceling pieces of her perfect life to take for myself. She practically told me her plans right there on the phone and I hung up. Hung up to meet her husband in Burlington—the halfway point between our homes, our families. Back then, of course, I told myself it wasn't cheating. It was easy enough to believe; our skin barely touched. When it did, though, those slight, soft strokes were everything to me. Amazing that something so small could be so erotic. I lived for the chance that we'd brush hands under the table. Even as it was happening to me I put myself above it. I'd scoff at other adulterous couples, consider them desperate clichés. Roy and I were doing things the right way. We were going to keep collateral damage to a minimum.

That last time we talked Laura was going on about Sue Stevenson, soon to be Sue Kristoff. She had just sent Laura an invitation to her wedding and Laura was micro-analyzing the handwritten postscript. Apparently "Vlad and I would love for you to come. We have so much catching up to do!" was code for "I married someone richer and want to rub it in your face."

"Maybe she really does want to see you and catch up. She was your roommate. You guys were close."

"We were not. Sue and all those white trust fund bitches don't make friends. They gather audiences. I could call every one of them right now and tell them I'm going to kill myself and they'd just laugh and ramble on about how they used to cut themselves in eighth grade."

I laughed, the way I always did.

"I'm serious. And it's really fucking sad when you think about it."

"Look, I got to go. I'm supposed to meet Tom for dinner in ten. We can trash all your old friends tomorrow. I'll call you around, say, four?"

"Oh. Okay. Emily?"

"Yeah?"

Something big was bothering her. She never used my full name. I could hear her ragged breathing as I feverishly applied red lipstick in front of the bathroom mirror.

"Speak now or forever hold your peace." I meant for it to be playful.

"Forget it. I'll talk to you tomorrow."

I don't remember what I ate for dinner that night, what I wore, what lie I told Tom to get out of the house. I don't remember anything that Roy and I talked about. But I remember the hollow of her voice, or at least I tell myself I do.

KIINT

BILL GASTON

I<small>F</small> A<small>RNIE</small> was honest with himself he would admit the fish farm job had saved his life and probably kept on saving it. Toba Inlet was an ocean dead end with no road in, no power, nothing. At night or in the sudden middle of a day it could get so quiet you could stand there—just stand there—and hear your heart beat.

It was just guys. Women need not apply. Arnie didn't know how they got away with that, these days, but no women, and no alcohol allowed. Almost like it was designed by someone with his best interests in mind.

The one link to the outside was a VHF radio, good only to call nearby boats or the company office thirty-nine miles by water in Campbell River, a one-room piece of shit across the road from the government dock. Hired there, Arnie could still picture that edgy guy at his metal desk, blaming him when some government papers didn't match up with what was on his stupid screen.

Some days were more isolated than others, no water taxis, no feed barged in, no fry barged out. Arnie called them Robinson Crusoe days, after one of his favourites. At low tide he'd walk the shore, out of hearing range of the bunkhouse, the guys yelling their video-game deaths. Away from gulls swarming the mort bins like junkies on a spilt bag. Away from the thump of the buried generator, the camp's beating gasoline heart. He'd walk until he could see and hear nothing but what had always been here. Toba was a mountain valley filled with ocean, dramatic if the clouds lifted and you could actually see above the trees, the mountains' rock shoulders and snow way up top. But even the cloud was natural, and a big part of the isolation. Socked in, was the expression. He'd stand on a barnacled rock, sometimes hearing his heart, still mostly glad he'd left the city, the bad kaleidoscope of people. It was easier here. At his feet, a simple current kept seaweed flattened to a rock. A stone's throw out, the sleek black dome of a seal's head. Then he'd be bored and walk back. He always had a book going, and industrial headphones for the bunkhouse noise.

The only real work happened by itself, in the salmon pens, under water. Arnie swore he could feel the fish down there, barely finning as they digested their food and swelled heavier with milt or eggs. Doing their job. They had no eyelids, and it was funny thinking of them down there big eyed in the darkness.

That was camp, and that was his life, until Kiint came to wreck things.

He arrived in the drizzle of late May, a newbie stepping off the water taxi with two other guys back from their days-off. He was medium height and thin. "Nondescript," would be the word. From the way he didn't pause on the dock to gaze up at his new home you could tell he knew this country. It wasn't just Arnie watching from the bunkhouse; only nine guys lived here at any one time and a new face in camp was news. Soon he'd be shoving food into his face across from you. Five feet from your head his nostril might whistle all night. You might get to know the smell of his towel.

He ate a prepackaged sandwich alone at the corner table, and they let him because he could have come to them. From his efficient chewing and the way he gazed at something far off but definite, Arnie saw he was different. Who knows why but he thought of a fox waiting in a den of mice. "Sated," for now.

When the guy finished and sat sipping coffee, Arnie wandered over. Arnie was both the biggest and the oldest here, forty-five to their twenty-five, which is maybe why he did the Walmart greeter thing. Or maybe he still wanted to think loneliness was a simple fix. The newbie's hair was oily and he looked tired. He was on the frail side for general labour, resembling more the pencil-neck university type who dipped test tubes in the pens or syringed juice from a salmon. But he was dressed in shit so general labour he must be. Arnie could swear guys wore the dirtiest crap on purpose, as if to show how hard they worked. If these camp guys paused at a downtown corner, people would drop change at their feet.

He shook Arnie's hand limply, but Arnie knew that meant nothing. When he said his odd name it brought to mind another guy here, a First Nations fellow who intro- duced himself as "B. Paul," leading to confusion he never cared to correct:

"Bee *Pall?*"

"Pleased to meet you."

"That's an odd name."

"No it's not."

Quizzical looks gained nothing and only later would you learn his name was Bob. Arnie didn't know if Bob found dignity using an initial or if he was just pissing off another white guy. He'd always been alert to names, because growing up a Bacon wasn't fun. He always wanted people to think of the actor Kevin, or even Sir Francis, who might have been Shakespeare, but everyone just thought of bacon, and in his school years he answered to Pig. When by some huge fluke he was the first in his crowd to get laid, for a while he was happy being called Makin'.

Introducing himself, the new guy had a faint accent, maybe German. Arnie predicted correctly to himself the jokes that would be made about him being a Norwegian spy. Every operation along the coast was Norwegian owned, so all new guys were of course Norwegian company spies.

The spy said his name was 'Sint.' Arnie saw that he wasn't drinking coffee. The tea bag was red, and you could smell its herbal sourness.

"'Sint?'"

"Yes."

"That's it?"

"That's it." Now he looked up. "Like Madonna."

Arnie asked him to spell it and he did.

"No way. A 'K?'"

"That's right." He was falsely smiling now.

"But can a K be, you know, an S?"

"The two 'I's do it." He held Arnie's gaze. His eyes were the light blue that feels too active. He was barely willing to be liked. "That kind of hard," Kiint said, "can't take that much soft."

Arnie waited a bit, but that was that and it was his turn. He got Kiint to smile for real at "Arnold Bacon." He said his folks were from the old country and couldn't have known what names might be hilarious in a new one.

Kiint asked, "Do you think you ended up here because of your hilarious name?"

Out here meant two grey buildings in a clearing hacked into the trees thirty-nine miles by boat from a wifi signal, flush toilet, or woman. For basically minimum wage. It was a job any guy could get. Arnie snorted at the question but wondered if it was five-percent true. It didn't bug him that Kiint might be right. It bugged him that this newbie thought he could know, in one minute, something about him that he didn't know himself. He was about to say, You probably *chose* your Eurofag name so fuck off and die—but he took a breath instead, an infantile temper being one of the actual reasons he was here.

A finger tapped his shoulder. It was Clarke, the super.

"Arnie? Since you're already sort of doing it, show him around."

It was a bit of a rebuke since he should have been outside brushing down E- pen ten minutes ago. Clarke told Kiint to come by his office when they were done. The office was a closet where timesheets were kept, but Clarke liked saying "my office." It wasn't easy being bossed by a guy twenty years younger than you.

In the mudroom they donned rain gear. Kiint shrugged off the offer of a spare floppy hat in favour of his own weird little cap, and as they walked past the land tanks and out the ramp to the first floating pen the wind hit and Arnie could see him pretend not to feel the cold drips down his back. The rain came so hard Arnie had to shout the age and size of the stock. Shouting that there were females topping a hundred pounds over there in D-pen, he was surprised to feel his pride. Shoulders up and stiffly listening, Kiint had no reaction to any of it.

Then they stood in the nice quiet of the feedhouse with the various pellet bins along all four walls. It smelled like ripe pet food and gave off a red dust that was hard to breathe. Centering the room was a computer station covered with plastic sheeting, which Arnie grabbed up to flap like a bedsheet and get the dust off. He'd heard it was red dye to turn their flesh salmon colored, which made sense. He watched Kiint take it all in.

Arnie took him through all the programs. He was mostly just avoiding work, but guys liked to hear about stuff. It was impressive gear. They had the new compressed air system where a computer key chose what food to blow down what pipe to what pen, where a carousel sprayer, like a robot spinning to feed a thousand pigeons at once, showered the water with pellets until the fish lost interest. Too much feed would sink through the fish and out the pen and be lost, like dimes through your fingers. Kiint stood patiently while Arnie scrolled through the codes that troubleshot clogs and spills. Arnie joked about salmon gluttons that fought their way up the dry pipes to gorge here in the bins, and Kiint either wasn't listening or didn't find it funny.

"Wanna see the morts?" You could smell the mort bins from anywhere. Morts were dead salmon and they were knee deep in them even here at a brood farm. At the market farms it was way more. Guys pretended the deformities were entertaining—fish with shoulders, or plaguey bumps, "buboes" was the word, which B. Paul called boobs. Some fish were skinny, little more than swimming spines that somehow stayed sort of alive. You didn't go out of your way to look at them. And it was nice to know they were working on that stuff, looking for answers. Fish farms really could maybe someday feed the world.

Before Kiint could answer, they jumped to the roar of a shotgun, not twenty feet from the door. Scare the newbie. Ha ha.

"That would be MacLeod," Arnie said. "He just fed a crow to the crabs." His heart was still going. "A headless crow." He looked out the window, but couldn't see MacLeod. "Or crowless head."

"Scared me," Kiint admitted. Rocking faintly, he gazed into neutral territory.

The fact was, guys killed birds. Next to video games it was the main fun. But only the noisy ones, the crows and gulls. A shotgun got used rarely because it made gulls disappear and not dribble back for a week. Guys got expert at slingshots. He once saw guys have a go with a paintball gun, hitting only the odd bird but screaming like little kids when they did, the gull flopping there, splotched yellow or blue. He saw guys invent DaVinci-like machines, and even for a non-birdkiller it was cool to watch an innocent-looking net fly down as hidden weights released, taking to the sea floor twenty gulls stupid enough to swarm a pile of morts magically served up to them.

Kiint didn't want to see the mort bins. He put his cap back on like they were done here, and fair enough, they pretty much were. Arnie reset the computer and yanked the plastic sheet back over.

"You have any questions about anything?"

Kiint looked around as if for a piece of gear he hadn't understood. "No."

It was strange that Kiint didn't ask a single question about the place. Not one. Newbies loved hearing about stuff. The predator cage, steel mesh that kept seals, whales, otters and sharks away from the soft-mesh pens, and how some, seals mostly, got stuck and drowned trying to get through. Or the bubble curtain that kept toxic plankton out. Or how algae and fish shit clogged the mesh so fast that each pen needed oxygen diffusers bubbling away down there at all times or the fish would suffocate. A fish farm was like a giant dirty aquarium.

"So this your first farm, or—?"

"Bella Bella."

"Didn't that one shut down because of the—?"

"They cleaned it up, they said. Now it's expanding."

"Really." The politics of aquaculture were beyond him.

Before leaving, Arnie opened the antibiotics closet to show him the arsenal and Kiint didn't even look—in fact he thought he saw him shudder. Arnie understood how, for some people, even fish disease might feel like their own.

Back in the rain, slogging up to the bunkhouse, Arnie was moved to shout a last fact, one Kiint probably knew.

"So this is one of five brood sites on the west coast of North America. All the salmon, for all other farms, for restaurants, groceries, everything—it starts right here."

Kiint said, "Cool."

Arnie wanted to yell that here was better than the market sites. All that butchering, all those morts. Humping all that bad meat to the bins, to be barged away under a spiky bonnet of screaming birds and dumped who knows where. Here there was less of that. Here it was all eggs and milt and helping a million silver darters grow.

Arnie did yell, "It's okay here."

At the bunkhouse door they smelled weed. Arnie turned.

"You know it's a dry camp, right?" He tried to say it in a non-revealing way. When the time was right Arnie might tell him he sought out dry camps for a reason.

"Yes."

"So everyone compensates by being high all the time. Everyone except me." He added, "Especially weekends." It was hilarious that even out here and in a job with no weekends they still used weekends as an excuse. They had a giant carved octopus hookah they called Mr Saturday Night.

He showed Kiint the showers and DVD players and what-not, and now Kiint was smiling sideways at him because, sure, anyone with a brain could figure out this stuff for themselves and, sure, he was taking work avoidance too far. But he still found it strange that Kiint didn't have a single question about the place. Simple ones, like, Does it always rain like this here? Or, How do you claim fridge territory or dib the stove? Or, especially, This is grizz country, right?

Kiint did pause to scan the books stacked in three towers beside Arnie's bed. Except for Bob Paul, who tackled an occasional thriller, he was the only one who read. And he was proud of it, though no one gave him reason to be. If anything they found it uppity. Kiint's eyes caught on several titles but Arnie couldn't tell which. His taste was eclectic and his aim was to educate himself. He saw he'd left in plain view his notebook for jotting his new words, and if Kiint bent to touch it he would get his hand stomped.

But Kiint wasn't curious and still had no questions. Now Clarke was in Arnie's face and hooked his thumb at the general outdoors, wordlessly ordering him back to work, wise enough to smile as he did so.

Kiint said an obligatory thank you and met Arnie's eyes for the second time that day. It felt like an icy insult. Kiint didn't exactly look through him. He saw him as part of the problem.

Arnie had no real suspicions until Labour Day itself, when Kiint went into action. Maybe he did have suspicions, but they were of the vaguest kind. One was Kiint's early request to stay onsite and work the Labour Day weekend, which besides Christmas was the one time the place all but shut down, only a barest skeleton crew staying on to make sure the stock got fed. When Arnie heard of Kiint's request, his eyebrows went up; it was the kind of request he made himself. Some people like to avoid holidays and go into hiding. In any case, it would be just him and Kiint working Labour Day.

There was also the way Kiint wouldn't talk about fish farms. He just wouldn't. Later it was funny for Arnie to recall telling Kiint the nasty secret that their salmon might be iffy, and that in fact one grocery chain was going to stop selling it, and Kiint, eyebrows up, saying, "Really?" And the time Kiint said "Yikes" when Arnie told him he'd read some-where about mercury in the feed.

There were other small clues. As when Kiint came back from his first days off with a wet suit, and the next time a scuba tank, but then never used any of it. Also the lack of an air compressor was stupid, because it would limit Kiint to a single dive. But Arnie figured Kiint wasn't getting around to it in the same way the rest of them weren't getting around to trap prawns or invent bird machines and ended up smok-ing weed and playing vids instead. Arnie would glance up from his book and watch them slumped there, bodies rigid only in the arms, faces an ugly blend of tense and dead, stabbing and jerking their controllers like what was left of their zombie lives depended on it. It made him think of, "Boredom is rage spread thin," from one of his quotation books. Sometimes they did go on hikes, but only after lots of "cajoling," and only in groups, shouting and singing to warn bears of their approach.

Kiint hiked by himself. He had been onsite a month when Arnie followed him. Not followed, exactly. The mountainside was impassable with underbrush and there was only one path, so he couldn't help it. Ten minutes out of camp he emerged from the dark tunnel of forest onto a mossy rock knoll and stumbled on Kiint just sitting there, cross-legged, some sort of yoga thing. Kiint looked irked to see him. Arnie said sorry and spun and turned back, which of course made it worse, and he thought he heard Kiint sigh. He felt like some sort of creeper, which is probably what he looked like. After a minute he heard, "Bacon." He stopped and turned and Kiint trotted up.

"Starting to rain," he said, short of breath, explaining himself.

"It is."

"You ever see Spirit Bears up here?" he asked.

"They aren't in Toba. They start next inlet up." Arnie waited. "There's grizzlies here, though."

Kiint shook his head. "No no no, they're here. I was just wondering if you've seen any." He glanced at Arnie, the brief ice of those eyes.

"Nope."

"The grizz will show up in about a month, right? At the river mouths? For the *salmon*?" Kiint snorted quietly. He might as well have said "for the real ones," this sort of sarcasm the closest he ever got to humour.

They walked. Arnie was angry-quiet because Kiint was walking with him like he was doing some loser a favour. Arnie had his own brand of humour and he asked Kiint if he was Norwegian. Kiint smiled but probably just thought this Canadian was stupid about accents. He said he was from Holland but he had lived all over, most recently New Zealand.

And so they became friends. Or "friends." Arnie knew it was more a case of two soloists falling warily into each other's orbit.

It wasn't like they didn't know there was something wrong with this business they were in, and days off be accosted in some bar by a health-foodie or commercial fisherman accusing them of sins against the world. Arnie used to live in these bars, he knew what yelled beer-spit looked like when it flew out a mouth a foot from your face. You know your farm spreads disease and kills wild runs? What idiot works for minimum and the profits go to Norway? Why you raising Atlantic salmon in the Pacific? Don't you know they're escaping, they're spawning wild, they're taking over?

This last one was definitely wrong and the guys knew it. If one of their fish blundered out a hole it wouldn't have a chance in the real ocean, let alone muscle miles upstream, get laid in the gravel and reproduce itself. The slobs in their pens were barely fish. If you had any doubts, troll up a fall coho and battle a twelve-pound silver bullet hard as a sprinter's thigh.

But so what? Arnie had imaginary arguments with Kiint even now. He considered writing him in jail. Fish farms might still feed the world. There were way worse jobs and way bigger sins. It was a *job*. Teachers keep teaching even though most kids don't learn a thing. The landfill is overflowing but garbagemen do their rounds. Are the workers part of the problem? It's a debate worth having, Kiint. Not that he ever said an accusing word. But Arnie had seen that look, more than once, saying he should know better.

When Arnie first got there he actually thought he was doing something good. And he hadn't done much of that, historically. Proof of this lay mostly in what wasn't: No friends, no family. No skills he could bank on. No credit rating. He wasn't even allowed a passport. He had told Kiint enough of this to imply that he was in Toba Inlet not just because his name was Arnold Bacon.

Anyway, after, the more he thought about it, the more he thought that Kiint had been only obvious. It was strange that more guys didn't suspect him. Or maybe they did, and just didn't care. Or forgot. Or were pleasantly puzzled by whatever unfolded. Weed could do all that.

Everyone worked ten days then waited for the aluminum taxi to come and roar them through waves and rain to five days of real life in Campbell River. The boat's arrival back was a spectator sport because guys climbing out told a story. Knowing he was watched from the bunkhouse, a guy might grab his crotch and hunch, feigning the rawness from epic screwing. Or mime a fatal headache, the epic drinking. Arnie saw guys wave bulbous bags of weed, hump the new porno vids in their backpack, wield a Canucks-signed hockey stick and fake slap-shots out to sea, or wave a chub of venison pepperoni they intended to auction. Mostly it was that: meat. They'd hoist heavy coolers onto the dock, give a thumbs up to say they filled the orders for chops and steaks and burger.

Except for Kiint. Unloading his cloth bags of salad and quinoa and whatever, he might flash a salute to their equally ironic hoots. He wasn't liked. Which was fine by him. They ignored him and he ignored them back. The point is, he was a card-carrying vegetarian. More than that, he was vegan— what sort of vegan worked for minimum at a meat farm? A *tainted* meat farm?

His oddities seem glaring now. He just didn't belong. He was a visitor from a wider world. He knew things no one else did. Things about this place. Things about them.

On one of their hikes together Arnie learned something about what Kiint knew. From the start they had wordlessly agreed to walk in silence, with only functional talking—Was that a marten? You sure that's a morel? This walk had begun in sunshine, now it began to pour, and Arnie had had enough.

He stomped and shouted in rhythm with his feet, "Fuck, fuck, fuck, *rain.*"

"No!" Kiint said. He stopped and he grabbed Arnie's shoulder. Eyes crinkled up in pleasure, Kiint yelled, "It's *rain*forest!" He laughed shaking his head, like they were in the arctic and Arnie had just complained about the snow.

"I guess."

"No! It's a *treasure!*" He put his head back, arms out like Jesus on the cross, and let the rain fall into his eyes.

As they walked on, Kiint described where it was they were. He was "sanctimonious" but Arnie let him vent. Pointing at the mud on the path he said they were at the southernmost edge of the largest temperate rainforest left on the planet. Almost chanting, he detailed how much it rained, why it rained, how that tied in with ocean currents, how it all might change and how the change might be gradual or "silent-spring sudden." There was still hope if governments were made to work together. It all came flying out as if under pressure. He described how the rain—*this* rain, he said, and he rolled his face under it to make sure every inch was anointed— created the icepack, which fed the rivers, which bore the tiny salmon out to sea. He spoke of a tightly knit drama. At one point he shrieked a single note of incredulous joy, describing something Arnie thought he'd heard before, which was that the sheer quantity of salmon dragged off by bears and eagles and wolves had over millennia fertilized the trees hundreds of meters up either side of the riverbanks, and today salmon was in the trees' DNA.

A minute after he'd finished talking and Arnie had said nothing to fill the gap, Kiint said, "I'm sorry."

"That's okay." He was stunned to hear a silent man talk in paragraphs.

"I love this place," Kiint added, unnecessarily.

This love might have been enough reason for this guy to be here, but Arnie sensed there was more.

In the bunkhouse, keeping mum, Kiint had managed to become a piece of furniture. He'd been onsite two months and it was another month till Labour Day. One evening a young guy, Kenny, was frying up some salmon he'd scooped from B-pen. It was verboten to steal stock, but if guys were too spaced out to get their meat order together, there it was swimming right outside the door. Clarke wouldn't do anything, since one salmon was so much less than a drop in the bucket.

As it sizzled, poking and worrying it non-stop with the spatula, Kenny asked no one in particular, "So when's this shit safe?"

He meant when were the antibiotics flushed out. The medfeed had ceased in B-pen months ago, and a few guys mumbled that it was okay. Bobby Paul joked that Kenny should go ahead and eat it and cure the gonorrhea he probably had.

This kind of talk was always floating around. So who knows why, but that night Kiint, quietly munching on his bowl of roots and fronds, lost it. He dropped his fork on the table. His hand hovered over it, his eyes closed.

"It's never *okay*."

No one said anything. Kiint didn't deserve a response. They were going to let it pass but Kiint wasn't. He actually smacked the table with his palm. You could hear the spice of his accent climb into the rest of what he said.

"The antibiotics are gone, Kenny." He waved his arm in the direction of the water. "The antibiotics are now in the crabs and shrimp and sea urchins. What's still in your piece of shit is mercury, lead, and dioxins. The Ruhr Valley is in your piece of shit." Shaking his head, he grabbed his fork and stabbed his greens. "Enjoy, Kenny."

It was Clarke who laughed, and then sang, "Whaaaat?"

Others were laughing too and Bobby Paul asked Kenny if he knew there was a valley in his dinner. Kiint ate quicker, wanting to get out of there. Clarke waved an arm at the same water and in the same way Kiint had, mocking him, and proclaimed there was no way any of that crap was in the air up here in Toba Inlet.

Kiint put down his fork down gently. "Where does the feed come from?" he asked.

"The big blue barge?" said Bobby Paul, who hadn't stopped grinning.

Kiint said it came from Norway. AquaCo bought it from themselves so they didn't have to pay taxes on it, but our country being stupid was beside the point, the point was that the feed was from North Sea plankton and fish waste that had absorbed "the air-borne hell of industrial Europe." In a gesture as theatrical as it was bizarre, Kiint pointed at Kenny's sizzling fish and listed off Mercedes Benz, IKEA, Volkswagon (saying the W like a V) and ten other companies no one had heard of. A guy playing video games yelled at Kiint to go back to fucking Norway if he didn't like it here, and Clarke shouted back that it was Norway Kiint appeared to be mad at.

Clarke added, "Well what the fuck." He seemed to think that, as boss, it was his job to win this argument, if that's what this was.

"No one's making you work here, right?"

Kiint appeared to come to his senses. "No," he said quickly. "I'm sorry." Then, "Eat your fish. It's good fish."

Emboldened, pulling on his coat, Clarke added, "Keep it to yourself for fuck sake. This place is bad enough without *your* shit in the air." He made a show of almost slamming the door. Being the boss, he pretended he didn't smoke weed by always going outside to smoke it.

Kiint wolfed his bowl. He looked angry, but Arnie wondered if he didn't also look afraid. Arnie was waiting but Kiint didn't look his way. If he had, he might have seen that Arnie knew something was up. There was just no way a guy like him was here by accident.

In the remaining weeks leading up to Labour Day Kiint kept his distance from Arnie, other than a few silent walks, and even then it seemed he was being careful not to show how much he loved the inlet, or the rainforest. When he returned the two Farley Mowatt books he'd borrowed he wouldn't even say if he liked them or not when Arnie asked. Arnie had to admit that he was a little hurt to be lumped in with the rest of them. It was difficult to admit to wisdom in a man so much younger, but Arnie did. Kiint hinted at a vaster, more intelligent world, one that Arnie had apparently let slip by. Something he saw in Kiint made him regret the puniness of what he'd chosen for himself. So it hurt to be shut out like that.

On what turned out to be their last walk, a week before Labour Day, when they stopped at the apex of Bald Head Rock and finished catching their breath and taking in the vista, Arnie was angry at the silence, angry at being shut out. One thing about fish-farm life was that he didn't get angry much, so when he did, it was easy to see it. And now he was angry that he was angry.

"Why are you doing this?" he asked. It sounded corny, like something a lover would say, so he hated himself now too and was about to stomp back down the trail.

Kiint turned to face him. Arnie sensed he was being read. But Kiint must have read him wrong because he answered a different question than the one Arnie asked.

"It's just a job. Right, Bacon?"

"Right," Arnie said, not knowing what he was agreeing to.

The Friday of Labour Day weekend, at low tide Arnie trudged the rocks to his Robinson Crusoe spot. It had been a year since he'd bothered coming out here. He stood and breathed. He held his breath and tried to hear his heart. Then didn't care if he heard his heart or not. He was surprised by his restlessness. He couldn't settle. Maybe it was the looming fall. Fall was when you started school again, and hockey. It was the time to stop screwing around, stop partying, time to get in shape, start projects. Arnie could feel the outside world beyond these mountains—big and busy, rumbling, buzzing, working, and though he hadn't forgotten that it was mostly bullshit, there was something out there he was missing. His life was easily half over and he had to admit he'd blown this half, first with trouble and then with hiding. He wasn't sure how but it was Kiint who had prodded him, who had lit this fire. Kiint who had checked him out and decided he wasn't worthy, lying here reading stupid books.

He scanned Toba Inlet. Its water, mountains and muffled sky were so familiar that he could be standing anywhere. He unzipped and pissed into the calm water at his feet. A slow and ignorant current moved the foam to the left. A crab the size of his thumbnail crawled back under its rock. Arnie laughed at himself, more sad than angry. No good book was pulling him back to the bunkhouse. For whatever reason, he didn't like fiction anymore. And he understood he'd been restless for years.

And that afternoon, not a minute after the water taxi picked up the crew and disappeared around the point,

Kiint destroyed the camp radio with a hammer. This was so nobody—that is, Arnie—could call for help, or whoever it was you called when the guy you were stuck with in camp methodically began smashing the equipment to pieces and burning everything else to the ground. Arnie liked to think Kiint did the radio first not because he thought Arnie would call, but because he knew Arnie would get into trouble for not calling. Arnie still wasn't sure if he would have called or not.

The following week, in whatever newspapers he could buy in Campbell River, Arnie read all he could about it and he learned Kiint's real name. All five brood sites on the Pacific coast were attacked that Labour Day Friday. One of the five "eco-terrorists," Andres Vandover, hailed from Amsterdam, so that had to be him. One was a New Zealander and another an actual Norwegian, which Arnie found funny because that made him a kind of double agent, and you could only imagine the weird ironies he'd endured, the bunkhouse jokes about Norwegian spies. The other two were women, a Canadian and a Brazilian, and how they got hired on he could only guess. They were at the sites further north and maybe they were more progressive up there.

There was mention of a "manifesto" that authorities weren't making public, in the spirit of not dealing with terrorists. Nor did the authorities reveal much else, since court cases were pending, and the news stories were littered with the word "alleged." The attacks were coordinated, but why terrorists would target fish farms was still a mystery. So ignorant and unclear were the stories that Arnie wanted to call and tell them that the only reason to attack just brood sites was to destroy how the salmon farm industry replenished itself. There was no other reason—it was appalling that they couldn't decide on even that much. Also, they said his site was located in Toba Strait, there being no such place. There were comma errors too, and more than one wrong "it's." Journalism had really gone downhill, and it was all the more obvious when you knew some of the truth of things yourself.

The reports said damage to the Toba Inlet site was the most severe. So Kiint had done the best job. The New Zealander had managed only some computer system damage, "fish mortality was minimal," and he got badly beaten up by the skeleton crew. (Arnie tried to picture the guys jumping on Kiint, and it was easy.) The other three sites were badly damaged but would "in all likelihood be made operational again." Toba could not.

In the manner of today's media they were dubbed the Fish Farm Five, another piss off, because somehow it cheapened what they did, and tried to cheapen the regard Arnie had for Kiint, for Andres Vandover, though Arnie wouldn't let it.

It had been truly amazing to watch this young guy work so hard, and nothing selfish about it. Because whatever Kiint believed—was he protecting the environment? Protecting the world from bad food? Chipping away at capitalism?—it was for others that he did it. This is what Arnie couldn't get over. In the outside world there were people like this. Sometimes they found their way up Toba Inlet.

Watching Kiint hustling to finish the job before they came and put a boot on his neck and took him away, Arnie wondered what Kiint's damn hurry was, he had all weekend. But unlike Kiint he didn't know about the other four attacks underway or that Kiint knew they would be putting two and two together soon and sending in the troops. As it turned out the cop boat didn't arrive up Toba until dawn. Followed by the coast guard—Arnie was surprised those guys were allowed to carry guns— and then, he couldn't believe his eyes at the overkill, a hovercraft. It was when they were putting the cuffs on Kiint that Arnie rethought the selflessness business. He was standing well away, in the first line of trees, pretending to be afraid, going with Kiint's advice to avoid resembling a friend. But the look in Kiint's eyes, amazing. He didn't know what to call it. It wasn't selfless. Kiint was just absolutely proud and loving everything he'd done, he was loving the cuffs, he loved that cop's shove, and he was loving it all so much that it had to, it just had to be selfish. It was a feeling Arnie recognized and wanted. He had no word for it yet.

He had run to the noise of Kiint smashing the radio, and hammer in hand Kiint came striding out the bunkhouse door, saw Arnie coming, and flashed a palm.

"Bacon, stay out of my way."

Kiint broke into a trot up the path to the generator hut, bouncing the hammer, testing its weight for a job bigger than the radio.

Arnie stayed out of his way. But he was thrilled and he had to move so he got himself away from there, and once up the trail and into the trees he couldn't hear anything from camp. It took only a half hour to get up to Bald Head Rock and when he reached the clearing, breathing so hard he brought his hand to his heart, he stood agape at the mushroom of black and brown smoke tumbling up from where he'd come. In this vista of giant things—mountains, ocean, sky—the smoke was a new creature that held its own. Arnie stayed up there as long as he could stand it. He wasn't scared of Kiint at all. Something spectacular was going on and he was missing it. He set off back, finding it hard not to run, enjoying the luxury and speed of the downhill stride. He did wonder if there'd be anywhere to sleep tonight.

He didn't know why he chose "Waltzing Matilda" but he broke into song when he emerged from the woods, not wanting to surprise him. But Kiint wasn't there and Arnie felt foolish and hoped he wasn't being watched from the woods. The feedhouse and generator shack were off the peak of their flames and were two collapsed heaps of hissing orange embers and metal, heat mirage throbbing over them. A grand old cedar next to the feedhouse was scorched halfway up its length. The feed bins were still releasing an odd smoke, the hint of black suggesting the gasoline poured in to help things out.

Arnie yelled, "Hey *Kiint*. What's *up*?"

Nobody answered, and Arnie could hear that silence behind the embers' hissing. It was that intense calm of aftermath, that stillness of a morning house that had been violated in the night. Kiint's absence was a presence.

He would tell Kiint to get over it, he was going to help. Or watch. Arnie didn't know what he wanted. But he was a lot bigger than Kiint, if it came to that. Arnie was still happy with this most basic of laws.

The sun was behind the mountain now and in the blue dim he walked past the dryland pens and, in their thousands, all the tiny fish were belly up. The pump was dead but they wouldn't have suffocated this quickly—he must have thrown some kind of poison in. Who knows what else Kiint packed in those bags of salad? The odd light helped make it stranger still, the tiny luminous pearl bellies forming an unbroken floating layer, a carpet of identical glowing shapes. "Tessellated."

He ventured out on the ramp to the pens, flanked on either side by still, deep water. Maybe Kiint had made a run for it. Maybe he'd stashed a kayak and supplies somewhere, though how he'd done that in this fishbowl was anybody's guess.

He walked the ramp to its limit, to D-pen, where the big ones were. With the bubble curtain off it was more quiet than ever, so quiet he stood still and tried to hear his heart. He couldn't. He thought he could feel the monsters under his feet, down deep, the hundred-plus pounders. On the east coast they used to grow that big in the wild and he'd seen grainy black-and-whites of rich Americans on guided trips standing beside their tail-hung trophies. As big as the ones below his feet. He stood over the black water, feeling the unseen gliding shapes, swollen with eggs and milt, bursting with so much future life. It was almost fall and they were ripening with the one thing they existed for.

Certain he could feel the immense parents gliding beneath him, something felt off. He could feel it. They felt badly alive. It tipped his guts. It was like seeing a turd on your mother's head. It was like a warm worm turning in your ear. Dumb giants bumping into each other down there. The giants had been brought here, from a foreign ocean, so we could grow and eat their sick babies.

The bubble curtain was off but he could hear a faint bubbling. Then he saw it, a green light, deep underwater, moving slowly. There was a moment when it might have been a sea monster, a demon, and then he knew it was an underwater lamp he hadn't seen Kiint unload. And there, scuba bubbles breaking the surface out along the rim of D-pen, slowly burbling his way.

He laughed, he hooted, he stomped his boot then caught himself. Kiint must be down there taking care of the oxygenators, so they couldn't be repaired. He had really thought things through.

That light, that little green light far below. It was like a quiet, tiny invasion from another planet, it was brilliant unlike anything else around here.

The bunkhouse had been left intact. Arnie went in and stood in the middle of it, in the coolness in front of the blank TV, and it all felt new and different. He couldn't stand still. There was no longer electricity but he knew of a propane campstove out back. It was unlikely that any of the guys would be returning now but he felt the thrill of theft as he helped himself to their food. He unwrapped the rest of Clarke's venison jerky and gnawed on it as he worked. He primed the campstove, lit it and fried up two burger patties, one of them Kiint's nutblend kind, which didn't smell half-bad as it cooked, and he built up two Mexiburgers, being mindful of melting no cheese on Kiint's. He toasted the buns on the blue propane flame, then plated them up surrounded by a decent salad. His he deposited on the table.

Arnie draped a white towel over his forearm to lighten the mood and walked Kiint's down to him, but stood off a ways to let him finish hacksawing the metal feed pipe. He was barefoot and had his wetsuit top off, but still wore the black pants. He grabbed a sledge to mangle the freed piece so it couldn't just be welded back on.

Arnie called his name from twenty feet away. Kiint turned bug-eyed, exhausted, head hanging forward off his neck. He gave Arnie a good stare before nodding that, yes, he wanted the food.

He took it and said only, "Don't tell them you did this." He waggled the burger.

"It's cool." Arnie unfolded the chair he'd dragged over and Kiint sat down with a gasp.

"Don't tell them we talked at all."

"Not to worry."

He wolfed his burger after first checking its contents. He smelled of extreme sweat, fish, and wetsuit rubber. As he chewed he quickly surveyed the damage he'd done, and what he had yet to do.

He seemed to remember Arnie standing there.

"Bacon. You have to leave." Kiint looked at him philosophically. "It goes bad for you if they know you didn't try to stop me." He nodded with a new thought. "And they think we're friends." He stood and thrust the plate at back to him, salad untouched. "Thank you, but."

Arnie hesitated taking it. When he did, he said, "Hey, I can help."

Kiint turned away, put the palm up again. "Don't joke about it."

"Who says I'm joking?" Arnie said, regretting it because it sounded whiny. And he had just understood what Kiint had said. They *think* we're friends. Kiint ignored him again, trudging off toward the ramps wagging his finger in the air, remembering something.

In the bunkhouse Arnie pulled someone's blanket over his legs and sat down to a solitary dinner, while starting Ken Kesey's *Demon Box*, apparently an unfinished novel plus other stuff he didn't publish before he died. The blanket smelled harshly of somebody's deodorant. The book wasn't that good and Arnie was bored by it. Fiction. And it was getting dark to read. He tried a flashlight for exactly five seconds before he threw *Demon Box* in one direction and the flashlight in the other, making a fantastic wobbling strobe in the room before it crashed through the window and fell out into the dark.

And then down from the ramps the clang of a hammer, the sound of which still made Arnie's heart race. He wondered where it was he should go, and if a city, what city it might be, and now Kiint's hammer sounded comical, a puny *tink tink tink* in the face of a world of steel and cement and big government. Arnie started to laugh, bouncing in his seat, mouth full of burger, ready to help take it on.

NEVER PROSPER

LIZ HARMER

One day, when Paul was practicing at one of the seven grand pianos in their winter home, the Palais Wittgenstein, he leaped up and shouted at his brother Ludwig in the room next door, "I cannot play when you are in the house, as I feel your skepticism seeping towards me from under the door."
　　　　　—from Anthony Gottlieb's "A Nervous Splendor"

O F COURSE there was no end to the cheaters. Evie prepared for the meeting by looking over the essay, which was so poorly cut-and-pasted that it contained several different font styles and sizes, and then the final sentence just ran off a cliff, no period, no final payoff to the opening promise: *After all it is clear that Wittgenstein believed.* She had now read the paper more times than it deserved, though it did have a strange beauty. *We have so far said nothing whatever*: a direct quote from the text itself but unattributed as such. Still, it was incredibly to the point.

She knew the name but not the face of the student who had produced such a mess. She had interacted with Steven Vandersteen only via email, emails that were also syntactically odd and sometimes even offensive in their illiteracy. *Be there at 3*, he had written, and despite the strange command of its phrasing, its keenness to keep her in this office chair, waiting, she knew that he really meant that *he* would be there at 3. She was sure she had never seen him. She knew the names of the twenty-seven who bothered to attend class regularly, and she knew the faces of those who never showed but sometimes came to her office hours as though their smiling manoeuvrings would earn them the grade they wanted. Steven Vandersteen, whose name had a performative quality as though invented for the sake of sound, belonged to a third category.

Teaching was a useless activity. Like torture as an interrogation technique it did not produce the effect it was meant to. Torture never delivered the truth, and teaching never delivered knowledge, regardless of methodology. Evie's disillusionment was nearly complete. *I am receiving a salary*, she told herself. *I have an office and prestige.* Meanwhile the students received the grades they needed, learning nothing. Only those already inclined to understand something did. She swivelled in the chair she'd picked out in the office furniture catalogue in a swell of optimism in August, and looked out at the few bobbing palm leaves along the parking lot. She hated palm trees now more than ever.

Cheating did not give her hives, but she was required to investigate and perhaps to punish those who plagiarized or stole. As someone who had never cheated—who had not even taken a shortcut or skimmed a book!—Evie had the illogical intuition that the principles of order in the universe would justly punish such people with or without her intervention.

It was ten after three. Steven Vandersteen was late. She left all the windows on her monitor open, each of her papers an attempt to untwist an elaborate knot, like a cop in those detective shows pinning up photos and strings to connect them on a board. Instead of working, though, she logged in to Facebook, where she saw that Natasha had just posted a few photos of herself in Queen's Park, and near Robarts Library, and in front of the Humanities building. Toronto with its trees flaming into colour and the olive green scarf Natasha wore loosely over her sweater were autumnal, and homesickness pricked Evie. She clicked *like* on the photos— they weren't selfies but there was no word on her companion—and then messaged Natasha: *Since when are you in TO?* Natasha seemed to be logged in but did not respond.

Natasha was the only one Evie could talk to about Tom. Evie had known him now for twelve years, since the Philosophy of Language class they'd both taken. He'd criticized her after the first session for nodding too much. "Your nodding does nothing to humanize you," he'd said outside the building in a drizzle, with a cigarette pinned to his mouth. His squint had a James Dean quality, but Evie thought she was immune to this, never having cared for James Dean. She blushed. Her nodding during class was a private movement cruelly exposed. To seem unperturbed she bummed a cigarette and smoked with him in the rain.

Later she discovered that she was exactly his type: straight blond hair, the body of a high-school athlete. He liked to make women blush; the other philosophy majors knew him well. The professor in that class, an eccentric whose glasses would often fly off his face by the force of his gesticulations, adored Tom. Tom got the only easy As in the class, drinking all night and then tossing off essays a few hours before class began in the dim lamplight of his dorm room desk, on a typewriter that he used instead of the computer labs like everybody else. Tom and that professor—Dr. de France—had a Wittgenstein/Russell dynamic. Bertrand Russell had once said of Wittgenstein admiringly that he was "destitute of the false politeness that interferes with truth."

For all her perky nodding, Evie really had to work in that class. Her notes included the sentences of encoded formal logic that Dr. de France scribbled on the chalkboard, muttering that the students wouldn't understand these but really they ought to be able to, and she sat there writing until her wrist hurt, hating de France and Tom both. Her ambition was as big as theirs was, but her naivety disguised her. That she liked Gottlieb Frege for asking the question they were all thinking: What is a number anyway? That she liked the verve of a philosopher called Quine who said that if we see a person pointing at a rabbit and saying "gavagai," we don't know if "gavagai" means "rabbit" or "undetached rabbit part" or "timeslice of a rabbit," and to assume that their language disclosed the same conceptual scheme would be shameful, despite the silliness of the example. By then, she had become utterly conscious of her every movement in the class (Tom sat two rows over and one back, and she felt the heat of his looking at her on the back of her neck), and soon afterwards she was sleepless in his bunk listening to the anachronistic type-tapping of his genius through the night, the dings and rolling, the chatter of keys a soundtrack so particular to their romance that whenever she heard it she rushed with feeling for him, like a person accused of nodding stupidly.

Her only contact with him was now on Facebook or over text. Men believed themselves to be unsentimental, but they were the worst of all. Sometimes he would text her, just: *the present king of France is bald*. It was a reference to this class, where they'd met and first read these essays by Russell to do with truth-claims and sentences that seem to have no meaning. He would text it only if they hadn't talked in a while, and it meant: I miss you, don't forget about me.

So she and Natasha talked too much about him. Natasha had appeared in grad school the way a fairy does in a tale. Evie had followed Tom to U of T, and he'd acted surprised that she'd gotten in on the same level of scholarship that he had. His disdain was almost as good as being treated roughly in bed.

Natasha was dark eyed and sleek with makeup, black hair long and shiny with care, and Evie was sure that Tom would sleep with her. Natasha's look of arrogant self-certainty and the intelligence in her eyes were, to him, nearly an invitation. The seminar they all took seemed to be just an occasion for the two of them to engage in foreplay while Evie watched. Blowjobs came up as illustrations of Hegelian dynamics more than once. Evie prepared herself for it, expected to find them in his bed, or to find one of Natasha's scarves hanging over a piece of his furniture. It wasn't as though Evie and Tom were together; it wasn't as though she hadn't found out he was sleeping with another woman before. But for about a year, her heart would race every time she had her hand on a doorknob for fear of what lay behind it.

"I don't like women who try so hard," Tom told Evie when she brought up Natasha, early on.

Years later, Natasha said, "I don't know why you like him. He's not likeable."

"It's not that I like him. It's force. Animal attraction."

"You want to be pushed around, but you should find a better man than Tom to do it," Natasha said. Grad school didn't turn Natasha's looks; not only did she not go ragged but her nails were still done. Evie became wan and cowed, blond hair limp, going brittle like an old book.

Natasha was now living in Germany on a fellowship. They were geographically triangulated, one on either side of Tom and Toronto. Evie relished any contact with him, which, at this point, tended to be criticisms of her Facebook posts. He was a man who had come of age in the nineties and still thought like Kurt Cobain, or like Ethan Hawke's character in *Reality Bites*—that one's every action must be perfectly consistent if one is to have dignity. He still believed in the concept of selling out. Smiling at a customer at the Gap or at the Dean who might give you a job when you do not feel like smiling is thus a form of lying. It was a maddening but deeply attractive quality, though now that he was on Facebook he was disappointingly knowable. He always liked her pictures, always criticized her for complimenting someone else, and could be counted on to message her whenever she complained about Southern California. These were Tom bait—she posted such updates when she craved an argument with him.

I'm not obligated to find this place beautiful, she told him. *It's a desert.*

You have everything you ever wanted, he wrote. *It's ridiculous for you to complain.*

I don't have everything. And I'm entitled to my feelings.

You need someone, he wrote. *You're no good on your own.*

The gall of this man! But she knew that he only meant that he was lonely, that he was no good on his own, that he needed someone.

"Maybe he wants to live in the desert with you," Natasha said later, during their phone-call debriefs. "Or it's just Tom being Tom. Some men enjoy knowing that women are talking about them, calling them asshole."

(Tom had once called Natasha a "femme fatale.")

"I think he's just immature. But he won't be gorgeous forever."

"He has a man-bun," Natasha said. "And he knows exactly what he's doing."

3:18. Steven Vandersteen had not yet shown. Natasha had not replied to Evie's message but had replied to various fawning comments to her photos, all variations of "what a babe," with the obligatory "aw, you guys are sweet" in response. They all pretended that this wasn't the game, this vanity, that the photos' sole purpose wasn't to attract envy and admiration.

Evie should know. She had not become threatening but more attractive to men since winning the position. Men turned around her like spokes around a hub. She had started wearing daring shades of lipstick—reds and neon pinks—and to admire herself in reflective surfaces when she passed them. She could not distinguish the feeling of attraction from the feeling of being attractive, her desire from her vanity. The better things seemed to get the worse they were: this was the hard truth.

Ludwig Wittgenstein's prosperity was a curse. Three of his brothers committed suicide, while the fourth, a pianist, lost a hand. Ludwig threw himself into the battles of World War I, spent his life plagued by the puzzles of philosophy and by his fortune, which he kept trying to give away, an incurable virus of wealth. The Nazis came and the Wittgensteins fled. Between the wars, Ludwig abandoned the work that made him famous and moved north to teach schoolchildren. As a young man, his aptitudes had been mechanical and he had worked on hot-air balloons as an engineer. The schoolchildren tromped behind him in the woods while he told them the names for things. He was an expert whistler.

He worked as a medic during World War II and tried to avoid his fans. By then, a circle of believers had formed in Vienna around his philosophy, and he had earned the raving admiration of Bertrand Russell. Ludwig hit the schoolchildren with a ruler.

"About which one cannot speak thereof one must remain silent," he wrote in the trenches of World War I. All purists wish that a word was a clean window, a direct line. All purists like stillness and singularity. In the preface to his final work he expresses his frustration at his results being "variously misunderstood, more or less mangled or watered down." This "stung my vanity," he wrote. As for his vanity, he "had difficulty quieting it."

At least she liked her office. The palm trees were not so bad from afar, the vista a postcard cliché, though she had since learned from her landlord that they were full of rats. "They live in the palms, honey," he'd said after she saw a dishearteningly large brown rodent on her balcony. "The palms are filled with 'em." Now she could see that their plaits of woven bark must be easy for a rodent to climb. And of course everyone talked about the smog. The dirty air—who knew on the particulate level what it really was?—blotted out, some days, all proof of mountains. Or created cotton candy skies at sunset.

Everyone back where it still snowed and rained in reasonable intervals believed she had won a jackpot, and now she needed to figure out how best to manage the envy of others. But Southern California was just like everywhere; people hated their lives here as they did everywhere else. She had opinions about the sky. Grey weather had not been the cause of her gloom, but had carried it like vapour. Gloom had a pressure system, too, and the blue sky was a taunt, cheerful as a sixties housewife. She longed for a downpour.

The glamour of philosophy, its sheen and its thrill, would soon dull for these students. It happened to everyone, except for madmen, maybe: the first dose of philosophy, which seems to question everything you thought you knew, is actually heady with illusions. A year or two of undergrad, three if you were lucky, and then you hit peak illusion, believing as you did that these thoughts mattered, that you were doing something both deep and important. But the end result was predetermined. What you thought was freedom landed you in an air-conditioned office somewhere, no better than a clerk. Type, type, tap. A person struggled to get up a mountain and, well, you know the rest. You can tire of a view.

She now had to manage the students' illusions. Wittgenstein thrilled them because of his renegade personality. He was a Jesus figure, toppling tables. So she told them his biography, she laughed over *gavagai*, she said, "What, we may ask, is a number?" and she did not tell them when they came to her office for advice about switching their major to philosophy that you only ended up becoming a desk-jockey if you were one of the lucky ones. She would not say to them, Look, you are headed to loneliness. If you even get a job, you will have to move far away from everyone you love.

Tom had once told her that he adored her strangeness, but she thought he only found her strange because he was prejudiced against blond women. But, then, being a genius often makes a person an asshole, and she pointed this out in lectures when she wanted a laugh. During his tenure as an abusive schoolteacher, Ludwig wrote in a letter to Russell, "I am still at Trattenbach, surrounded, as ever, by odiousness and baseness."

3:23. She refreshed the feed. Nothing from Natasha, but a new photo from Tom. Tom Abstract (he had of course invented a bullshit name)—with Natasha Balay. It was a picture of the two of them fairly close up—definitely he was holding the phone that took the picture—in Queen's Park, surrounded by trees gone gold, dropping leaves in a glitter. Their faces were nearly touching. "Philosophers in Autumn," he'd titled it. She cringed at the attempt to be ironic that read as gravely sincere. They think that they're philosophers, she thought. It was like calling yourself a poet when you'd never published a thing. But after her cringe came another set of facial expressions, which she did not see in the reflection of her screen, because she was so focused on the photo. The *likes* were pouring in. Someone had commented: *look how cute you are together.*

Eight months ago, she'd been checking into the hotel here and saw Tom coming out of an elevator with his duffle bag. She looked away, since she often hallucinated familiar faces while travelling, but he spotted her and came right to the front desk and watched the concierge give her a key. "It's a beautiful hotel," Tom said. "Quite a town."

The hotel was built to look like an old mission (she'd thought it was an actual converted mission and was not disabused of this until after she'd accepted the job), and the cool Mexican tiles alone were enough to convince a person that this would be a wonderful place to live.

"What are you doing here?"

They were frozen in the lobby, staring at each other. A breeze from the bronze, old-timey ceiling fans tossed his shoulder-length hair. He was looking craggier every year, long lines where his dimples used to be, eyes a bit blood-shot, though through the alchemy of his charm all of this made him seem more beautiful.

"Did you think you were the only big shot with a campus interview?"

It was then she understood what was meant by the phrase *I was floored*. She gathered herself and tossed back to him: "Oh, you have a secret interview. You must be taking this very seriously."

He liked it when she hit him with things she herself would have hated to hear. The meaner she was to him, the warmer he was to her. "Let's have a drink. I've got a few hours before I have to catch my flight." He led her to the bar, which, since it was the middle of the day, was mostly empty. She was still crumpled as the clothes in her suitcase. "Pretty soon they'll know everything about you," he said.

"Just like you do, I guess," she said.

"I do know everything about you."

She sipped her old fashioned through the tiny straw. "What do you think I want to do right now, if you're so smart?"

In the hotel room, in bed with him, she felt as she always had in all those years of letting this happen. It had happened a thousand times; it had been six months since the last time; it was always the same: just at their moment of greatest intimacy, his warm flesh against hers, absorbed by hers, his moaning and sighing marks of vulnerability, she felt that she could not trust him. His mouth was on her until she couldn't bear it, until she was almost in a trance, hallucinating a third party as though her suspicions were made flesh. So, now, against the door, lifted onto the bathroom counter, him pulling her open with his hands, and then on the bed, distrust flicked through her. "What are you doing?" she cried out as she came. He wanted to distract her before her interview.

"You romanticize my despair," he said. But the magic had gone out of him. In all those years, Evie hadn't slept with anyone else, as though a silent commitment could stand in for monogamy. He said, "Let the best man win," before letting himself out the door, and she nodded, decided that though he'd hoped to throw her off her game she'd use the fuck to her advantage. She was desirable, powerful, the sort of person who could shake off an intense encounter and go into a room full of strangers and charm them with her poise.

"Whatever you do, don't drink, no matter how much you want to," her advisor had told her. She downed a black coffee and then another. She rinsed out her mouth with tepid water and brushed her teeth. She zipped on her nicest pencil skirt.

Now it was Evie who'd started drinking. She was not an alcoholic and could admit that she was drinking excessively, watching bad reality TV and *Dr. Phil* and going through a twenty-sixer of Wild Turkey every week. This is not the outcome we expected, she thought he'd say if he were here with her and not with Natasha in Toronto. Now it was Evie who was drinking and Tom who was in love. There was a language to these photos. She knew it was post-coital and then also pre-coital. Now, 3:29, Natasha had finally replied. *Yes! I'm in Toronto!* Then *How are you?*

Go fuck yourself, Evie thought, trembling like a palm. Before she could think better of it, below the photo of the two of them, she copy-and-pasted a quote from the lecture she'd been writing. *"I know that human beings are on the average not worth much anywhere, but here they are more good-for-nothing and irresponsible than elsewhere."* Take that! The slim moment of triumph was followed by terror, but before she could figure out how to delete it, Steven Vandersteen walked in.

Well, it turned out that Steven Vandersteen wore a top hat. She was in no mood to laugh, and, trembling still, Evie looked calmly at the hat and the bearded face beneath it and gestured at the chair for him to sit.

"I assume you are Steven Vandersteen," she said. "Nice to finally meet you."

He smirked at her. Then, he lifted his finger and thumb to the brim of the hat and tipped it at her. "Likewise."

"So, I've got your essay here, and I just wanted to consult with you before I send it down the channels."

"Yeah."

"I mean, you didn't write this, right?"

"I wrote it."

"You arranged it."

"If you think about it," he said, with such an emphasis that it was clear he thought she hadn't thought about it, "that's all every essay is. An arrangement of various invented words."

"I have to disagree with that," she said.

"There is nothing new under the sun. Who said that?"

She stared at him. Men always taking it upon themselves to teach her.

"Marcus Aurelius," he said.

"Actually, it's from the Book of Ecclesiastes."

"I can guarantee you," he said, seeming not to have heard her, "that Wittgenstein wouldn't care one way or another whether he received attribution. He was purely interested in the truth."

He pronounced the "W" in Wittgenstein as a "W," and for a moment she felt sorry for him. He was the sort of kid who thought that genius was worth something, the sort of kid who wants to find out that he is a genius, or, rather, the sort of kid who is certain that he is a genius and is just waiting for someone to discover it. Like a tall, thin woman waiting for a modelling agent to come along.

"You never come to class, and you've committed several shades of academic dishonesty. Not just misattribution but outright plagiarism. And regardless of the possibility for novelty on this Earth, there are rules and consequences in the university, and—

"Man, I feel sorry for you," he said.

She was still trembling. She took a deep breath. "What are your plans? I saw that you're a philosophy major."

"Yep."

"Well, you're wasting your money and your time if you don't bother learning the ropes here. You want to just think your own thoughts, might as well drop out."

"Yeah, I wish," he said.

"Guess what?" she said. "The world's your oyster. You can just drop out and work with your hands and learn how to build hot air balloons or whatever. Spare the rest of us this nonsense."

"What the fu …? Hot air balloons?"

"You aren't a child," she said, though he was, though he looked like one. "You like the truth so much?" (I'm not a liar, I'm just kinder than you are, she had told both Tom and Natasha, who thought she was soft just because she was pretty, because she was blond.) "You want me to tell you the truth? If no one else will?" He's a cheater, she thought, but he's also a child.

"Lay it on me," he said.

It would feel good to punch a person in the face. Sometimes it would. "Everybody is putting up with you. You think you're a renegade surrounded by phonies, but those phonies are just being kind. Wearing a fucking top hat."

Now she felt breathless, as though she had run into him and beat at his chest with her fists. She laid her hands palm down flat on the desk to stop their trembling. Out of the corner of her eye she could see that her phone was flashing with a message, but Steven Vandersteen showed no sign of getting out.

"Whoa, lady, I don't know what your deal is, but—"

"You are supposed to address me as Professor."

He stared at her, eyes banded by shadow below the brim of the hat.

"It's very disrespectful." She thought maybe he'd take the hat off and clutch it to his chest in apology and humility.

"So, what do you want me to do about this essay?" he said.

"You're going to take this home and you are going to rewrite it." He nodded at her. "If you don't want to fail," she said, and he continued to nod. In this case, nodding did a great deal to humanize him. "You think you're such a genius?" She smiled at him. "Okay, then. Prove it."

FOR WHAT YOU'RE ABOUT TO DO

BRAD HARTLE

I'VE DRIVEN out to Selkirk Mental Health Centre to be with my dad. He's about to be taken to Winnipeg for his trial and I've been asked to wait in a holding room while the staff get him ready. Waiting with me is a peace officer named Rodney. Rodney's heard I'm in from Toronto and we're making polite conversation about the Leafs' goaltending woes when Dad shuffles in, arm in arm with a nurse. White slippers and an orange jumper is his outfit for today, and the nurse is in almost-matching orange paisley scrubs. It could be a strategy, the near-matching clothes. Maybe she's putting him at ease? Saying, yep, I dress silly sometimes, too. We all do here. Not just you murderers.

The name on the nurse's name tag is Alice and I tell her my wife's name is also Alice.

"It's a common name," she says.

Rodney smirks and taps Dad's arm. "If she seems prickly it's because I've been turning her down all week."

"Oh!" Dad's eyes beam with his old clowner's joy. He looks from Alice to Rodney and back at Alice. "You could do better than this brute!"

"And I regularly do." Alice licks her thumb and gives Dad's mangy eyebrows a straighten. To me, she says, "Sorry. Overtime hour six."

I tell her no harm done.

She glares at Rodney. Rodney winks. "Such a pig," Nurse Alice says, but when she places her hand on Dad's shoulder she's all business. "Now, Mr. Wakefield, we're gonna send you on a field trip today. That sound okay?"

When she addresses him as "mister" I smile in an unexpected way.

Dad looks at Rodney, then me, not seeming to recognize me. "I'm not up for it."

Rodney says, "But we've got your boy, Ira, here with you, all the way from Toronto. He's gonna be with you the whole time. Right by your side."

"Hey, Pops, look what I brought for you." From my pocket I pull his old ruby-red clown nose.

"What am I supposed to do with this?"

They all look at me. "I hoped it would, well…"

"What Ira's getting at," and Rodney looks at me to make sure it's okay if he comes to my rescue, "is we have to visit some gloomy folks who need to see what a kind fella you are."

Nurse Alice rubs Dad's arm. "And they're gonna see right away, aren't they?"

Dad pushes the nose back at me. "Foolish."

Alice says, "You don't have to wear it if you don't want, but Ira should hang onto it in case you change your mind." She mouths to me, He'll change his mind, then says, "I'm gonna leave you boys to it."

Dad wide-eyes Alice. "You're not coming?"

"You don't need me." Alice's hand makes slow circles on Dad's back. "I'll be here waiting for you, though."

"I'll be with you, my friend," Rodney says. "And Ira, too."

Dad looks at me and then Rodney. "But you." He points at Rodney. "You're coming for sure, right?"

"Yes, my friend. For sure." Rodney lays his hand on Dad's shoulder.

It occurs to me I'm the only one in the room who isn't in some way embracing my dad.

Last night at the airport there were no hugs waiting. Mom tore up her driver's license decades ago, so I cabbed to her place, our family home in West Winnipeg. She's lived alone since Dad went into a care home a year ago.

As always, the front door of my parents' place was unlocked. Lights were off in the doorway and down the hall. I stomped the snow from my boots and yelled into the dark, "Mom!" She hollered back that she was in the kitchen, where I found her hunched over her laptop. When she stood to hug me she seemed creaky, aching. I noticed what looked like a lesion at her temple and pushed back her white hair. "What's this?"

She shook her head away. "A bruise that's not going away fast enough."

"From what?"

"Had a little fall in the walkway. It's nothing."

I tried to get a better look, but she jerked away. "You're falling apart."

She reached into her mouth and removed her dentures, the whole top and bottom rows. With her sunken-face smile, she said all slobbery, "I'm a picture of health. Now, give me a kiss."

"I'm not kissing you, you old hillbilly." But of course I did, a wet one on her forehead.

She put her teeth back in and pointed at her computer. "How do I create a profile?"

"A profile for what?"

"Hear this. They should have locked the old drunk up when he got his DUI." She was on the *Winnipeg Free Press* website. "I want to tell this guy, this guy named," she leaned closer to the screen and squinted, "JetsPrideBaby, that he doesn't know his asshole from his word-hole."

I hadn't taken my coat off and the heat was getting prickly.

"It's a story about your father." She scrolled up. The head-line read: "Personal Care Home Assault Kills Woman, 87."

"We figured it would hit the media at some point, right? Don't overreact."

"It makes your Dad out to be a drunken murderer!"

I took off my parka and set it on a chair back. "It really mentions his DUI?"

"Yes! For no good reason!" With her hands in the air, the frilly arms of her nighty fell to her shoulders in bunches.

All the pertinent information was in the article. Tomorrow my dad faces a judge for the first time since a fellow resident at the care home, a woman named Penny Whallen, came up behind him and he turned around and shoved her. She fell, struck her head and died. The subhead read: "Accused has criminal history."

Mom said, "That DUI was over twenty years ago!"

"They're in the business of selling news. Controversy sells."

"How would they even know about the DUI?"

"Record check."

"How are you so cool about this? This is your father. It's not who he is. It's slander!"

"It's not slander if it's fact."

"Why didn't you bring my grandson? I could have ordered him to help me."

What I didn't tell her is Tim and I hadn't talked in days. That when Tim heard of the trouble with his grandfather, he laughed. "What an old retard," he said, and I threw the TV remote I was holding at his head. Without a thought. A reaction from some violent depth. It cracked against his forehead, batteries flying out, and I was over him, pinning him against the couch, my forearm against his throat and my wife yelling, trying to pull me off. Tim left the room swearing over his mother's demand that we calm down.

"He's studying for his midterms," I said to Mom. "And he'd say the same thing to you: commenting on this will plunge you deep into the Internet's sewer."

"How did you become such a pushover?"

That one stung and my look must have shown it.

"I'm sorry," she said. "I didn't mean that." I saw the slightest quiver in her lower lip. "Ira, I don't know what else to do. I don't know how to help." I hugged her and could feel her warm breath on my neck. "I don't care if I'm being stupid. Let me be stupid for your father." She pulled back and gave me those teary eyes. "Because I am stupid for your father. I love him so stupid."

I'm a suck. I set her up with a profile. When it came to creating a username I asked her what she wanted to call herself.

"My name, of course. I'm Angela Wakefield, not some coward."

With Mom fighting it out on the comment board I went to my old room to call home and check in. Alice answered and I said, "I've arrived at the killer's lair."

"Yes, well, this family is full of criminals." She let that statement dangle for a moment, then said, "Tim was arrested."

"Arrested?"

"He had a bag of pills in his locker, which he's been selling. A grand worth of Oxycontin." She said Oxycontin slow, navigating each syllable like she had just learned the word.

"That asshole."

"Yes." She breathed deep. "Yes, he is."

"Is he there? Should I talk with him?"

"Nope, you shouldn't. And you know that."

"But he's there?"

"Yes, police released him a couple hours ago."

There was a decorative doll on the bed, nestled between pillows. With a backhand I sent the doll flying, its hard head hit the wall with a thump. "I don't know what I'm supposed to do from here."

Alice exhaled into the phone. I pictured her taking a seat at the kitchen table. "I don't know either."

"Is he expelled?"

"I meet with the school tomorrow."

"I've never seen drugs around the house. He doesn't look like he's doing drugs."

"Doing. Selling. What's the difference?"

"Right," I said. And there was silence.

"How's your Mom seem?" Alice asked.

"She's fighting for her husband's honour on the Internet."

Alice giggled. "I love that woman."

I stretch out on the bed. "It's madness."

"No, it's all she can do at the moment and she's someone to do all she can. It's admirable."

"I didn't marry my mother. I didn't marry my mother. I didn't—"

"Tell her I say not to listen to you."

"She invented that advice."

If I had to guess, I'd say Alice had cracked a brief smile, which I took to be a minor victory. Then she asked, "What's tomorrow hold for you?"

"The term 'paddy wagon' is actually a slur against the Irish," Rodney says. He's across from Dad and me in the back of the van taking us into Winnipeg. We're seated on a cold metal bench and so is Rodney. Protocol is Dad's supposed to be anchored to the floor by shackles, but when we got settled in Rodney said Screw it, I won't tell if you don't. "Whenever anyone calls this a paddy wagon, I try to correct them."

"My apologies," I say. Dad's dozing and, with every bump, his head clunks against the van's metal side. I stuff my gloves inside my toque and place it behind him as a pillow.

"My uncle has Alzheimer's," Rodney says. He looks at Dad all sorry. "Last week he booted my cousin in the gut. She was trying to light his smoke for him. Drives to his care home nearly every day to sneak him a smoke." He looks at me with a dismal smile. "And what does she get? A kick in the gut."

He's got this tone like he wants to have a serious chat, which I owe him, given how nice he's been, but I can't bring myself to talk about Dad as though he's not here, napping beside me. All I can do is shake my head.

"Was your old man really a drinker, like the paper said?"

"No." I chuckle for posterity. "Furthest thing from." But there it is, talking in the past-tense like he's dead and gone. I tell Rodney the story of the DUI. Dad was curling with buddies he had curled with for twenty years when, mid-game, his skip had an aneurysm and dropped so fast and hard, his head cracked open on the button. Dad and his buddies got carried away after the wake and Dad drove into a lamppost. He cried in the court, even before the verdict came.

"This is all such garbage," Rodney says.

"Tell that to Penny Whallen's family."

"No, not that. I didn't mean that. I mean more that this is how your dad will be remembered. That anyone down the road, searching him out, putting together a family tree, stuff like that, they'll see all this and think it's the man he was. It's garbage."

None of what Rodney said had occurred to me. I tell him that.

"Sorry," he says. "I didn't mean to bring you down further."

"I think there's still a ways to go." I've taken the clown nose from my pocket and I'm rolling it between my palms.

"Yeah, well, that's true for everyone." He drums his palms on his lap as he sits up straighter and breathes deeper. The Jets beat the Blackhawks last night and before I can shift us onto the inane topic of that hometown win, Rodney asks, "What's with the clown nose?"

The name of the clown who got it all started was Dr. Feel Good. Surprise, surprise, Dr. Feel Good was a creep, eventually fired for groping a nurse. But that seedy side of him wasn't apparent when I was seven years old. What was apparent was Dr. Feel Good was hilarious and could make the pain and worry slip away from my older sister's face like nobody else. Tabby was nine and losing to leukaemia. When she would hear the squeak of Dr. Feel Good's shoes she would jolt up all smiles from her hospital pillow. Dad would have to hold her back so she didn't tear the IV from her wrist.

"I want him here every day," Tabby once said. She would spend over three weeks in the kids' ward before she died and on her second last day, the last time she saw Dr. Feel Good, she told him he made her feel stronger.

But he was a volunteer, a Shriner. And he was the only one.

A few days after Tabby's funeral I caught Dad in the garage making balloon animals. His workbench was covered with dogs and pigs and a pink jackrabbit leaning against his band saw. "Check this out," he said and from the car he pulled a white suit with thick rainbow pinstripes.

I called for Mom and he sushed me. "Not yet. It needs to be right."

And I guess it was right later that night, because his unveiling was in our living room. He had Mom and me sit with the lights dimmed. From around the corner his voice boomed, "Ladies and Gentlemen, I present to you the silliest, most stupendous specimen of super smiles, guaranteed to make the grossest hospital food bearable and the best hospital food gross."

I giggled. Mom didn't. I looked over at her on the couch beside me. She had her hands clenched between her knees. I put my hand on her back. She felt so tight.

"Albert?" she said. "What is this?"

And with that Dad leapt into the room, wearing his rainbow suit, a red felt top hat, and the ruby-red nose, his face painted white with red diamonds around his eyes. He broke into a march, a finger pointed in the air, and circled the room. The shoes he wore were massive, like red flippers, and when he stepped they squeaked.

"I present to you, the one, the only—"

"Stop this." Mom said to him. "Stop this right fucking now."

He halted with an unfortunate squeak, but he didn't stop smiling. "Angie, babe, this is a good thing."

"She's gone. This isn't going to make her not gone."

"Yes, it will." It was his smile I won't forget, its rock solid sincerity.

"Stop."

"No." He put his thumbs in his ears and made his gloved hands into antlers, then stuck out his tongue.

Mom began to cry into her hands and as she did Dad started up again with his marching.

"I'm sorry little lady, but there's no crying allowed around Mr. Pickles." He glanced at me and winked.

Mom asked, "Did you say Mr. Pickles?"

Without breaking stride, Dad said, "I certainly did. Mr. Pickles, Pickles the Clown, at your service."

Mom fell back into the couch. "That's the worst clown name."

Dad stopped. "It's a fine name."

"Absolutely the worst," Mom said.

He looked at me and back at Mom. "Pickles will make you tickles."

"What?"

"Pickles will make you tickles. It's my—"

"You! Can't! Tickle! Her!" Mom had her eyes closed as she yelled.

"Yes I can." Again, he winked at me. "And besides, we've moved on from whether or not this is happening. It's happening. Now we're onto the name. Mr. Pickles."

There was a thought my parents seemed to share for a moment, staring at one another. A tear was about to drip from Mom's chin and I reached over and touched it. She looked at me, confused, like she forgot I was there.

She said to Dad, "It's the worst name."

"Ira, come on, what do you think? It's not so bad, right? Mr. Pickles?"

Mom looked at me. When she spoke, her voice cracked. "It's the worst."

But I didn't think it was so bad and said so. Mom asked if I was crazy too and I said, "Tabby's favourite food was pickles."

Mr. Pickles was a hit, the kids and the staff loved him. Dad still worked his regular job as a carpenter, but after falling from a roof and busting his shoulder, he couldn't swing a hammer the same. And right around that time Dr. Feel Good was fired for following a nurse to her car and pressing his polka-dot pants against her, so the hospital was clownless. To help Dad out, they created an extra janitorial position. Part of the time he worked maintenance and the rest of the time he clowned for the sick kids.

"Sometimes I change in the janitor's closet." Dad kept staring at me when he'd said that, like I was supposed to pick up on something impressive. "You know, from my janitor's outfit and into my clown gear. Who does that remind you of?"

"I have no idea."

"Think of a phone booth instead of a janitor's closet."

Mom was in the other room and she hollered, "Ira, the answer is Superman. He wants you to tell him he's just like Superman."

"Superman doesn't change beside a bunch of mops."

"Well, yeah, I know. But, same idea."

"Dad?"

"Yeah, bud?"

"You're just like Superman."

I've stepped out into the cold. Dad's still seated in the van and I've reached up to help him shuffle over and step down. But instead of taking my hand he stares out behind me. There isn't much to see, just dirty snow swirling from snowbanks. Rodney's holding open the steel door to the courthouse.

Dad's eyes dart around. Something is happening, he knows it.

I smile and tell him I love him and those words grab hold of him. He looks at me, hyper-focused. "Dad, I'm gonna be right here the whole time."

He's breathing heavy now. "Okay, that's good to know."

I ask him to come on out so we can get things started.

He nods, takes one of my hands and with the other finds a grip on the van's wall.

"And this, you've done all this before?"

I'm about to lie to him, to tell him I'm an old pro, only because that's all I can think to say, but when he steps down onto the ground it's like he doesn't trust me and in his panic his knees buckle. He slips, back and over. I have him by the arm and try to keep him up, but the full weight of him is too much and he pulls me down. As he falls on his ass I land on him.

The fall wasn't hard, but my elbow got him in the gut. He's winded and makes this horrible groan. Rodney runs to us as I try to get off Dad, but Dad has my arm clenched high and I struggle to rip it away. Rodney gets his hands between us. Right before Dad releases me, his eyes lock on mine, terrified.

Rodney pulls me from him and I slide on my back across the hard snow. "It's okay, Mr. Wakefield," Rodney says. "The air's coming back. Just relax." And from the ground, propped on my elbows, as the air returns to Dad, as he moans what seems to be unintelligible questions, he wraps his arms around Rodney's neck and Rodney lifts him.

When they're standing, Dad's arms still wrapped around him, Rodney looks down at me in the snow. "Do you need a hand?"

Dad's lawyer is a man name Jack Harris, who I've yet to meet in person but have spoken to on the phone. He was nice enough to pick Mom up at home today and bring her down to the courthouse while I went out to meet Dad in Selkirk.

Jack, Dad and I take our seats on the defense side. As the proceedings begin, Dad leans over to me. "I don't even know whose funeral this is."

"It's not a funeral. Something sad happened and we're gathered to talk about it."

"Talking doesn't help. Laughing helps." He straightens up and is looking for something on the floor near his chair. "Where's my clowning duffle?"

"It's not here, Dad. That was a long time ago."

He pats at his pockets.

"Dad, you need to settle, okay?"

"I can be helping. Don't you tell me to settle." And as he spoke those words he shoved me, clawing at my face and jamming a finger in my eye. I had to grab hold of the table so I didn't topple over.

Rodney and another sterner looking guard come at us. Rodney says, "Mr. Wakefield."

Dad sunk into his chair at Rodney's show of authority, mumbling to himself as I blinked through the pain and told Rodney it was all my fault.

Jack was about to give his opening statement and decided Dad's enraged act of confusion helped. He said into the record that Dad thought he was a clown and that he could help us all by doing a goofy routine. There was something flippant about his tone, and with the way he started to almost twirl around the room, like he was showing us how ridiculous someone would have to be to think clowning could help anything, let alone a court room and a murder trial. Even the judge and the prosecutor smirked. It was so cute to them, the old brain-dead clown.

Court rises. I leave Dad with Rodney and tell them I'll be right back. My hope is to catch the Whallens in the hall and have a quick word. They're already standing outside the courtroom, conversing with their lawyer. Mrs. Whallen's son is about my age and from what I've pieced together he's with his wife and teenage son. Their lawyer sees me approaching and says, "This is a private conversation."

"I want to introduce myself."

The lawyer is about to speak when Mrs. Whallen's son raises his hand, hushing him. "My name's Jaime." We shake for a wordless moment. I look away first. Jaime says, "I know what you want to say and how hard it is to say it."

"That's decent of you." I smile at the three of them, though Jaime's son won't look at me. "But I'm going to anyway. On behalf of my family, please accept my apology. I can't imagine what this has put you through."

"This is my son, Dominic," Jaime says, nudging Dominic toward me. I extend my hand but he keeps his hands in his pockets and refuses to look at me. "What Mr. Wakefield is doing takes balls, Dominic."

Dominic doesn't care.

"It's okay," I say. "I don't want to cause more trouble."

Jaime Whallen shakes his disappointed head and introduces his wife, Marie. Marie and I shake, though she seems too timid to say much of anything, which Jaime doesn't take issue with.

"I understand the legal steps you'll be taking," I say. "We don't intend to lodge any big fight against you."

Their lawyer interjects. "This is an entirely inappropriate conversation."

But I keep going. "We have every intention to settle this and move on."

The lawyer squirms in his suit. "You can't make a statement like that without counsel, Mr. Wakefield."

Jaime says to his lawyer, "Hal, shut up." And Jaime and I both smirk. "Ira, if I can call you that, you seem like a good man. I appreciate you coming to us, but I can assure you I have no interest in letting this fade away. What happened to my Mom could happen to anyone's loved one and I intend to drive change." I try to chime in but Jaime keeps on. "I'm sorry, but this isn't going to go away. I want politicians held to account. I want more staff in these homes so people are protected. I want big systemic change. Our parents, they're casualties. But they can be martyrs. This can all result in a better world, but we have to make that change happen." He points at me and back at himself.

"My father is still alive. This isn't who he is. This isn't his legacy. This is a tragedy. It's a horrible tragedy."

"And it will stand for something." He places his hands on my shoulders and I catch myself wondering how Dad did it, when he hit Mrs. Whallen: was it just a shove and she fell or did he deck her good?

"Ira, we can make this stand for something. Don't you want this to stand for something?"

After seeing Dad back to his room—or cell, or whatever the hell they call where he's stowed—I drive back to Winnipeg. My phone's hooked up to the bluetooth in my rental car and I've dialled home to fill Alice in and get an update on

Tim. Snow falls in thick flakes that glow red in the press of brake lights. The phone rings through the car speakers.

"Hello?" It's Tim. A horn honks. The lights have turned green. Cars move. "Hello?"

"It's Dad," I say, easing off the brake.

"Mom's not here. I'll tell her you called."

"Wait! Just, just hold on."

Tim's breathing into the receiver. It sounds like he has me surrounded. "What?"

"Are you expelled?"

"Mom's not sure. She's meeting again tomorrow."

"Do you think you'll be expelled?"

"Probably not. Mom's good at this stuff."

It's true. Maybe too good. "Do you care if you're expelled?"

He lets out a lippy huff. "No."

"Yeah, who cares, right?"

After a moment he says, "Anything you want me to tell Mom?"

"You can tell her your grandfather hit me today, in the courtroom, in front of everybody, and you can tell her it's taking everything in me not to tell my son that I couldn't care less what happens to him."

"Well," he says. I no longer hear his voice around me.

"Well what?" I say. The windshield wipers whoosh as they push away snow.

"I hope Grandpa hit you good."

This gets a laugh out of me. "The lunatic eye-gouged me."

Tim laughs. "Good! Reminds me of a time my dad threw a remote at my head."

"I should have thrown it harder, knocked some sense into you." Then I ask, "How's your mother seem?"

"I don't know. Fine, I guess."

"I bet she's been crying."

"I couldn't tell you."

"You probably could, you just don't like what it means for you."

"Sure."

"Could you do me a favour?"

"I thought you didn't care what I do?"

"That's not what I said. I said I was trying not to say that and I think I've been successful."

"One way to put it."

"For real. A favour."

"What?"

"Find your mother, hug her and tell her you'll be there for her."

"Be there when?"

"It doesn't matter when. Just promise her."

He's silent.

"Tell me you'll promise her."

"Fine. Anything else?"

"I'm going to tell your grandmother you love her and miss her. Is that okay?"

"Sure, why not?"

The answer to that question—"Why not?"—is because it feels like a lie. "Be sure to hug your mother. Sell all the Oxy you want. Just hug her."

He doesn't respond right away. I hear a choked inhale. "I'm gonna hang up now," he says.

"Tim," I say, but he's gone. So instead of getting the chance to tell him I love him, or I'm sorry, what I hear is the call click away and the sound of teeny pop rise from one of the pre-set stations.

"They're saying I'm heartless! Ira, how can they say I'm heartless?" I can't see Mom from where I stand in the doorway and kick snow from my shoes. My guess is she's deep in the septic sludge of the comments section.

"I told you, it's a deep, stinky sewer."

"Oh, save the I-told-yous." She's where I found her yesterday, with her laptop at the kitchen table. Draped over her chair back is the suit jacket she wore to court. "They're saying nobody cares about who he was." She points at one of the comments and says, "This asshat is pretending to be a doctor. Alzheimer's just brings out a person's true colours, he says, like this violence was always in your father." She rests her elbows on the table and pulls back at her hair. "How do you fight back such imbeciles?"

"Have you tried writing in all capital letters?"

She looks at me and looks away, then closes the laptop. "That pleased little grin of yours is the same as your father's, otherwise I'd smack you." Then she stares off at nothing.

I say hello and she snaps out of it.

She says, "Do you remember my friend, Fay Wheeler?" I tell her I don't and she says it doesn't matter and starts into a story of Fay's granddaughter, a girl named Caroline, who died when she was nine of a cardiac condition. Mr. Pickles visited Caroline in her final days, though Caroline was terrified of clowns.

"Your Dad came into the room doing this dipping dosey-doe shuffle, tipping that top hat of his and smiling with his wacky face paint. But poor Caroline starts screaming and on a dime your Dad stops and does that same happy shuffle backwards, like he hit reverse. He didn't break form and his smile didn't wobble, but he knew he shouldn't be there, that he wasn't helping. I think others might have forced it, tried to prove something, the power of laughter or whatever. But for your Dad, it was never about him. It was always about the kids."

"Why do I feel like that was a lecture?"

Mom gets up and when I go to help her she waves me off. "There's a plate in the oven for you," she says. "I'm gonna lie down."

"I'm trying to help. You, Dad, everything—I'm trying."

"You're here, that's true."

"Yes, I am. What else what you have me do?"

She looks past me. "I really do need to lie down, honey." As she makes her way to her bedroom she frowns as she glances out the kitchen window, where snow falls harder than before.

"I'll shovel before I eat," I say. "We can't have you falling again."

Walking away, she says, "Do what you do."

Mom gets a neighbourhood kid to clear her snow, so she doesn't own much in the way of shovels, just an old rusty one that weighs as much as a sledgehammer.

I'll clear the front first. As I jimmy open the gate, edging away some snow that's got it stuck, I see the taillights of a car stopped at the curb in front of Mom's house. The car's idling, the tailpipe pumping cloudy exhaust. Moving down the walk I see the driver's door is open and can hear dinging coming from inside. The overhead light is on, but the driver's seat is empty. A couple more crunching steps forward and I hear the crash of shattering glass.

I stumble as I round the corner of the house. There's a man in a green parka standing where the sidewalk meets Mom's walkway and he and I make eye contact. He seems young and surprised to see me. He turns to run to his car and slips.

Mom's front window is broken and jagged. The boy gets to his feet and bolts for his car. As the recognition of what he's done comes to me, so does the urge to hurt him.

I huck the shovel at him. The blade clips him at the hip and he drops.

When I get to him I grab the shovel. He's trying to stand up and I cross-check him back down. When he turns over, he has a gloveless hand raised to me, protecting his face. It's a face I recognize. It's Dominic.

We're both breathing heavy. Dominic is holding his hip and sucking in air.

I ask if he's hurt. He looks up at me, then away. I say, "You're alone." Though I meant that as a question, it sounded like I was pointing out a menacing fact. "I mean, do your parents know you're here?"

He shakes his head no, for which he seems proud. The pain he's trying to stifle seems to be worsening.

Back through the broken window I see Mom in her housecoat.

"I'm leaving in a few days," I say to Dominic. "Do I need to worry about you?"

"Fuck you," he says, though he does so in a guttering way, on the verge of crying.

I extend to him my hand to help him up. At first he doesn't take it, but then he does and I help him. "How do I make this better?" I ask him. "Tell me how and I'll do it?" His eyelashes are hardening into crystals.

"You have no idea what you took from me." He glances over my shoulder at the house.

I give him a moment to get his nerves in check. "And this is what even looks like?"

"This is the beginning."

"The beginning?" I check him again with the shovel. "Here." I press the shovel into his chest and when he's got hold of it I drop to my knees and pat my hand on my cheek. "Here, right here, this is where you wanna connect." I lift my arms up at my sides and wait. He's turning the shovel in his hands now, his grip harder, like maybe. "Do it! Do it like my dad did." And I lower my head to him, giving him the whole of the back of my skull to crack. I can hear him breathe, heavier and heavier.

The shovel falls into the snow. Dominic has made a break for his car, getting inside and slamming it into gear. But he's not moving. The car's stuck in a snowy rut.

Mom's in the window, clenching her housecoat at the neck. Dominic's tires whiz and whir. Cranking the wheels one way, then another. Hammering it into reverse and lunging forward, but it's no use.

Mom calls my name and I tell her it's okay, that she should go to her bedroom. Then I go to Dominic's car and knock on the window. I make a cranking gesture and he slackens into his seat and lets off the gas. After another knock, he rolls down the window.

"This didn't go as planned, eh?"

He's breathing to the point of hyperventilating.

I say, "This seems like the time a guy in my shoes should call the police."

He tries to muscle out the tough-guy phrase, "Go ahead," but a pubescent squeak in his voice betrays him.

"How about I give you a push?" Without forcing him to look me in the eye and concede, I walk to the back of the car and place my hands on the trunk.

He's watching me in the rear-view. The snow caught in his eyelashes is melting in the dashboard heat. I yell to him, "Promise you won't jam it into reverse?" And in the rear-view I see it: I've made him laugh.

An old blue tarp, duct-taped to the window, is what's protecting us from the winter night.

I've told Mom it was all an accident, that while shovelling the walk, I somehow lifted a chunk of brick and sent it flying though the window. And the car out front, well, just as I broke the window a car got stuck and needed help.

"You have your father's sense of priorities," she says as she makes her way to bed. "And now it's freezing in here."

I've made her some tea and brought it to her in the bedroom, where's she seated on the edge of the bed, shivering. The furnace is struggling to keep up with the burst of cold. Mom asks me to get her some pain meds for her hands from the bathroom.

"It's a pharmacy in here." There's about a dozen pill bottles in neat, front-facing rows.

"Nothing too strong," she says. "Just Tylenol. Everything else makes me woozy."

"Why do you have Oxycontin?"

"From when they yanked all my teeth."

"What's it like?"

"Made me numb, and stupid. Why?"

I twist open the pill-bottle lid. "Saw a program about kids crushing it up and snorting it."

"Idiots."

"Yup." Then I say, "I'm going to use the washroom. Be right out." I close the bathroom door and turn on the fan for some sound.

There's at least twenty white pills. I shake one out onto the sink, beside a mug with a faded Children's Hospital logo, that smiling teddy bear in scrubs. With the mug's flat bottom I crush the pill into as much of a powder as I can. Surprising how much powder a single pill crushes into. From the trash I take an old toilet paper roll, tear a strip, and roll it into—whatever it's called—a nose straw. Takes a couple swipes to suck up all the powder.

It doesn't so much burn my nostril as it does flare it. And the taste of it down my throat is the same dusty, medicated taste as every powdery pill I've ever swallowed.

Mom calls my name from the bedroom. I tell her I'll be right out. After a mirror check to make sure I'm not all white-nosed, I flush the toilet and run the sink. When I'm out I bring her some Tylenol. "I can't even hold this cup my hands hurt so bad," she says. She takes the pills from me and drinks them down, holding the teacup with her stiff hands. Then she pops out her dentures and places them in a glass. It fizzes.

"Let me help you into bed." I tuck her under the covers.

"It's so damn cold," she says, toothless and juicy.

When I've got her tucked in I tell her I'll stay with her, which she doesn't protest. I turn off the light and crawl onto the bed beside her.

As Mom asks me to hold her tighter, the Oxy kicks in. My arm is draped over her and my hand, holding her, feels like it's blooming, expanding with an easy heaviness. The only sound is the tarp in the living room, billowing against the wind like a sail, and I can't tell if my grip on my mother is loosening or tightening. Tightening or loosening. I snuggle closer. It's like I'm bobbing atop the sheets, rocking along the softest cotton current. It's wonderful. This is exactly it. The tarp on the window keeps whipping against the snowy night. I'm holding on and I'm floating away.

SIX SIX TWO FIFTY

DAVID HUEBERT

THERE'S A tap on my shoulder and Coach tells me I'm up. I ask who but he just nods out towards the ice where Scab Benoit's lining up on the left wing. So I hop the boards, skate out into the crowd's feral purr. Scab opens his busted picket fence mouth into a grin and wiggles his mitts as if we needed a signal to start what's about to happen. Eyeing his teeth, I ask if he'll get some implants with this year's PIM bonus and he starts beaking faster than a ravenous seagull. Starts about my skating, saying I'm dragging my knees on the ice, saying I've got a stride like a lame jackrabbit, asking whether I need to borrow some tape for my ankles. I tell him to cool his jet stream, tell him to wait until Stripes drops the biscuit before he lets his hairy knuckles fly. Scab says something about the snatch of the sister I don't have and the ref drops the puck and we're tossing mitts and cocking elbows and squaring up in the bright white open.

The arena a seashell, conjuring oceans. The strange hissing emptiness of twenty thousand screams.

Scab keeps his fists close but I can see they're yellow and bloated from his scrap last night in Buffalo. He's taking his time so I unclip my helmet and toss it off. Then I tell him he'd be wise to keep his bucket on for this one. When he reaches for his chinstrap I clutch his sweater and wail, clap his jaw once, twice, glance his helmet on the third swing.

The crowd whistling and shrieking and my heart pattering wild. That glow in my fist meaning pain later and strength now, and Scab still standing, breathing hard.

"You're a fuckin' jizzrag," Scab yells over the crowd and then he fakes one and lands one, opens the old wound above my left eye. Quicker than I remembered. Scab keeps hailing and hailing and it's all I can do to grab his sweater and hold him off with a stiff-arm and thank fuck I have reach on him because my socket is fast filling with hot bright darkness.

That stun ended by another: Scab's fist clacking my chin. Half the world red and missing as Scab keeps hammering, the refs closing in to stop it. I tug him in and turn my face away and we both land a few more body shots and then I drop, yank him down to the ice, pull him close and hold him there.

The sweet cool balm of the ice under me while the crowd howls above. Scab's body curls into mine and the heave of our lungs gradually merges. We hold each other, breathing in synch. A drool of my blood leaks down onto the white of his sweater. The lovely warm clarity of it.

"Good fight," Scab pants, and I tell him same.

I'm sitting at the bar with a beer and a bourbon and my right fist stuffed in a wine chiller, the ice melted into salty gazspacho. Three new stitches in the braid of scars along my left eyebrow and according to the team doctor I can't fight for a month. Not fighting for a month meaning four weeks as a healthy scratch and the live possibility of getting traded or sent down to ride the bus.

The place is dry even for a Tuesday and Sudsy and Moose have already ghosted home to their wives. Smithy and Taylor are the only others left and they keep stacking rounds of Petron in front of me, rounds of Petron I pour into the wine chiller when they're not looking. Smithy and Taylor calling me a beauty, calling me Swamp Thang, saying how that scrap was so ferda and there's nothing better than a man bleeding for his team.

I know they mean it but I also know I'll never score a pro goal and they'll never fight on my behalf and I'll likely retire with five career points and CTE. Two cup rings and zero recorded playoff minutes and I'd have to be pretty dull not to realize that I'm the guy who takes punches for the guys who score goals. That I'm a fighter on a team of hockey players.

Smithy and Taylor tell me I'm a fuckin' beautician and I nod and grin and dump another tequila into the chiller and find myself hunching over my phone, searching for Tinderella. Find myself turning into Mr. Swipes Right. I get a reply from a girl named Stacey who has a pug licking her neck in her profile pic which I guess is meant to show she's got a sweet side. Stace tells me she's tired of the bar scene and I tell her I'm tired of dominating the bar scene and she sends me a Noah's ark of emoticons and then I'm popping a Cialis and climbing into my truck and heading for the Loop, city lights slurring through the dilute dark.

Suiting up for practice Smithy and Taylor are asking me where I skedaddled to last night. "Slay the dragon Wessy?" "Hit the clinic this morning?" "The slipper fit?" It's all chuckles and high fives as we head out towards the ice but then Coach pulls me aside and asks if I saw what Taylor was tweeting last night. Coach wiggles his rat-grey moustache, bald scalp glowing womb-pink under the rink lights, and asks if I saw my mug all over the *Tribune* website, a dozen empty shot glasses twinkling on the bar. I tell him no I didn't see it but I can imagine and he says you better smarten up unless you want to head down to Rockford. Says he likes me and I'm a good dressing room guy but I'm a lot easier to replace than Smithy or Taylor and I tell him "yes coach" because I'm not eager to sell my house and move to the fifth new city in ten years.

Coach doesn't care that I played regular minutes for five years in div one, that I led my team's defencemen in points two of those five years. Doesn't care that I was the only student athlete at Penn State to graduate *magna cum laude* in kinesiology and he seriously doesn't care that I anchored the power play on a Midget AAA team that won the New Brunswick provincial championship. Coach genuinely doesn't know that I have a harder clapper than half our d-men, doesn't care that I have an ex-wife and a little girl. Coach has won two cups in the past five years which means he is not obliged to care that most of the league is moving away from keeping pure fighters. To him I am a giant fist with skates on. Yes, Coach gives me the odd pity shift as a seventh defenceman when we're up by a few but he still clearly thinks my only real skill is face punching. Thinks and is not scared to vocalize that there are plenty of guys in the league who will punch face without complaining or causing media shenanigans or asking for ice time.

It gets hard thinking of yourself as a hockey player when you get one non-fighting shift every five or six games, which is why I like practise. Shooting pucks at pro goalies who know I can snipe my portion. I get a sweat going and gradually forget about Stacey and Coach and just get into the rhythm of active sticks and hard strides and crisp passes. Coach hollering his mantra: "It's all about economy of motion." Yelling "economy of motion" over and over until I start hearing it as a story about a girl named Connie Demotion, a girl I have to dig deeper and deeper to resist.

What happened with Stacey was she mentioned something raunchy, something dark. Something I wasn't expecting from a soft-faced nurse who'd admitted she'd been watching *Gilmore Girls* when I messaged her. I told her I don't do this particular dark kink and asked why she didn't mention this before I was in her living room with my bare feet on her zebra print rug. She said it wasn't a big deal, said she was still up for whatever and then I saw this look in her eyes like Rebecca used to have when she wanted more from me but didn't have it in her to ask. Then Stacey's pug, Gorgonzola, came over and I started rubbing it around the neck and I guess the gorgon got really excited because his eyeball jumped out. His eyeball scooted straight out of its socket. Not like I saw the little tendrils connecting it to the brain or anything but it just sort of deked out in a way that was clearly not right, perched at the cusp of the skull like an orange held in a mouth.

Stacey was not concerned. She said he'd had three surgeries and there was nothing she could really do so she leaned down and pulled his eyelids out and over the ball and then just popped it back in with her thumb. Which how could someone not find that hilarious? Stacey popping her pug's eyeball straight back into its socket and the dog sitting there panting and snorting and breathing louder than a snoozing bear and all of it was too awful so I shot back on the couch laughing. Stacey got into it too and soon we were both cackling. Sitting there wheezing in a condo on the thirtieth floor, looking out over the river and the city lights, a belligerent hard-on going numb in my pants.

When you're six six two fifty everyone in the league wants to fight you. When you're this size guys can make a name for themselves by landing a knuckle in your personal space. Dusters become fan favourites in a slick instant, even if all they do is hug and block and throw little body jabs that couldn't bruise a rib. The other thing that happens when it's your job to hurt people in front of twenty thousand spectators is that people notice. People watch. People record and tweet and blog. Joe Nobodies come on Twitter and beak off about how you're a skeezbag because you ran their team's goalie and can you really write back that you were just doing exactly what your coach told you to, exactly what you get paid for, exactly what someone else will do if you decide to turn your hairy nose up? When you make your living throwing punches, sometimes you get heated. Sometimes you tell someone that if he doesn't drop the mitts you are going to shove your thumbs through his nostrils and watch them come out his eye sockets. Sometimes the stupid hanging microphone picks up the comment which then circulates on social media and you end up with a two-game suspension and a $5,000 fine. And how to explain that you are not actually a particularly violent person when what circulates on YouTube is a shot of you skating across the rink at full speed, holding two halves of a stick you've just broken over your knee, the ends like mouths full of jagged splintery fangs.

What happened with Stacey, after the eyeball incident, was that I told her about Rebecca.

After that fit of laughter I said I had to take off and she gave me that same look again, like wanting some wordless more, and I opened easy as a twist-off Chablis. Told her about Rebecca the gorgeous and brilliant and funny publicist for a women's health magazine. Rebecca with the single snaggled incisor and a smile like a grade school secret. I told her about the diagnosis, a year after Lucy was born. Told her about Rebecca's double mastectomy, how they found a colony of cysts on the uterus, meaning full hysterectomy plus radiation. How there was no sex for two years and then Rebecca went to the doctor concerned about something hanging out of her vagina and the doctor said it was her bowel. Seven hot nights hardly swallowing thinking over and over what kind of a man leaves the ovarian-cancer-surviving mother of his two-year-old child. Puking at practise and for the first time in my life unable to stomach food. I told Stacey all of it. Told her how Rebecca had calmly lowered her voice and said she'd always suspected I was a monomaniac and at least now she knew. Told her how Rebecca took the house and the child and half the bank account and though she'd always been against them she had new implants by the end of the week. How she called them a gift to herself. I told Stacey how that was three years ago now and my daughter was five now and begging for a baby brother and I'd had this perfect chance to make a good family and had failed. I told every stained and sneering truth and she asked what my name was, my real name. Then she said we didn't have to do anything but could we just go to bed and she took me there, wrapped her fingers around my drugged, exhausted cock and just held it there, whispering "Wes, Wes, Wes" until we both fell asleep.

The plane lands in Boston at 4:00 which means straight to the bus because the puck drops at 7:30. On the ride to the rink Moose tells me coach is probably going to ask me to spar with Anderson which both of us know is a bad idea. Not because me and Anderson were a regular d-pair for two seasons in Tucson—you fight your friends more often than not in this line of work. It's a bad idea because Anderson is soft. Because he got called up last month and he's won two fights and so his coach is foolish enough to think he can scrap. Because it's my first game back and there's no way, contract-wise, I can justify holding back but if I don't hold back somebody could get hurt. Somebody who's not me.

So I sit in the bus looking out across the river and thinking maybe that's Harvard on the other side. Moose tells me Anderson texted him saying I better get a broom because I'm going to get dusted which I'm not even sure makes sense. I try not to think about Anderson and eventually it works. I start thinking about Harvard, thinking maybe Lucy will go there one day, wondering what my daughter will think of me five years from now. Wondering if I want her to watch me wailing knuckles for a living. I'm thinking, not for the first time, that maybe retirement is my best option. Maybe I could try journalism or get a nice office job with the player's association. Maybe I could get into training, use my kin credentials. Maybe it would be nice to throw towels at guys and lay guys on spinal boards and stitch them up on the bench.

There are few things as lovely as the sight of blood pooling on white ice. No red has ever seemed more red—like a rose blooming out of a snowbank. It is this sight, I sometimes think, that keeps me going. Not the ocean hush of the crowd, not the salary or the sense of belonging, not the elite level gear or the hundred thousand Twitter followers but the sight of a man's liquefied essence spreading out before him. The gentle wisp of steam as it leaks onto the indifferent slab below. The pattern never the same and something so simple and vast about those spattered archipelagos on the cool, stark ice. Recalling, always, the same shrill memory. A childhood pond, a whirl of lazy snowflakes. Flakes like little white insects bobbing after each other and never quite getting there. Sweat-damp pant legs clinging to calves. The shred of skates *skirring* over ice. Cardinals fluttering through a winter sky.

What happened with Stacey, eventually, is that she doesn't date hockey players. It's always been a rule of hers. An age-old prohibition she chose not to bring up until three weeks in. A steadfast embargo that did not prevent her from sitting in the special box reserved for wives and girlfriends and saying afterwards over rye and Cokes that she could get used to that kind of treatment. A hard-and-fast rule that did not deter her from joining me on one of my twice-monthly Sunday afternoons with my daughter. Did not discourage her from playing miniput at the mall with me and Lucy, the three of us afterwards drinking Orange Julius in the food court, singing along in Kermit the Frog voices to the late-November Christmas music—"He sees you when you're sleeping, he knows when you're awake." This alleged rule didn't stop Stacey from coming back to my apartment and eating spaghetti while watching *Frozen*. From holding Lucy's hand under the blanket and then saying "I hope so" when Lucy asked whether she'd see her again. But it did cause her, a week later, to suddenly cease communication. To leave all texts and phone calls unanswered for three days and then finally write back, "I'm sorry Wes, I can't date a hockey player. It's been fun but please don't contact me again."

There are times when there are no good choices. There are moments when you have to choose between your own happiness and your duties, your vows. What you may have to realize is that "sickness and health" can become very literal, very mundane. "Sickness and health" can mean you spend ninety percent of your waking life cleaning vomit and changing your baby's diapers and helping your impossibly pale wife stagger from the bathroom to the bed, her body like an apple tree in winter. It can mean walking over to a lump of covers and body holding that screaming infant several times a day and the child's mother always groaning back, "I can't I'm sorry I just can't," a morbid whistle wheezing through the back of her mouth where the chemo had rotten the teeth out. It can mean that since you have a decent salary you can afford a part time in-home caregiver for when you have to practise and play and sometimes her mother comes down to help but none of this stops you from feeling terribly, constantly, excavated. Feeling like a grave that has been dug up and left open, exposed to the vagaries of sleet and snow and wind. A grave who has to rise up each morning to smile and bounce his never-silent child up and down the vicious beige halls.

And of course you know it's worse for Rebecca. Of course you do everything you can to imagine her side, to consider how she must feel when she can't feed or snuggle or even really touch her own child. You reach into every deepest reservoir of empathy but at some point it doesn't change the fact that something in you is faded, almost lost.

You may get through all of this because you simply couldn't gather the strength to leave in the middle of the sickness. You may come through everything to discover your beloved partner is weary and sexless and she is not making any promises because her underbits are all sliced up and swollen which you are sympathetic but some nights you dream her saying "just go," saying "it's okay." And you can't anticipate that it will never be okay. You can't predict that leaving does not, in fact, mean relief.

How could you know that after leaving you would wake up each morning to find your tongue turning fuzzy and your stomach a mangle of rage and shame? How could you know you would look into your daughter's planetary eyes and wince with shame each time she said the word "mummy?" That the shame would thrill through your bloodstream and you would lie awake at night fearing the You your daughter will come to construct as she grows older. The You that has left his diseased and broken wife alone with their daughter and the ravage of her body. Fearing this future You because it is also present You and nothing, now, can make that otherwise.

One of the worst things is the waiting. Waiting through the plane ride and the bus from the airport and warmup and the pregame speech and the national anthem, knowing the whole time that you are going to have to get violent. Sitting on the bench listening to the crowd turning frenzied and knowing you've got to face a professional fighter who will open your face in an instant if you have a lonely second thought about pounding him first.

I sit on the bench feeling a little ridiculous wearing all this gear. I sit through the Megacard National Anthem, sit through the Mite-T-gel puck drop and the Trinity TV tim-eouts, wondering when I'm going to get my nudge. Moose scores a clapper in the first and then they bang in three quick ugly ones and I'm sure I'm going to get the tap but I don't get the tap. At the start of the second we kill off a double-minor and there's a long stretch of play with no whistles and then I see Anderson taking the ice. He's lining up on the wing and he's got his little weasel eyes on Taylor which is when Coach grabs my shirt and basically hurls me over the boards.

At the faceoff circle, standard banter: "Let's get some Windex on that glass jaw." "Nice fuckin' lip sweater." "How're your glutes bud? Picking up a few splinters from the pine wagon?"

Then Anderson goes personal, goes dark. "Shame about Rebecca," he says, nodding iceward. "Heard she got shredded down there, basically went through the blender."

Words that send the world listing.

A blast of light and a dentist's drill, sans anesthetic.

Everything red and blue and all cares and friendships wilting and who the fuck did Anderson hear this from? My chest and biceps flickering and a slurge of vomit in my throat. A smell like oil and before I can swing the puck drops and Anderson skates away chuckling and I'm lost out here with the horn-blare and the crowd-howl and everything noisemakers, everything glare.

Bodies whizzing around and the *schwick* of skates on ice and I find myself with the puck even though the puck means nothing now. Thinking about shooting just to get rid of it but then I see Anderson and I simply leave the puck where it is, skate towards him dropping my stick and gloves.

What happened with Stacey, eventually, is that I went to her house late-night. I drove over to her condo six and a half deep, fully ready to rage into her intercom and send some golf balls through her window. Expecting her to be in there with the latest Justin Tinderlake but no such luck or whatever else you'd call it. Because it turned out she was sweet, deadly sweet. Turned out she answered the intercom and said hey, said she'd half expected this, said she'd been thinking a lot about it and she supposed I deserved an explanation so come on up. So I came on up, mussed Gorgonzola until his eyeball made a move and then I sat there on the couch with my feet lost in zebra-print plush. She brought me a peppermint tea which I did not remotely drink and told me that although she'd told herself she wouldn't do it a friend had send her a link which brought her down a YouTube rabbit hole. Hence she wound up watching me pommel guys. She spent a fierce half hour watching me flatten Denis O'Neil's nose and concuss Ryan Armstrong and blind Todd Salinger in one eye. And after seeing me batter people like that, she said, she could no longer look at me the same way. She just couldn't get those images out of her mind and that's why she hadn't responded to my texts—when my name came up she saw visions of me leering and ramming my arm down another man's throat, flashes of me skating down the ice holding two composite plastic scythes, my beard bright with blood. All of it made her squeamish and fear-ful, she said, and how could I possibly object? She saw me as a barbarian i.e. saw me as myself and I could not argue with that so I walked out. Walked into the elevator and plummeted down. Fell slowly through the city with my feet on the floor.

Anderson turns and smiles for a second then sees that I'm bare-knuckled and drops his mitts. I'm swinging before they touch the ice. Two swings before he can even get his fists up and he's already down and tucking. I sit down hard on his chest and start beating, feel the teeth slough loose under my knuckles and keep going, opening his nose.

A hiss in my ears, someone far away whispering *monomaniac*. A flash of a woman in silhouette, stark and bald at the bathroom sink.

My fists churn faster and as I look down Anderson's face becomes my face too. I'm torqueing my fists against my own face, watching my skull tock against the ice and my eyes go distant. I find myself split in two and know this can't be right but it does not make the warmth of the blood between my fingers any less real. And even as I keep pounding I know that none of this is reversible, that this choice cannot be undone, and so there is nothing to do but keep swinging, keep trouncing, keep mashing this mask until it curdles, leaks the matter of its making.

A TITAN BEARING MANY A LEGITIMATE GRIEVANCE

REG JOHANSON

By New Year's Day I was back in Vancouver but my daughter was still visiting in Edmonton. Over Facebook Messenger I found the courage—suddenly, I surprised myself—to say what I couldn't at Christmas: "I felt like we didn't really connect in Alberta," I wrote, "and that you didn't really want to talk to me or spend time with me. Is that true?" I held my breath. She wrote back and said yeah, that's true. At the age of nineteen she could finally write:

> I don't feel comfortable around you for long periods of time. You have the same blood as me but I don't know you. It's not like after this trip we will be all peachy and it will be as though you were always there. No way. Spending 6 days together isn't going to make it all better. This is really stressful for me actually. This isn't easy. I look at you and I see the face of the dude who didn't want me. I don't care anymore but after all these years I can't just be normal and stuff. I was really mad at you for a long time

and it's not just going to disappear. I didn't even want to come to Canada to get to know you or anything like that. I don't want that to be what this is based on.

I have to stop here. I want to rush past these words—I mean continue rushing past them, as I rushed past them when they were written—*Give me time to say it*, she wrote, *because I don't want to be mean and my nails are too long so I'm not as fast*—because she wrote so many other things that distracted me, that I felt needed responding to, needed answering, needed explaining, defending, apologizing for, denying, refuting, that I ran by these words until I tripped over them just now. I was telling the story and something told me I should check the record to make sure I was remembering the conversation accurately. I wasn't. I had made up another conversation very different from the one we had. Or—the conversation we had, that is on record, was simultaneous with another one, that is unrecorded and much, much longer. The story I wanted to tell—so that I can continue the story—the story continues, many days have passed, many more days, life has been lived, there have been developments that I would like to narrate—but just now in recounting it I can't move past this. When she wrote them it felt like the beginning, and I wanted to begin. Now we were getting somewhere. Now we were connecting. Hurry up let's get somewhere, let's get that connecting going. Let's, let us, do or go. Let us not stay here, with these words—even though it's not every Christmas that I receive such a gift, of speech such as this, that lifts us out of hell as the Greeks imagined it, where the dead repeat the same gestures for eternity (she wrote: *Can you be more personable? you seem so cold and offended right now ... I know you are online but you can add more personality?* And that's what got me started). If we hadn't spent

Christmas together we might still be stuck in our distinct modes of resentment. Her apparent indifference, that broke out into open contempt only in moments of exhaustion, when she was maybe surprised by anger and forgot for a second that she wasn't giving a fuck, then come stabbing out like a stiletto. My guilty conscience, that made me pathetic and contemptible to both of us, the judgement of which I internalized until I wanted to kill myself. This mood is the thing I hate most about myself. It lifted only when I could very clearly feel <<*I don't like her*>>. I mean it lifted when I could *accept* this thought. Then it relieved me. It cleared the air of moralism and sentimentality that keep out the real feelings, out of which I had made awkward gestures, like sharing a meme, something like, Share This If You Are Just So Proud Of Your Wonderful Daughter, or some other such bullshit. It felt like the whole Internet went *WTF?* She wrote: *I have no intentions of being a bitch—please don't take it that way. But I'm not going to sugar coat it either. I'm going to say exactly how I feel.* And none of this would have happened if it wasn't for Facebook. We could not have said what we said face to face. Facebook was the right platform for these ugly feelings. Our first conversations were on the telephone, starting when she was about five. We talked on the phone most weekends until she was ten or eleven, when our talks became, for the first time, stilted and one-sided—me asking a lot of dull questions, withering a little more with each of her shorter and shorter answers. Which was a reversal of the situation in our earlier conversations, in which she did all the talking. So we didn't talk much for a few years, and then Facebook. About age sixteen she popped up one day with a confession: she was in love with a boy—a white boy she met in the Christian private school her mother—who was the daughter of Muslim parents from Fiji—had sent her to, because she thought it was a good compromise between the state school's racism and violence and the too-conservative Muslim school, where the girls wore hijab. She was sneaking around to hide this white boy from her mom, who she was certain would not accept the relationship. Also, she had become a Christian, just like her boyfriend and all her friends at school. Her mom would for sure not be accepting that. The situation was coming to a crisis. She had run away for thirty-six hours a few weeks previous. She was desperate and didn't know what to do or who to turn to, so she reached out to me. And for me this was so rich. It was a plenitude. It gave me an opportunity to act responsibly, and I relished it. At this time in my life I was grateful for every opportunity to be good. So just for the record, in case her mother should hack our messages, I advised her to tell her mother everything, and then I sat back and enjoyed being her confidant. She swore me to secrecy and I accepted to be sworn. Because the other thing about it was that it was a repeat of the circumstances of the way her mother and I got together. She was living our story again, in so many of the particulars: a brown girl and a white boy, hiding from her parents, running away, seizing the long-awaited opportunity of each other to force the irrevocable transformation of her life, and his, after which they would be free from all constraints. Even down to the religious conversion: she had become a Christian just as I had become a Muslim, though she claimed to be an actual believer, whereas I did it to help her mother's parents save face in their community after the scandal of our running-off. But her crisis passed. It all came out and her mother accepted her boyfriend and even the religious conversion, which did not last, as mine did not. She is still with her boyfriend. I'm not sure where he's at with religion now. Nobody's asking him to become a Muslim, I do know that.

GRAVITY

AMY JONES

THE DEER flies through the air almost elegantly as it ricochets off the hood of the car, its long, slender legs stretching out like a dancer's. Time stands still as fur and flesh rotate around the still point of the deer's eye, focusing on Jonah through the windshield with a look of pure terror. Then, as if time were completely irrelevant to begin with, everything speeds up, the deer landing with what Jonah can only imagine is a sickening splat against the pavement as the car continues down the stretch of road like nothing has happened, Jonah staring in shock at a small patch of fur-covered skin caught in the hood, flapping in the wind.

Jonah pulls off onto the shoulder and rests his head against the steering wheel, his whole body juddering with the force of his heartbeat. There is a fine spray of blood across the windshield, and he turns on the wipers, watching as they sluice indifferently through the gore, leaving red streaks across the glass. He turns to Brie in the passenger seat. "What do we do?" he asks.

She looks at him, and her face is a blur of freckles and skin and eyelashes. The sound of her voice doesn't come from her lips, but instead originates from somewhere deep within Jonah's subconscious.

"My dad's going to kill you."

At work Jonah takes the lunch his mother has made him and scrapes it into the garbage. Nancy works at a health food store and tries to make him eat quinoa and tofu, drink puke-green smoothies with omega-3 supplements. But Jonah has only been working at the call centre for two weeks, ever since he got fired from his job working security at the mall, and he doesn't want to be known as "that loser with the disgusting lunches" again. He'd much rather just eat chips from the vending machine, or chicken from the KFC next door. He has just finished rinsing out the Tupperware in the sink when Matt, who has the desk next to Jonah's, comes in and immediately pulls his hoodie up over his nose.

"Dude," he says, scrunching up his face. "What is that *smell*? Is that *you*?"

"What smell?" asks Jonah.

"You don't smell that, dude?" Matt is small in all the places he is supposed to be, the same way that Jonah is not. He looks like the kind of guy who uses the body wash from those commercials where the girls all chase you. Everyone likes him—or, at least, they pretend to.

"Oh, yeah, totally," says Jonah. "What *is* that?" Then he adds, "Dude?"

Jonah lives in Nancy's attic, his choice of storey solely based on his reluctance to become a cliché. The attic is too hot in the summer and too cold in the winter, but at least when people call him "that loser who lives in his mother's basement" he has some basis for rebuttal. In his attic room, Jonah paints Warhammer figurines and sometimes makes up D&D campaigns even though he doesn't have anyone to play with. He chats online with his friend Vikram, who lives in California and who he met on a Japanese manga message board, or with one of the women he pays money to have describe their lingerie to him while he jerks off. All of these things he imagines Matt can see just from looking at him, his prodigious shortcomings written on his face as plainly and indelibly as the JOJO DESMOND scrawled in Sharpie by Nancy across the bottom of the Tupperware he holds in his doughy hands.

"Hey, Savannah," Matt says to a pretty brunette with short hair who has just walked in. "Five bucks to go stick your head in that garbage can and tell me what smells."

"Fuck you," says Savannah, and bites into an apple.

Matt shrugs. "Chicks," he says, looking at Jonah.

"Totally," says Jonah. He tucks the Tupperware under his arm, making sure to cover up the writing, the one thing he knows he can actually hide.

Jonah hasn't seen Brie since the mall. Back then, he would be in her store every day, checking up on things, asking if she had seen any suspicious activity—and then, later, if she had seen any good movies lately, or if she was going to spend the summer in town, or how things were going with her grandmother, who has Alzheimer's or Parkinson's or some other kind of old person disease. But he reads on Brie's Facebook page that she has gone back to running outside, so Jonah has gone back to joining Nancy on Saturday mornings at the marina, sitting on a bench and listening to his iPod while she does tai chi.

"You should try it sometime," Nancy says the first week, pulling back her greying curls into a ponytail. "It might help you restore some balance in your life."

"I have balance," Jonah says. He stands in front of the bench on one foot and puts his arms out to either side.

"Be careful," Nancy says, touching his hand. "You have a low centre of gravity."

Jonah extends his leg, grinning. "Oh, and you'd just let me fall?" As soon as he says it, he loses his balance, and grabs onto Nancy to stop himself from tipping forward. "Whoops," he says, sitting back down with a thud.

Nancy sits down next to him and wraps her arms around him, nuzzles into his shoulder, like she has been doing for the past twenty-seven years, the cartilage in her delicate nose pressing into his soft flesh. "Oh, my Jojo, what am I going to do with you?" she says.

Jonah is hit with a sudden, sharp image of Brie in a sundress stripped off to the waist, straps pooling around her hips, purring "What am I going to do with you?" He can actually smell the lemony scent of her skin, her hot breath on his neck, rummy and sour; he can see the light blue fabric of her dress, delicate eyelets marching in a line along the curve of her pale thigh. They are sitting in a lamp-lit room on the edge of a bed covered with a pink striped duvet, pink flowers dancing across the wallpaper behind them. There is the faint sound of a party coming from beyond the room, music and voices and laughter, but there on the bed all he can hear is the whisper of Brie's hand running through his hair, his own breath coming in quick, staccato gasps.

Then she is gone, and Jonah is sitting on a bench at the marina with Nancy's arms around him and an erection pushing against the zipper of his jeans. He wrestles himself out of her hug and lurches to his feet, pulling his duster tight around his waist. When he closes his eyes, he sees pink stripes lashed across the insides of his eyelids, pulsing to the faint thrum of his heartbeat.

The next Saturday Jonah waits again for Brie on his bench at the marina, Nancy and her classmates all moving slowly and silently through the space behind him. But all he sees are a flock of Canada geese, flying in unison, their wings dipping low towards the water, and in his mind sees Brie brushing her teeth while humming "Yellow Submarine," dropping a splotch of toothpaste onto the front of a Montreal Canadiens T-shirt.

"I think I'm having someone else's memories," Jonah types to Vikram, later.

"Maybe they're your own repressed memories," Vikram types back. "Have you tried therapy?" Vikram is all about therapy, ever since his parents split up last year. It's been tough on him, but he is only thirteen, he has time to get over it.

"Is it normal for repressed memories to be *good*?"

"No, those are fantasies," Vikram types. "Start watching more porn, they'll probably go away."

When Jonah was young, he used to daydream about rescuing Nancy from aliens or zombies or sometimes Spiderman, who he was inexplicably afraid of. Now that he is older, his fantasies about women always revolve around them being held up at gunpoint, or being kidnapped by terrorists, or being trapped in a burning building, with Jonah the hero racing in and saving them at the last second. These things with Brie, they aren't fantasies—they are everyday life, and they *happened*. To someone.

Jonah's screen flashes and he sees that Vikram has sent him a link to a website featuring Big Busty Bored Housewives with Vibrators. He wonders if there is anyone out there who really knows him at all.

Tuesday is KFC day, and so there are a dozen people in the lunchroom at work when Jonah goes in to dump out his lunch. He stands there awkwardly for a moment, unsure of what to do. "Have some chicken," says Savannah, waving her hand towards the bucket. Jonah tucks his Safeway bag full of health crap under his arm and reaches for a piece. The shape of the drumstick in his hand brings back a memory—because that's what it is, a *memory*—of Brie's bare calves draped across his lap as she reads him his horoscope. "Let your instincts point you in the right direction, and don't hesitate to follow where they lead," she says. She lowers the paper, raises her eyebrows coyly. "What direction are your instincts leading you in?"

"Which direction are you in?" he asks, and Brie shakes her head, arching her back against the arm of the couch they are sitting on, orange and itchy, in someone's basement where they are trying to escape the heat. Jonah can feel the dampness of the room, smells something that reminds him of old Christmas decorations.

"You Virgos, such sweet talkers," Brie says.

"I'm not a Virgo," Jonah says out loud, and he is back in the lunchroom leaning against the counter and holding the drumstick. Everyone is staring at him.

"Could have fooled me," Matt says. A few people laugh. Jonah laughs too, thinking maybe it's better that way.

Back at his desk, Jonah thinks about how it would make sense if he were part of some kind of secret memory implantation experiment, maybe by the government, maybe something to do with his previous access to surveillance equipment at the mall. He dumps the contents of his Safeway bag into the bottom drawer of his desk, and the top of the Tupperware pops off, spraying curried lentil soup across a stack of folders like a stream of baby diarrhea. Jonah closes the drawer with his foot and logs back into his computer.

Nancy invites a man to dinner, something she has done on and off since Jonah's father died five years ago. This man, Ray, is thin and pale and exceptionally tall, a shiny bald head inside a ring of white hair pulled back into a ponytail. Ray is an art therapist, Nancy has informed him, prompting Jonah to ask why art would need therapy, in turn prompting Nancy to tell Jonah to stop being such a smartass.

They all stand around the kitchen island while Nancy makes tapenade. "I hear you're in the customer service industry," Ray says to Jonah over the roar of the food processor. "A noble profession, to be sure."

"I answer phones," says Jonah.

Ray nods knowingly, looking at Jonah as though he has just said something incredibly profound. "I'm sure you answer more than phones," he says, pressing his fingers together under his chin.

"Nope," says Jonah, rolling an olive across the countertop. "Just fucking phones, okay." The noise stops as soon as he says it, and "fucking phones okay" echoes through the kitchen in the ensuing silence.

"Jojo," Nancy says quietly. She puts her hand on his shoulder. There is no memory of Brie this time, just Nancy, standing in that underground parking garage with Jonah's old supervisor, promising that Jonah wouldn't come back to the mall if the girl didn't pursue the restraining order. The two of them looking over at Jonah, leaning against a concrete pillar with his hands in his pocket, his duster hanging open around his soft, womanly hips. No knight in shining armour, just a creep in a dirty Minecraft T-shirt waiting for his mom to take him to East Side Mario's, as if all-you-can-eat pasta and breadsticks could make everything all right again. All of this coming to him now like a hot rush of adrenaline to his cheeks, bright red in the kitchen as Ray and Nancy watch him back out of the room, tripping over his feet and cursing his stupid low centre of gravity.

Safe upstairs, he wonders if there really is someone out there whose memories he has stolen, and if it's true, why that guy couldn't have taken Jonah's memories in return, the prick.

The next Saturday, Jonah finally sees Brie. She is running, little earbuds pinched into her ears, ponytail bouncing behind her. He has to run to catch up with her, feeling like a pervert huffing and puffing past the playground, wheezing along behind her until he is close enough to tap her shoulder.

She pulls the earbuds out of her ears, keeps jogging on the spot. "Oh," she says. "Hi."

"I waved," he says, trying not to sound out of breath. He can feel sweat pooling under his collar, bleeding out of his armpits. "I guess you didn't see me."

"Nope," she says. She toys with the earbuds. She is beautiful, with flushed cheeks and no makeup, her bright blue sports bra. She looks sinewy, strong, like he could pluck on any of her exposed tendons and it would sound out with a twang.

"So, uh, crazy running into you like this, right?" he says. Brie just looks past him at the lake, at the boat masts rising out of the morning mist, at nothing. "How have you been?"

She rolls her eyes. "What's up, Jonah?" she asks.

"Nothing," he says. "I just…" She puts one earbud back into her ear. "Wait, Brie, hey," he says. "Do you remember that time we hit a deer in your father's car?" The words just appear, and he grabs onto them, like a man tumbling down a cliff grabs onto a passing branch.

She blinks, the other earbud suspended in the air just outside of her other ear. She has the volume turned up so loudly that Jonah can hear the music. Taylor Swift. He didn't know she liked her.

"Jonah," Brie says, finally. "That wasn't you. I just told you about that."

"No you didn't," says Jonah, suddenly knowing she did.

"I'm going now," Brie says. "Please don't follow me."

She jams the earbud into her ear. Out of desperation, Jonah shouts, "Brie! Which direction are you?"

Brie doesn't say anything, she just pushes past him, and Jonah feels his feet separating from the earth, feels the sky changing position above him. And although at first he thinks his fall must be metaphorical, when his knees hit the grass he realizes it is not. He looks up and sees Nancy watching him, her head cocked to one side, her mouth formed into a perfect O. Jonah has seen that look before, that look of poorly disguised pity. But he has never seen it on his mother before.

Et tu, Nancy, he thinks, before he rocks forward from his knees onto his hands, then spread-eagles across the grass, cheek to earth.

Something is happening at work. Matt is on the other side of the office, talking quietly to one of the managers, Todd, who keeps looking at Jonah. Jonah tries to concentrate on what the customer is saying, but he can feel his palms begin to sweat, his voice begin to crack. When he hangs up, Todd comes over and asks him to log out of his computer and step away from his desk.

Jonah stands in the middle of the aisle while Todd opens his desk drawers, one by one. When he gets to the bottom one he takes a step back, letting the drawer hang out like a tongue. The spilled lentil soup is still in there, as is the quinoa salad from the next day, and the tempeh patties from the day after, and the baked kale chips and hummus from the day after that. There are even a few KFC chicken bones thrown in there from when Jonah snuck some pieces back to his desk, and some stale potato chips that he had found in the bottom of his bag. All fermenting into a brown, putrid soup.

Everyone around his desk gets to their feet, clamping their hands over their faces, making small grunting noises, backing away from what certainly must be some sort of catastrophic biological warfare. Todd's face has turned a pale shade of green, and two desks over, Savannah retches into her garbage can. On the other side of the room, Jonah sees Matt standing with a girl he doesn't recognize, and they are laughing, without sound, their faces scrunched up with the effort of containing it.

When the smell hits Jonah, he closes his eyes and suddenly he is standing on the side of the highway, staring down at the deer. The car is still running somewhere down the road, Brie leaning out the window calling after him to come back, just leave it for fuck's sake, there's nothing he can do. Jonah kneels down next to the deer—twitching, bleeding, but not quite dead. He places his hand where he imagines its heart to be, somewhere beneath the coarse fur, the shattered ribcage, and holds his palm against it until he feels the deer's pulse begin to weaken, and finally fade away to nothing.

CANDIDATE

MICHAEL LAPOINTE

S PENCER SHOWED me the margins. The symbol cart-
wheeled down the page. We'd seen it in a movie. The
bad guys wore the symbol on their arms. Spencer was
the only other boy who'd seen the movie, so we could laugh
about it together.

At my desk, I tried drawing the symbol, but the pencil
sometimes went the other way. For a while, I forgot how
it was meant to go. Then I thought about the guys in the
movie, and it came.

I laughed and looked to Spencer. His head was down,
pencil working on the page. I made one symbol after
another. Every time it worked, it was exciting.

I wondered what else Spencer was drawing. What else
had he seen?

The teacher stood up. Spencer's head stayed down.
Now she came up the aisle. In the movie, we'd seen what
happened to the bad guys. I rubbed out my symbols and
brushed the dust away.

The teacher asked for Spencer's paper, but I guess
he'd erased his symbols, or maybe it wasn't so bad after

all. She just handed back the page and told us to keep working.

Spencer and I tolerated other shows but only really liked *The Simpsons*. *The Simpsons* taught us the culture. For years, we'd see something in a movie or on TV and finally understand the reference from *The Simpsons*. When we encountered the actual source, we already knew how to make it funny. The only other thing we watched was a tape of Spencer's sister getting thrown from a horse.

Everything Spencer said was funny. He talked like *The Simpsons*. You didn't have to know why.

One time, he said, "Ask me if I'm a tree."

"Are you a tree?"

"No."

That was the funniest thing we'd ever heard.

"You thought we were joking with this campaign," I remind the woman from the CBC. "But Dom is reaching people outside the bubble. If I were trying to reassure a certain bloc, I might point to his charitable donations. Go ask SickKids about Dom Crossman. But we aren't motivated by reassuring moderates. There are people who don't pick up when you people call. There's a country out there, unlike the one you carry around in notebooks. Dom's for them, all the way. At this point, he can't be denied the nomination. I think the party knows that."

A few months into our campaign for the nomination, reporters started interviewing Wei and me, "the millennial brain trust of Dom Crossman's candidacy"—a label that annoys Wei, who's forty. They started asking how a retired hockey coach could work his way into federal politics, apparently not realizing their questions drew him further in.

I give credit where it's due: Wei polishes the Dom Crossman product—broad shoulders, double Windsor knot, white sideburns shading into black. She strictly limits his vocabulary, runs the lint roller down his breast; she makes him viable to the casual eye gliding over a TV screen.

My role is different. Reporters call me a strategist, but it's not like I'm hunched in some tent, moving armies on a map. To an outsider, my day-to-day would appear laughable: I scrutinize memes; I dragnet comments; I absorb varieties of anger. Where others hear nothing, I detect a mood. And when I finally speak, people lean in to hear me. The results of what I say aren't quantifiable, except, of course, we're here at the convention and no one wants to talk about a candidate unless his name is Dom Crossman.

People thought Spencer was Trench Coat Mafia. It wasn't a hard category to fall into. All you had to do was point a french fry at somebody. Call the principal's office and breathe heavy—everyone got the day off. But Spencer really did fit the profile, pale and stubby and delaying his first shave. He had this weird flair for slobbiness. He'd wear one collared shirt on top of another; he'd stalk the hallways in fingerless black gloves and supermarket shades. Everyone knew he played *Counter-Strike* at an elite level.

Spencer was my best friend, but we weren't treated with the same suspicion. I was taller, cleaner, able to pass into groups without projecting a suffocating air. I knew the names of the people around me.

Spencer and I were fascinated by Columbine, by anything fucked up. We downloaded scraps of video off Kazaa.

"Check out this fucked-up takeoff."

"Check out this fucked-up crackhead."

"Check out this execution."

On the Hewlett-Packard in Spencer's basement, I saw a Chechen rebel getting stabbed in the throat; I saw a man getting fucked by a horse. Child soldiers ran through a minefield in some distant civil war. Then we'd alt-tab back to *CS*, or turn our attention to TV, or take a break and defrost something to eat. When another video finished downloading, we watched it.

We liked the idea of being desensitized. It was something to be cultivated by subjecting yourself to constant imagery, like a game of who can hold a burning match the longest. We hoped our curiosity would lead us to a place out of reach; that was where we wanted to be. We could look at people and know we'd seen things that would disgust and horrify them.

That was the aura of the Trench Coat Mafia, but I knew Spencer, at least, wasn't a killer. The thing with so many of these massacres was that, in the end, the shooters killed themselves. It was real for them in a way it could never be for Spencer. He didn't want to die. Name something worth dying for.

Spencer said, "How do you kill a thousand flies?"

"How?"

"You hit an Ethiopian in the face with a frying pan."

Jokes had to be on the margins. We made jokes about Jews, jokes about blacks, jokes about women. Gay sex lurked behind all our innuendo. Being monstrous was the funny thing. It said more if you just made the other guy go *wow* than if you made him actually laugh.

Only we could handle the material. We performed at a very particular frequency. We'd never want to be overheard. Yet I always pictured a woman—white, respectable, like Spencer's sister—hearing our jokes, and she became the final object of ridicule. Her face contorted; she was afraid of laughing.

Spencer and I considered ourselves fluid. The final safeguard against monstrosity was that we didn't have a sense of self at all. In fact, we'd mastered what we'd been told was the basis for all morality: to put yourself in other people's shoes. So we could be bigots, wife beaters, lovers one instant to the next—a shuffle of reference. If you thought we were serious, the joke was on you.

Wei worries about disgrace. She says it's the natural conclusion of most candidates with the volatile momentum of Dom Crossman. The great fear is of exploding just as you're taking flight. She's described a vision of Dom blowing it here at the convention. He could succumb to his confidence, as if the game were in hand, and start slaughtering some of our campaign's sacred cows: jobs, God, the intrinsic goodness of the people. All in an instant—evaporation. "You'll look for me," and Wei pats me on the shoulder. "But I'll be gone."

Despite her genius, it's possible that even Wei doesn't realize the roll we're on. She might be just a little too last generation. She still really feels every scandal.

And our campaign has weathered its share of them: tax discrepancies, plagiarized college papers, an off-script joke about Mental Health Awareness Month. But I encourage Dom to shoot from the hip. Sometimes I tell him: "We're pushing out from the centre." He internalizes that kind of strategy, force confronting force. I've been spoken of as a hazardous influence by members of his inner circle, and I understand. Their curse is that they have to worry about every last vulnerability.

I'm not like them. I accept that Dom is an imperfect vessel; it wouldn't surprise me if he had brain trauma from his playing days. I dream of a candidate who steps out of the margins already complete—fluid and faceless, a total negation.

The Ontario Teachers' Federation picketed in our first year of middle school. Spencer and I welcomed the strike, which dragged on for weeks. But we also became aware of our status, in the clash between the union and the government, as the lowest priority—chattel, basically—and this formed the first occasion of our taking political offence. We began to frame ourselves as marginal.

In our view, they were all morons—our teachers and our government—though the teachers were slightly worse, because they complained directly to us. How many times had class been interrupted so the teacher could bemoan how there weren't enough supplies due to government cuts? It was laughable how small our teachers were willing to appear in their efforts to turn us against the government. Cuts, cuts, cuts—like the school was bleeding out from a billion wounds.

Politics now became a central topic for Spencer and me. Political knowledge was something you were expected to acquire when not around each other. When it came to news of the world, we liked stories of war and terrorism. It was adult to imagine what would happen if, for instance, Pakistan leaked a nuclear weapon, one you could fit in a briefcase, to religious fanatics. When it came to domestic issues, we took a general stance against welfare and taxation—people leeching off hard work. We pictured our teachers, who barely knew our names, always craving more.

At our high school, you could take comp sci. Spencer and I sat side by side in the computer lab and worked on all the projects together. I wasn't very good at programming, but Spencer covered for me. I think he was glad to have me as a partner; he could do the work alone. He coded a tank warfare game that hooked up between computers, so two players could go at it from across the lab. Despite a bunch of bugs, the game impressed everybody. Spencer called it *Napalm Sunburn*.

Comp sci ended up one of my highest grades, and I took it as a natural fact that Spencer would design games for a living. But he wasn't even the best student in class. We kept an eye on a girl named Meera, who bused in from another district so she could attend a school with a computer lab. Meera never looked away from the screen; in her glasses, the blue light glowed. When we fell silent, I could hear her keyboard chattering. Spencer called Meera the Muskrat because of the wild eyebrows, the matted hair, the dark down on her cheeks.

Meera's projects were totally clean and actually useful. Spencer hated watching her presentations. She seemed aware of functions that adults needed performed and designed sharp, intuitive interfaces for just those purposes. Meanwhile, we couldn't imagine anything outside *Napalm Sunburn*.

The school organized an annual plant sale to supplement its budget, and our comp sci teacher gave Meera the special assignment of programming an online ordering system. Parents who used the system could get their plants a day early. This particular program was Meera's masterpiece. We did a beta test in class, and I remember feeling like her system somehow made the computer itself run faster, like a glass of water in a marathon.

The night the system went live, Spencer messaged me on MSN. He said the Muskrat had made a big mistake. There wasn't a character limit to the ordering fields, so you could submit unlimited amounts of data to the system. By the time I got to the site, Spencer was already copying hundreds of thousands of pages of text into the fields. He told me to help, and I did it for laughs. We forced reams of text down the throat of Meera's code. I'd never used a computer that way; it was a creative act—compulsive, unconscious. After a dozen submissions, the site was taking forever to load. In another minute, it was gone.

Monday morning was when parents who'd used Meera's system were supposed to collect their orders. The plants were kept in a small gated area against the side of the school. When I arrived that morning, the gate was locked. No one was around. Under the tarp, the plants were in shadow.

Our comp sci teacher gave a speech about hacking. Computers were a liberating force, he said—by which he meant a force for good. We could be the vanguard of all that, if we wanted. I looked over at Meera. Her computer was off; she was staring at her hands. Beside me, Spencer had already started on the next program.

At first, people saw the Dom Crossman campaign as obviously right, then possibly left, then hopefully centre, until finally it depended on where you stood. I tell Dom: track along the spectrum. I tell him: wait until they've found the face they're searching for.

Lately, I've observed a kind of delirium in our supporters. They actually dance at our rallies, swaying together and laughing.

The weekend of the convention has been building up to Dom's address. But when, in the first movement of the speech, he mentions border security, a woman unfolds a sign: WELCOME THE NEWCOMERS.

I can't hear what she's yelling. Some members of the party boo; others applaud. She's drowned out. I look over at Wei, who fretfully awaits the moment of disgrace. Is this it?

Everywhere we've gone, the Newcomers are the fixed idea. I don't have a strong feeling on the matter, but to the extent that they embody the borderless flow—of jobs, capital, culture—I advise Dom to maintain a stance of general antagonism. That comes naturally to him; he was a bruiser for the Leafs in the '80s.

"I boarded Hartford's top prospect," he once told me, plucking his eyebrows in a pocket mirror. "And he got this burst fracture in the spine. Put an end to his career, like that—fresh-faced youngster. And people called me all sorts of things, but my family never went hungry."

Vis-à-vis the Newcomers, we're only absorbing the spirit as we find it. "You'll do something about them," a woman told us at a rally. "I've got three families in my neighbourhood alone. Nobody's working. The women are pregnant. You can see them on the steps. Our local boys are scared to go by the building."

Dom said, "You'll feel safe in your own country, ma'am."

And he held her small hand. Her eyes beamed up at him with gladness.

Now he stands at the podium as the protestor is strong-armed off the convention floor. But Dom's in a magnanimous frame of mind. Wei can relax.

"It's good, it's good," he says. "This is democracy, folks, pure and simple. She has the right to yell. And we have the right to yell. Show her some courtesy on the way out, will you? Don't let her trip. I don't want anything happening to her."

From the edges of the room, at just the right moment, Wei strikes up a chant. Dom exhorts: "Strength! In! Numbers!"

I don't like the mob, but I love to see them like this.

I went to Vancouver for university. Spencer chose to wait a year. I figured he'd get up to something that would make further schooling redundant. In fact, it was a minor source of shame that I'd trace a more conventional path, majoring in some vague humanity and wandering into the job market. I read about the office spaces of developers in California, where you lounged poolside beneath the fronds. That's where I envisioned Spencer, with an XL black T-shirt and knock-off Oakleys, drinking from a coconut.

The Americans invaded Iraq in my first year. Over MSN, Spencer and I pored over the details. He took a zoomed-out view of it. In quasi-biblical tones, he spoke of civilizations clashing, historical cycles churning, epochs disintegrating. I didn't know where he was absorbing this rhetoric. For me, it was a lot simpler: war was expensive; it had to have a point.

Spencer blamed the balmy west-coast atmosphere for softening my brain.

I wrote, *Isn't it obvious that Rumsfeld is lying?*

And Spencer answered, *Yeah of course.*

For most of my peers, Iraq was the refining flame, solidifying positions on the left or right. Somehow, it worked differently on me. I remember the February 15 protest. I got stuck in a crowd of hippies re-enacting memories of Vietnam marches—walking on stilts, sparking cannons of weed, dressed up like Uncle Sam. The march seemed fun for them, light and playful and nostalgic. Someone on a megaphone read out numbers from protests all around the world: Berlin, 300,000. Barcelona, a million. Rome, another million. There in Vancouver, an estimated 25,000. Everyone cheered; a global passion flowed together. Yet, with startling clarity, I thought we were in error. We were inhabiting a reference, a received idea of dissent.

The protest briefly splintered while a faction, clad in black with red balaclavas, smashed in the windows of a Starbucks. This, too, gestured toward a precursor—I pictured them laughing behind their masks—but I fixed on the desire for violence. The desire was real. That was the spirit, finding its occasion. As the march surged on, I hung around. Broken glass crunched beneath my feet.

After the invasion, I watched Iraqis overrun the statue of Saddam. The media said Americans staged the event, but the violence was ecstatic. The crowds were laughing. No one cared who was behind it or what came next.

Not long before I finished my poli sci degree, I got an email from someone named Kim. I had to stare at the name awhile before I realized the message was from Spencer's sister, Kimberley.

She asked if I was coming home for the summer. She said she didn't know how aware I was of the situation. Spencer had been laid off by Bell; he wasn't leaving the basement; she thought he had a problem with his lungs— what their mom once had. He was tired all the time and his legs looked swollen.

I felt embarrassed by her familiar tone, as if, in her mind, I'd only been away a week or two, whereas my entire adult life had unfolded out west. Not that I was avoiding Spencer, but I didn't have time to chat anymore. When I thought about him, that ancient picture in a Palo Alto pool was still parked in my mind, and it came as a shock to realize I might be doing the more remarkable thing with my life.

By then, I was organizing municipal campaigns and advising several provincials. Because of my strident views on foreign intervention, I was generally received as coming from the left, but our campaigns merged affiliations in unclassifiable ways. Push against the edges of the political spectrum, I discovered, and they reach a vanishing point. We never won anything, but we claimed victory whenever another candidate had to answer a question raised by our campaign. Invade the prevailing discourse, we reasoned, and before long, everyone would be living in our world.

But this wasn't a campaign year—I didn't have a candidate—and, in fact, I was planning to go back east that summer. Kim invited me to the house, which their mom had left to them. We had coffee in the living room. I'd never sat there before, always just breezing through on my way to the basement. Every few minutes, I heard Spencer's coughing. Kim said she didn't know what to do anymore; she had to get out of the house, get on with her life. She asked about Vancouver, then seemed to lose focus as I described it.

In a few minutes, I went downstairs. Spencer had the lights off, the room dimly blue from two computer screens. He greeted me as if it hadn't been four years, which made me feel loved. I sat on the edge of the bed. On one screen, he had some chat open; Russian MMA streamed on the other, two women in a bloody knot. He offered me a beer from a mini fridge and coughed.

I asked after his health, and he said, "Black lung."

"Seriously?"

He laughed.

I said that if he was sick, he should've told me sooner.

"Animals hide weakness," Spencer said. "Come on, sit here. I've been wanting to show you something."

One woman drove her knee into the other's spine, but Spencer pointed to the second screen. It was a simple interface, white text clipping down a black box. I recognized certain proper names interspersed with the usual *fap* and *fag*. They were talking politics.

We watched. We laughed together. Sometimes, his laughter ended in coughs. He kept a blanket over his legs.

"We start things here," he said. "Out west, did you ever hear about that third-line goon we got into the all-star game?"

My eyes were trained on the text, as if discerning starlight.

"How many of you are there?"

And my best friend said, "More all the time."

The following year, when the Russians beat us in the World Championships, a retired hockey coach named Dom Crossman would make headlines by suggesting that Canada's national vigour was diluted. He singled out certain players; he cited ancient Roman history. Reporters had trouble suppressing smiles. When the *Toronto Star* ran an editorial against him, he said there should be a referendum to decide if the writer should keep her job. Within minutes, the paper's site had crashed.

New faces appear in the green room. Before the convention, they spoke of our campaign as an act of vandalism. Now the president of the party pops an oversized bottle of Veuve Clicquot and toasts Dom Crossman, our nominee.

Even in victory, Wei never stops working. She monitors how many flutes Dom's finished. I bask in the news online, where there's a clearer sense of velocity, even destiny. By contrast, the faces in the green room are as worried as they are celebratory. I only worry they won't go far enough, that this marks the moment Dom becomes one of them. All of a sudden, we've gained a lot of old weight.

"Always on the phone," says the president, who clinks my flute. "Tell me—what are people saying?"

"They're laughing."

"Laughing." She searches my eyes. "I can't tell if you're serious. It's not a pleasant feeling."

I'm about to say, "I had a friend like that," but I keep it to myself.

"Don't sweat it, chief."

The president empties her champagne and looks across the room at Dom. The candidate's face has reddened. Wei hovers at his elbow.

"I've been doing this a long, long time," says the president. "Let me enlighten you. Crossman isn't really one of us. In a federal campaign, people will see that. Be serious for a second—you know he can't win."

I can't hold it any longer. Spencer is here; he's bursting out of us. I break into a smile, and the president reflects it, and now the room fills with laughter.

TWINKLE, TWINKLE

STEPHEN MARCHE

T**HE FOLLOWING** *story was algorithmically generated. I call it an algostory.*

Two researchers named Allan Hammond and Julian Brooke have spent the past few years developing software that analyzes literary databases. Their program can identify dozens of structural and stylistic details in huge chunks of text, and if you give them a collection of great stories—stories that maybe you wished you had written—they are able to identify all the details that those stories have in common.

Hammond and Brooke agreed to collaborate with me on a simple experiment: Can an alogorithm help me write a better story? I began by giving them a collection of my 50 favorite sci-fi stories—a mix of golden-age classics and some more recent stuff. (We decided I'd write a science-fiction piece, both for the obvious reasons and because sci-fi is easy to identify.) They used their program to compare my stories to a mass of other stories. First they came back to me with a series of stylistic guidelines that would make my story as much like the samples as possible—things like there had to be four speaking characters and a certain percentage of the text had to be dialogue. Then they sent me a set of 14 rules, derived from a process called topic modeling, that would govern my story's main topics and themes. All I had to do was start writing.

Hammond and Brooke created a web-based interface through which their algorithm, called SciFiQ, could tell me, on the textual equivalent of the atomic level, how closely every single detail of my writing matched the details in my 50 favorite works. (I'm talking "nouns per 100 words" level.) When I typed in a word or phrase and it was more than a little different from what SciFiQ had in mind, the interface would light up red or purple. When I fixed the offending word or phrase, the interface would turn green.

The key, obviously, was the texts that I selected: "Vaster than Empires and More Slow" by Ursula K. Le Guin, "The Father-Thing" by Philip K. Dick, "There Will Come Soft Rains" by Ray Bradbury—I can't list them all, but you get the idea. I wanted to write something incredible, so I picked stories I thought were incredible. Whether that's what I got might be another story.

The machines sat empty in the dark. Only a single light was on when Anne and Ed entered. A lone searcher was staring at the Other planet[1], his face half-swallowed by the viewer and the empty banks of blank screens[2] sloped into the room's vague emptiness.

---

1   "Topic modeling," Hammond says of the process he and Brooke used to create the 14 rules, "is mathematically sophisticated but otherwise stupid. The algorithm looks for words that tend to occur near one another in a very large corpus of text." Based on how frequently the words appear together, Hammond determined what my story had to be about. For instance, after finding clusters of words throughout the texts that suggested extraterrestrial worlds and beings, he gave me rule number one: "The story should be set on a planet other than Earth."

2   The algorithm affected the story much more than I thought it would. Rule number one above seemed to conflict with rule number nine: "Include a scene set on a traditional Earth farm, with apple trees and corn fields." The only way I could figure out how to follow both rules was to have someone on Earth viewing another planet. Which, I have to say, I like—the feeling that you're watching helplessly as faraway events transpire. That suits our time, doesn't it?

"Profitable and marketable," Ed said. "I cannot stress that enough."

"Profitable and marketable," Anne murmured in agreement.

The man at the viewer sucked out his face with a faint squelch and, with no acknowledgment of either Anne or Ed, began to pack up as quickly as possible. Anne had over-dressed for her first day, obviously. Ed was night supervisor, but he was wearing blue and green overalls. The guy at the viewer was in head-to-toe sweats. His sallow eyes were exhausted[3]. He emanated a grotesque odour of off-brand bleach, and it burned the inside of her nostrils. And she was wearing her best outfit, the pencil-skirt outfit she'd bought for her dissertation defence.

"Once upon a time," Ed continued, "people were interested in the Other world just because it was another world. There was discovery. Then there was building the telescopes, carrying the mercury to the translunar observatories, constructing the antigravity bases, the discs within discs of whirling silver the size of cities to capture the light."

The sallow man Anne was replacing misted the inside of the viewer with antiseptic spray, and gently rubbed the screen down with a paper towel. Nodding curtly to each of them in turn, he half-jogged out the door. They were apparently not to be introduced. Her coworker couldn't wait to be gone.

"If you're curious, go to the archives. I know, you're a full prof, full xenologist. I know you've spent ten years in the archives already, but you've got four hours tonight, well, three

---

3   What most writers and readers consider style (a recognizable way with words) is not what the algorithm considers style. It was developed to analyze average sentence length, variance in paragraph length, verbs per 100 words, and dozens of other statistics and patterns that my story would have to follow.

hours and forty-two minutes. The archives have a hundred million hours cross-referenced. Your job is to keep looking to find something so we can justify keeping the lights on here."

"I understand."

"This light here," he said, tapping the lamp.

The glow from the viewer that no one was looking into unnerved Anne. The Other world, 1564 light years away, was flowing brightly[4] and glamorously[5] into the machine, unobserved, while Ed concluded what must be his boilerplate orientation speech.

"Nobody cares. That's the thing to remember. While you're here, I'll be making phone calls to the South China coast begging for cash. Help me out. Keep the lights on here to keep an eye on there. That's our motto now."

"Curiosity isn't enough," she said.

"Curiosity isn't enough. Exactly. You're starting to understand. When people with money, people who matter, think of the Other, they think of aliens who have been dead for fifteen hundred years. It's a nightmare, in a way, a planet of corpses who don't know the oblivion they have momentarily escaped with us. Everybody knows. If they were ever going to find their way to us, they probably already would have. And if they're looking at us, which they probably aren't, what would we have to say to them? So it makes everybody sad, that there's intelligent life out there and it doesn't matter much. And sad is a hard sell."

Ed was obviously wrapping up.

---

4 I wrote a rough draft, based on the rules and guidelines, and dropped it into the interface. The first thing SciFiQ told me was that I used too few adverbs. I've always been taught to cut anything ending in ly, and I had to go back over the story putting in adverbs. Absurdly, good science fiction has a lot of adverbs.

5 It wasn't just adverbs either. It was adverbs per 100 words. So they had to be sprinkled throughout.

"You're here to see, not to have insight. You will no doubt be struck by the reality of a planet so similar to ours, so distant from ours, and you will think deep thoughts about the loneliness of the cosmos. You may come to think even about the fate of a universe that is probably one of many universes, exemplified only by the fact that the universe that we happen to reside in happens to have to have created observers. Don't bother sharing these digressions. They have already been written down by people who are ten thousand times more perspicacious than you and I and still managed to die in comprehensive obscurity."

"Profitable and marketable,"[6] Anne repeated.

"That's correct. So tonight you have fewer than four hours to look at Othertribespeople on a ring of the lesser Chekhovs. Nobody knows much about them. They might have some new medicine. Anything that might have saleable value, report."

"So I should call you if I see something new?"[7]

"Call me if you see an Other holding up a sign that says, 'Hello, earth. It's us up here.'"

At its peak, the Institution for the Study of Extraterrestrial

---

6   The algorithm also told me what percentage of text should be dialogue and how much of that dialogue should come from female characters. This is where things get embarrassing. Turns out that, based on the stories I chose, only 16. 1 percent of the dialogue could be from a woman's point of view. Which is a crazily low number. Female writers historically write 40 to 50 percent of their dialogue for female characters, male writers about 20 percent; so even by the shitty standards of male writers and history, this is appalling. It meant I had to make Anne shy and scholarly, and I had to make all the men around her bloviating assholes. Otherwise the dialogue numbers wouldn't work out.

7   The female dialogue thing is still bugging me. If I had chosen a different 50 stories, or even changed one of the 50 stories, there would be a different outcome. I need to start reading better science fiction.

Life had employed 264 fully trained researchers at the banks of screens. The mania for the Other had gripped the world and every school devoted a class a week to its study. Universities all over the world had Other departments. Biologists handled the various pockets of life discovered in the rest of the universe, slimes mutating fiercely but drably on dozens of freezing or burning hells. The Other was its own field. The similarity had come as an existential shock to the earth. A planet 1564 light years away had forests that were not dissimilar to earth's forests. They had animals that were not that unlike the remaining animals on earth. And they had the Others, who lived in cities, with streets, or in villages, or in tribes, just like us. The Others wore clothes. They fell in love. They wrote books. They kept time. They had laws. The odds of two worlds being conjured by chance at such similar points in their development—the Other was roughly at Earth's 1964—had to mean something. The anthropic principle was considered proven. The universe could only exist under conditions in which ourselves and the Others were there to witness it. Those were the day when children, like Anne when she was a kid, wore pyjamas with patterns of glublefrings gamboling among the tzitzi-glug trees, and everybody called it The Yonder. But all novelty eventually wears off. The natural market for the shock of recognition is perishingly small.

Alone in the vast[8] dark room, Anne wiped down the viewer again, just to be sure. She understood why there had been so many conspiracies in the days after discovery. It was like the machine fabricated the planet. Anne placed her face inside. The sucking in of the face curtains sealed

---

8 Rule number 11: "Engage the sublime. Consider using the follow-ing words: vast, gigantic, strange, radiance, mystery, brilliance, fantas-tic, and spooky."

her. She was hovering over a planet on the other side of the galaxy, twenty feet over a small group of Othertribespeople at night fishing.

The quality of the screen was so impeccable that the sense of her own body dissolved, and she was a floating dot. There was no comparison to watching a tape; this was live, or rather it was live 1564 years ago. The tribe grouped tightly around a mountain stream. The males held torches up to the water, where a flurry of small fishes roiled on or under the surface, and a female Other poised, a spear in her hand, waiting for a Gallack. They were huge, the Gallacks, nearly the size of an Other. A single fish could feed a group of tribespeople for a month of desert season.

Anne wanted to look a bit more closely. She reached down and her screen went blank. She had zoomed too far. She pulled up with a clenched fist and an elbow curl, and she was among the clouds above the mountains. The fire of the tribe's torches made a rosy-red[9] and blue dot in the centre. She pushed down slowly, adjusting. She had asked one of her dissertation supervisors what it was like working on the screens and he had told her it was like being an impotent god, and the description was precise. Delicately, tentatively, Anne focused on the face of the Other woman holding a spear. Sometimes a Gallack might not come to light for hours, and when it did, it offered maybe three seconds of its purple-streaked skull bone for a strike. The Otherwoman's eyes had narrowed sharply in concentration, her eyes small, even for the eyes of the Others, who had no nasal bridge, and

---

9   The algorithm distinguishes between the "literariness" and "colloqui-alness" of any given word, and I had to strike the right balance between the two kinds. My number of literary words was apparently too high, so I had to go through the story replacing words like *scarlet* with words like *red*.

whose button noses, like tiny dogs, were considerably more powerful than a human nose. A horrific violence lurked in her gaze.

The Others stood so still, so intently and contentedly waiting for a slimy mammoth fish to rise out of the waters. Why was she watching this? The hope was that someone would hurt themselves in the hunt, and that the tribe would use a herb that had found an analogue in the surviving jungles on earth, to repair the damage. That's how they had found the bark of the Amazonian gluttaree had curative properties for Bell's Palsy. That was profitable and marketable. Only the leaves on the Other trees—she thought they were hualintratras, or maybe grubgrubs—moved at all[10]. The shimmering and the stillness were so different from the recordings, somehow. The recordings were always significant. That was the difference. Something had always happened to make them worth watching, worth preserving. The Othertribespeople, were just waiting around for a Gallack. Maybe the Gallack would come, or maybe it wouldn't.

It wouldn't really matter if she snuck off to the city for twenty minutes, would it?

She marked the place of the tribe, flicked up with a curled fist, saw the planet whole for a second, found the biggest dot, centred herself visually, and pushed down.

She landed accidentally in a funeral, right in the middle of the green twigs. Curling up, she could see that a ritual was in its final stages, the morbid consummation. The funeral must be the Middle Space, off the straight avenue. Soon they would have a horrible shattering, a grandiose

---

10   I loved writing descriptions of the Other planet, but I could only include a few. My story had to consist of about 26 percent dialogue, so every time I wrote a bit of descriptive non-dialogue, I knew I'd have to make up for it elsewhere with some talking. It was like working out probabilities when you're playing poker.

howl, an unconditional prostration. The crowd was small, six Others, so a prominent Other must have died. The body was already under the branches though, so Anne couldn't quite tell.

She pulled up, too quickly, and she was once again too high. She hovered over the whole of the OSC, the Other South City, momentarily dazzled[11]. There were twenty-four million Others in the city, more than any city on earth had held for fifty years, and that was without counting however many were living in the subterranean tunnels. Even at night, glowing with torches over the large avenues, the circles within interlocked circles, orbs within orbs which were so typically a figure of the Southern part of the main Continent, the City Center sprawled haphazardly. So much life. So much life to see.

But all that life was none of her business. Her business was back on the lower Chekhovs. Anne flipped back to the saved locale. The Othertribespeople were still waiting patiently for a big fish to come to light.

Back in OSC, she floated over the Coil, the central avenue of the biggest Other city. The flashes of the running Others, the tumult of their flat faces. Who to follow? Who to forget?

She followed one Other licking his lips anxiously. He turned off the corner and was gone. She followed another Other woman before she dipped into a store that sold texts. The universe is crammed with fascinating irrelevance. Anne was just watching now. All the work had already been done on the main streets, although it grew out of date so rapidly. When she had been a

---

11   Rule number four: "The story should be set in a city. The protagonists should be seeing the city for the first time and should be impressed and dazzled by its scale."

xenosociologist, she had studied some of the commercial patterns, the gift and theft matrices that seemed to be their version of exchange. That was before her department, and all the other departments except xenolinguistics, had been folded into general xenology. They were all just xenologists now.

She widened her gaze and drifted into one of the neighbourhoods halfway or more than halfway if the city was still spreading since she had last read about it of the Uppertown Stage. The harsh tangerine dawn was rising on Other children as they played the string game in its labyrinthine star patterns laid out in the sand. She had written one of her first papers in grade school on geometrical erudition in Other children games, an A+. Her teacher, Ms. Norwood, had said, not quite believing it, that she might work at ISEL some day.

She remembered that Ms. Norwood had been a devotee of Wodeck's theory of distant proprioception, though it had been defunct as a theory even then. By virtue of the Heisenberg principle, Wodeck argued, we must be altering the Others in our observation of them. The idea was too Romantic for the academy or the public, both of whom thought Heisenberg was fine for electrons but not for aliens who had been dead for 1500 years and whose remains had long since rotted to ashes by the time their light had arrived. The idea was doubly distasteful, because who knew who was watching us, and from where? Who wanted to believe their lives were shaped by alien eyes?

Anne saw another Other girl, to a side of the players, reading pages, so she pushed in, focused, and caught a corner of the text, and cut and pasted into the archive comparer, on the off-chance it might be new and viable, a late entry into the now mostly unread library of the Other.

Then the book, in the middle of being copied, fluttered from the Other girl's hands. The Other girl's face was up, staring, in horrified confusion. Anne flicked over to where the Other child was looking. A smouldering hole had formed in the sand lot beside the children's play space. A bizarre machine, unlike any devices she had seen in any xenology class, careened[12] at top pace down one of the lesser coils. She looked down. An Other man and an Other woman were riding in it, driving. The machine was large and silver. It would fit a bed. The thing must have ripped through the surface. She had never heard of that. She looked closer, and the Other man and the Other woman were carrying a baby, and they had a look of terror and tenderness on their haggard faces, pale from the cruelty of underground life. Anne pulled out with a curled fist and they had no chance to escape. The restraint work of the Other authorities was always impressive in its brutality. The Others were monsters when it came to crime and punishment and angrily excised any difference with savagery. A remorseless circle of exexalters, at least thirty of them, were coiling in on the fleeing Others. How long did they have? She looked back, flipped up. The Other man smiled at the Other woman for some obscure reason, cooed over the infant. She flipped back and the round group of the sinister exexalters crept in, and then they all slowed, out of screen. She flipped back up and the strange machine had vanished. She curled up more. The machine had crashed into a boulder, and the Other woman with her baby were burning horribly inside the wreckage, and the Other man, thrown clear,

---

12   Rule number six: "Include a pivotal scene in which a group of people escape from a building at night at high speed in a high tech vehicle made of metal and glass."

lay dying on the grey sand. The Other man was looking straight up. He was looking straight up at Anne. He was staring at her across the galaxy right into her eye.

Anne's face, as it sucked out of the viewer, pulled slightly on the flaps, gently squeezing her eyeballs in their socket[13]. Two hours and seventeen minutes had passed. Time was always distorted by drifting over the Other, what with a thirty-six hour, seventeen-minute, fifty-four-second day. Culture shock is always worse coming home.

"Ed?" She called up the professor's visuals from control. His face, on Skype, was the haggard face of a begging administrator on one call after another.

"Hi Anne, did they hold up a sign saying 'Hi, earth?'"

"I saw something."

"Is it profitable and marketable?"

Was there profit in that rickety old machine somewhere? Was there some kind of profit in that? Or in the look of sadness on the Other's face?

"There's lots of wonderful things to see, Anne. Nobody needs us here to show them a new wonderful thing. The moon shines wonderfully every evening. Nobody needs seventy-thousand-ton telescopes in the sky to show them a place they have never seen before. If we want to keep an eye on, we have to find useful, profitable Otherness. Not the new and wonderful. Got it?"

"Got it."

"Profitable and marketable."

"Profitable and marketable."

---

13   Rule number 10: "Include extended descriptions of intense physical sensations and name the bodily organs that perceive these sensations." The first part of that rule is generally good writing advice (make 'em feel it), but the second part is innovative: It's not just the description but the organs that matter.

The wreckage was still smouldering gruesomely on the viewer. The corpse of the Other man had already been cleared away. The machine, which must have been cobbled together in the underground, chuffed and spluttered smokily. And there was no way any of it could ever be profitable and marketable.

Anne called Lee, a colleague from graduate school who had worked on subterranean history, and if she was recalling it right, even something with machines. He was living in Cairo these days, she thought, some kind of assistant professor at the uni there.

"Is that Anne?" he asked[14]. He was older, more slovenly than she remembered, but it had been nearly ten years. She reached him at a Shisha bar on Tahrir Square. "Is that the Anne who is working, I heard, at ISEL and who is actually looking into the sky?"

"That's me."

"And what can I do for Anne who has a good job at ISEL where she is looking into the sky?"

"You once, long ago, studied the subterranea right?"

The hitch in his voice swelled awkwardly, stringently into a silence. The envy reached through the phone. Anne remembered. Lee had only managed a lousy archival job[15], rustling in ten-year-old tapes for culinary elements. All the best dishes had been transferred years ago.

---

14   This guy is here—this whole scene is here—because there needed to be four speaking characters and I needed more dialogue. If I were just writing it myself, I would probably cut the whole section.

15   Ordinarily, when I'm writing and I'm stuck with a line I don't like, I work on finding the right way to write that line. The adjective sucks? I find a better adjective or cut the adjective altogether. But, in this case, that's not enough. If you cut an adjective in one place, you have to put in an adjective somewhere else, and putting in that adjective somewhere else alters the balance of sentence length, paragraph length, paragraph length variation, and so on. It's a bit like doing a Rubik's cube. You fix one thing, you've messed up the side you weren't looking at.

"Wow. You're actually at ISEL asking me a question about the subterannea, aren't you?"

"That I am."

His voice hitched again. "You didn't see a real breakout did you?"

"Well, I'm not sure. I just want to know if there's any history on the machines used in breakouts."

Lee paused, recognizing that his scholarship might matter, realizing that the Other existed, was existing, and he understood it, understood it usefully.

"Well, a big book on subterranea as a prison system is Nguyen's Other Underground, but that was forty years ago or more even. The subterannea's only had maybe a thousand hours of inspection over the past twenty years."

"Why is that?"

"I guess they figure if the Others don't care about it, why would we? People get bored with mysteries after a while, for sure. And then there was an article a couple of years ago, out of the unit at Oxford. 'Otherness among the Other,' but it was general xenosociology. Wasn't that your field?"

"Before it all folded."

"Right. We're all xenologists now. Also, there's a footnote in my last paper in Otherism on the first escape but you know all about that. So what can you tell me about your breakout?"

She would be fired for a leak, even with Lee, even for a story no one cared to hear. Systems grow stricter as institutions decline. If there is nothing profitable or marketable in a thing, it must remain a secret or it has no value at all.

Her parents were still up when Anne, sick from the train and suffused with an indefinable and all-suffusing disappointment, rolled through the portico of the family farmstead. She found them in the viewing room, watching a new storm[16] roll ferociously over the cornfields and the apple orchard. Mom was lying down, asleep, with her head on dad's lap. The lightning from the storm was continuous enough that the room needed no other illumination, and Anne's skin tingled furtively[17] with the electricity in the air. She sat beside her father in the noise of the rain that filled her ears like a cloying syrup.

"How was the first day at ISEL?" he whispered.

"Everything I thought it would be."

"And what did you think it would be then?"

It was the first time that day that anyone had cared what Anne thought. And at that very moment she didn't want to see or to record. At that very moment she just wanted to listen to the rain.

"There's just so much of it," she said.

"It is another world."

"And what are we doing looking at it?"

"Keeping an eye on, right?"

"Keeping an eye on what?"

Anne's father ran a hand through her mother's hair a few moments.

"This morning I was weighing in my mind that first book of the Other plants and animals we bought you. Remember that?"

"Sure."

"And those bedroom sheets you wanted so badly, the ones with a little kangaroo-like Other thing on it. What are they called?"

"Calotricks."

---

16   Rule number five: "Part of the action should unfold at night during an intense storm."

17   One way of looking at this algorithm is as an editor. It's commissioning a story with guidelines and then forcing me to write it the way it wants. If I don't do it right, the algorithm makes me do it again, and again, until I get it right.

"And now you're a grown-up woman, and they're letting you look up in the sky from the big machines at ISEL."

The storm ripped the sky, harsh as a lash against her eyes. Her dad was proud of her, but she could tell he cared less for the Other world, the distant miracle, a sign however remote that we were not alone in the universe, than whether she would be able to move out now that she had a job. She was about to tell him about the nightmare chase of the burning woman and the dying man and the baby they took with them when her mother roused, and Dad shushed, and began to sing:

Twinkle, twinkle[18], little star
How I wonder what you are.
Up above the world so high
Like a diamond in the sky
Twinkle, twinkle little star[19]
How I wonder what you are.

He picked up his wife and carried her out of the viewing room to bed. Anne was alone, more alone than before.

The exhaustion of the day accumulating inside her, she was glad of a half-dark room and a storm. As a child, to be even a cog in the celestial machinery would have been enough. She loved a whole other world, miraculously reflected in a skypiercing eye. She was middle-aged now: there was only light, moving through emptiness, trapped by machines[20].

---

18   I chose the title of the story. Some things the algorithm didn't get to decide.

19   Did you know this poem was actually written by a person? A woman named *Jane Taylor (1783–1824)*. And it's so famous that everybody assumes nobody wrote it, that it just kind of appeared. That is the ultimate achievement of writing, that it's so good that no person could have written it.

20   "The fact that it's really not that bad is kind of remarkable." That's how Rich, my human editor, described the story. I'll take it.

VISITATION

LISA MOORE

I STARTED having visions in late July, just as things were starting to heat up. The visions were preceded by the kind of optical disturbances many people experience. Floating prisms in my peripheral vision. Unaligned rainbows, or shimmers that sometimes drifted in front of my eyes as if carried on a light breeze. They were radiant but opaque splotches, so if I were looking directly at someone's face, the mouth might be obscured. If I darted my eyes, fast, to the right or left, I could sometimes shift the spot so I could see the person's mouth, but then an eye would be obscured, or a cheek. I thought early migraine symptoms, or detached retina, but there was no firm diagnosis.

I began to experience these floaters, or whatever they were, a month or so before the first vision. I don't know if the man I saw was in any way connected to the minor visual disturbances that preceded his presence. I say man; he was corporeal. But that is all I can say for certain.

The vision was accompanied by the stink of rot; it smelled like our dog after he had rolled in the remains of a moose carcass someone had dumped in the woods. It was a stink that wafted in—simultaneously piercing and blunt, like a hammer that hits a thumb—but the smell was whipped away when the wind changed direction. I didn't think supernatural at the time. I didn't think evil. But I felt uneasy almost at once, a fluttering in my gut. And after only a moment, I was very afraid.

The first time I experienced the vision, or visitation, was at the Low Point beach. I thought stress. The collapse of my marriage. My husband and I had been separated for a little more than a year and had recently finalized the divorce. Psychotic episode, I thought. I hadn't been eating very much. I was working long hours. I thought fatigue. Though at first I thought the man was an ordinary stranger who had stopped at the beach because of the strange phenomena with the fish. The bay was thick with cod. Half the community had come out to see. There were cars lining the harbour, people standing around in small groups, trying to get a good look.

A marriage is this: My husband likes the glasses with the glasses, the cups with the cups. Every morning I unload the dishwasher and put the cups and the glasses together. He comes down and moves the cups.

The bath running, pipes shuddering, lolling surges of water, the scrudge of a calf or buttock along the white enamel of the cast-iron claw-footed tub we salvaged from an abandoned house in Low Point, a house collapsing into the long grass.

We are: Daily walks along Duckworth Street in the late afternoon together; occasionally, change for the homeless of downtown St. John's, mostly kids with dogs, sleeping bags draped over their shoulders and cardboard signs that say they're trying to get home; lattes from Fixed; past the Devon House, raku pottery in the window and hooked rugs, up to the Battery where there are seven black cats, mostly on the picket fence or the porch of the last house before you get to the lookout. We are the dog let loose in the Anglican Cathedral on the way back home, rippling through the chest-high snow at dusk. A mutt, mottled like an old mirror, an undulation, sniffing the graves; and my husband, with the black nylon leash wrapped around one of his puffy Gore-Tex gloves, letting the metal hook of the leash slap against his thigh.

We are roast chicken dinners with chicken seasoning that we bang out of a tin can with the flat of our hands. The chicken from a frozen package of three, purchased at Costco, frost-burnt and plump. We cook with haste. Long as it isn't raw. We buy the jumbo Party Mix and shovel handfuls into our faces while we cook and do the dishes.

We tell each other stories, outrages from my husband's office, flecks of pretzel flying as he says about this one or that one. Or I talk about the customers at the store; the new Excel spreadsheets I'm using for inventory, glitches in software.

I type, I say. Then there's a delay.

These are fillable forms?

A delay and then the letters and numbers flick across the screen, meanwhile I'm not doing anything. These are fillable.

You're not touching the keyboard?

And the letters pour across the screen, seconds later, like, thirty seconds maybe.

My husband doesn't like the gloves I use for washing the pots and pans. Yellow rubber gloves.

You leave them all over the place, he says. Put them away at least.

They're gloves, I say. Grease, what do you call, globules in the water.

You leave them on the counter.

Clots of dog food, pork fat, a soggy toast crust. I don't want my hands touching that.

The feel of those gloves inside, he says. Wet, icky.

And then, I say. Like, a half sentence of text ticks out all by itself across the screen.

Turn the machine off and turn it back on, my husband says.

I do.

Do you turn it off?

I do, I tell him.

Marriage is: you buy a cabin (a "cottage," they'd call it on the mainland, with a veranda and garden, a lilac and an apple tree, blossoms all over the ground) in outport Newfoundland, maybe an hour or two from town. Canoes, barbeques, an ATV. Before long, you invest in a small business, buy a convenience store down the road from the cabin. A commercial property with a gas bar, soft-serve machine, beer; sell firewood to the crowd who come in from town for ice fishing on the ponds.

When the store came on the market we saw it as extra income to supplement my husband's retirement, maybe six or seven years away. We thought: opportunity. We thought I could commute for part of the week, manage the store from town the rest of the time. An hour and a half drive.

We thought when my husband retired we'd live around the bay most of the year. Solar panels, maybe even thermal heating, a greenhouse for tomatoes, basil. He'd apply for a moose licence; get one of our neighbours to take him out. We thought off the grid, maybe. Or partially off the grid. Turn our house in the city into an Airbnb.

We are: a box comes in the mail. Something rattles around inside it; I have to slit the packing tape with an X-Acto knife.

Here, let me get you a knife. I got it. No, use the knife. Okay, give me the knife.

Even then, I have trouble ripping open the heavy cardboard. Present for you, my husband says. Guess what it is. No idea.

What's the occasion? No occasion. You can't guess? I've no idea.

A dildo, bright purple with ridges, a smiley face at the tip. Hilarious.

Set in a bed of Styrofoam S's. I twist the wheel on one end and the vibration is industrial. The S's squeak against each other, writhing in a pelt of static electricity. Twist the dial back the other way, a gentle hum.

Give it a whirl, he says.

We are the neighbour's snow blower at dawn. Trips to the dump. We are the new surveillance system I have installed at the store. A camera pointing in every aisle. The simultaneous feed on a flat screen at the cabin and the video footage, three months after the system was installed, of the first break-in. A young woman with long dark hair and a round rabbit-fur hat, pixelated and flaring white like a halo. A young man loading cartons of cigarettes into an army surplus bag, cleaning off the shelves with a sweep of his arm. I'd phoned the cops by running out onto the road with the phone until I found reception. Only two bars, halfway to the river out back, but they answered. They blocked off the highway on both ends, the only two ways out of Low Point if you're driving.

Marriage is: You should get that windshield wiper fixed. I will. Don't go on the highway with it like that. I won't. Stop at Canadian Tire. I will. Did you stop at Canadian Tire? No. You drove like that? Yes, I did.

The wiper with the rubber blade torn away from the metal arm so that the strip of rubber wiggles over the glass like a maddened eel. The metal arm scratching an arc in the glass.

Sucking his cock; the vibrator on roar.

How was it? Oh my god. Was it good? Oh my god.

A marriage is: remortgaging the convenience store in Low Point after the divorce and the condo fiasco. I work more shifts at the store and live in our cabin, to which you say: Okay, until we figure out something else.

You got the cabin in the divorce. We split everything down the middle, the accretion of a life, the worst being the doodads; the worst being the Aerolatte from Bed Bath & Beyond for milk foaming; the worst being the Dirt Devil, and all the handheld devices for cleaning to which I'd inexplicably formed an attachment.

The glass decanter your mother gave us, and the popcorn maker; the worst being the Christmas decorations, dragged from the basement in the heat of summer, the needlepoint Santa my sister did which naturally went to me, the pewter reindeer.

The very worst was the tin salamander from Mexico City with plastic jewels on its back and you could put a tea light behind it. The salamander you bought after we'd stood over the graves with the Plexiglas covers embedded in the stone of the courtyard outside the Metropolitan Cathedral. Unable to see what was below because of the condensation on the Plexiglas, the murky depths of the graves, and the febrile moss of decay.

And the wild fucking in the hotel room behind the cathedral and the bar when the Mexicans stood, one at a time, stood up from tables squashed with relatives, maybe fifteen at a table, all ages, and sang out folk songs, and the enchiladas and old grandmothers.

You took the salamander. We fought over the salamander and I threw a plate at your head but I missed, smashed it against the cupboards. You got the salamander.

I had lost my entire share in the condo fiasco; that was not us, it was me. But after thirty-two years of marriage what could you do? You would not have me say I was put out on the sidewalk. For a time, until I got on my feet, I could stay at the cabin in Low Point. You refinanced the convenience store. Of course this was not us. This was my lawyer and your lawyer.

I was a dancer until I was twenty-seven. Once I performed in a dance that began at dawn in the graveyard of the Anglican Cathedral. We dancers lay face up on the graves. Many of the headstones in that graveyard lie flat on the ground, and the words and dates are smoothed away, gouged by centuries of rain and sleet.

We were wearing long gowns and petticoats, the colours too brilliant for period dresses. A troupe of fifteen young women. We rose from the graves as the sun came up, yawning, stretching our arms in the air. We each had a big silver tray with heaps of cut fruit that we offered the audience. Fog crawled around the graveyard. The trains of our dresses left streaks of bright emerald in the dew-greyed grass. I was wearing a ruffled dress with a stiff lace bodice; the smell of baby powder and the comforting scent of some other actress's stale underarm sweat; lying in a faint depression in the earth because the coffin below me had rotted through and collapsed.

Dancers live by their bodies; they know the muscle and gut, ache and attrition. It's a short stint, dominated by youth and strength, and sexual appetite. Ungovernable hunger. When we accept the idea of decay we are no longer dancers. We hold the simple tenet: everything moves.

The divorce had come through, and then, at the Low Point beach, the vision. I hadn't been to town in more than two weeks. I had to be at the store when gas was delivered for the tanks, to see the Atlantic Lottery rep, the Central Dairies delivery, the man from Labatt's restocking the fridge. I was discovering discrepancies in the accounts: small sums, sometimes significant sums, but I could see no pattern, make no sense of what was missing. Almost everyone in the community ran a tab, and everything they bought was written down by hand in Hilroy exercise books. I was transferring the accounts to spreadsheets but there were glitches in the software. Some customers complained they had been charged for things they hadn't bought. They said things like this had never happened under the former owner. One woman said it was as simple as the nose on your face. If it wasn't written down you never bought it.

The man at the beach was in a too-tight plaid jacket and jeans with the crotch hanging low enough on his thighs that it seemed to pinch his gait. He walked with a cordoned strut. He was standing with his phone out, trying to take a picture of the water.

The ocean was teeming with cod. They were so dense near the shore I could see their backs breaking the surface, piled on top of each other, their violent writhing. They formed a solid sludge. Some had been left on the beach when the waves withdrew. The sun was setting, turning the water a streaky orange, and close to the beach it was a bloody violet. All the windows in the houses along the shore glowed deep yellow. It was only a matter of minutes before the sun disappeared into the horizon. Fish were dying all over the sand, flinging themselves up, sometimes as much as a foot in the air, and wriggling.

I smelled the alcohol off the man, and the stink of rot or sewage so strong it made my eyes water until the wind changed and the smell was gone. His face was slack except for a ridge of cheekbone, high and sharp under his deep-set eyes, the corners of which radiated white lines in his tanned face as if he had been squinting into a permanent glare. His forehead swooped back, a receding hairline. The pate spattered with brown patches. He had a beard, tufts of thin hair, almost colourless. He was bone with hard knots of stringy muscle and very short. I'd never seen him before.

People said with the downturn in the economy, strangers were coming from St. John's to cause trouble, break into homes, vandalize, steal what they could get. This was new in a community that slept with their doors unlocked.

What's happening? I asked.

Fish, he said. I saw that there were cars lined up on both sides of the harbour with their headlights on. People standing at the edge of the cliff. I had never seen anything like it. It was unnatural. The water churning.

I was trying to post a picture, he said. But you got no reception here.

Sometimes you get one or two bars, I said. Up near the church.

You don't belong here, he said. What are you? From town? He ran his eyes over me and slid his phone into the back pocket of his jeans. He started to walk beside me toward the road, where his truck was idling. He took a flask out of the inside breast pocket of the jacket. The bottle was in a paper bag, soft with thousands of fine wrinkles from reuse. He tilted the mouth of the bottle toward me. A truck up on the hill pulled out of the line of trucks and headed down the dirt road. Its headlights, for a brief instant, made the man a silhouette. Light punched through his crooked elbow and between his legs and over his shoulders and when the truck had gone past there was a shimmering floater hanging over the man's mouth. I blinked hard but I couldn't get rid of the blinding spot of light. Then my stomach flip-flopped like the fish on the beach and I felt very afraid of him. It was a paranoia that I recognized, even in the grip of it, as being entirely unreasonable. But the fear was a quickening, solid and instinctive; I could neither make sense of it nor stand another minute in the man's presence. He was befouled. But it was only later that I understood he hadn't existed. That he was a visitation, a violation.

A few weeks after the first vision there was the fire at the Bay de Verde fish plant. Down the shore a few miles from my cabin—the cabin my husband was letting me stay in free of charge until I could get back on my feet, until his good will ran out—a whole community went up in flames.

The smell of fresh paint in the condo; fifty-six people defrauded of their life savings. A chalky vanilla scent. They are scenting interior paint these days. But I'd stepped inside the one-room condo in St. John's with Marion Sullivan that day and I'd felt nothing out of the ordinary. I am not a good judge of character. Even in hindsight it is hard to believe that Marion is not the well-meaning, never-stops-talking but canny person I thought she was.

She intuited the divorce when we were getting a coffee at Tim Hortons, though I hadn't said. But at Tim Hortons, the pressure I'd felt. Preparing to sign the papers for the condo at the bank. My husband would have known about

Marion Sullivan. He can smell a false, bright confidence as surely as I could smell that vanilla paint.

I had my son, Kevin, with me the morning I signed for the condo. He'd been skateboarding outside the bank with friends but the security guard came out to make them leave. All Kevin's buddies dispersed with the slump-shouldered lag of kids who don't respect authority but would find anything other than sluggish compliance unstylish.

Kevin stepped on the tail end of his board so it seemed to leap into his hand, and then he followed me into my meeting at the bank without a word.

The day before, I'd let myself in the front door of our downtown house after one last, confirming visit to the condo with Marion Sullivan and I'd looked down the long hall to the kitchen where Kevin had been standing at the counter making a sandwich. He was lit up by the setting sun from the patio doors at the back of the kitchen. He winked out of view; I heard the kiss of the rubber seal on the fridge door as he pulled it open, tinkling the jars and bottles, and he winked back into view.

Kevin had sprouted during the divorce. He'd shed a stunting dormancy, arms and legs telescoping out, shoulders broad and muscled. The growth was accompanied with unexpected elegance, loping grace.

In that instant, while he was backlit with blinding sunlight, I thought Kevin was his father. I thought my husband had come back, or more accurately, had never left.

What's happening out there, I asked the man at the Low Point beach. A lockjaw wince stole over his face before he spoke.

Fish, thousands of fish, he said. He was one of those men who deliberately pause too long before answering.

That kind of subtly coercive silence that counts on you to be polite and wait it out.

I saw that there were lots of people around. It looked like the whole town had stopped to take in the leaping bodies of the fish. Cautious stories on the news, lately, of a return in the cod stocks. But cod don't usually do what I was seeing. They don't behave that way under normal circumstances.

Percy Strong picked me up from the beach that night and drove me up the hill to the store. Percy owns the only other house on my lane, his lights visible through a stand of whispering aspen and a few birch. Percy's daughter, Jocelyn, lives behind my cabin, an acre of hay between us, and a row of high white rose bushes. Jocelyn has put in one of those motion-sensitive halogen lights and it pierces the cabin's kitchen in the middle of the night. A car or a coyote will set it off. The bright things in the kitchen flash, the chrome kettle, the stainless-steel fridge. When I flick on the light to get a glass of water, after a bad dream, the picture window in the kitchen goes black and reflects everything in the room. Even the panda bears on my flannel pyjamas are visible. Perfectly delineated bears, little white chests, each chomping on a branch of leaves. Sometimes, I've wandered out to the kitchen for water just in my T-shirt and underwear, and there I am, lit up, but pale.

On the day I thought Kevin was my husband: we had a stained-glass fish, a sculpin (mouth hanging open, protuberant saucer eyes) made by a local craftsperson, suspended in the window transom above the front door. The reflection of the fish was visible on the wall, red and amber, floating without moving, as though the fish were working against a current too strong for it. Kevin has his father's posture, his voice.

The illusion afforded a reprieve so tender and dream-like it weakened my knees. I stumbled over the boots in the front hall and had to hold the bannister.

Part of the reason I was buying the condo was that Kevin had decided to live with his father and his father's girlfriend; they were renting an apartment on Waterford Bridge Road. Kevin was moving out of his bedroom on the second floor, full of dirty dishes smeared with hardened ketchup, the wall-sized flat screen for video games, the blasts of pseudo-automatic rifles, the way he talked (too loud because he couldn't hear himself with the headset) to people all over the world, somehow sounding in command, offering strategy, logistics, in a voice both calm and full of intelligence, cajoling, instructive, often playing through the night; the hole in the wall where he had smacked a basketball hard against the Gyproc, the posters of rap artists smoking joints, the electric guitar and amp, the pile of laundry.

The house was too big for me if I was going to be living alone. Selling it for a condo was also a fuck-you to my husband. I expected him to intervene. I expected him to decide to come home once there was no home to which he could return. I wanted him to think I'd moved on.

At the bank, Kevin had sprawled in the chair beside mine, his legs flung wide. He shot questions at the manager. He finagled me a lower interest rate by threatening to go to another bank. But the threat was so pleasingly articulated, amid banter about the relative advantages of investing in lithium or cannabis, the young manager complied without argument.

Once we were back outside, Kevin dropped the skateboard and put one foot on it to keep it from rolling away.

What will you do with your life? I said. He told me that a friend's dad, driving them from a field party at four in the morning, kept saying that Kevin should do communications.

I want a job where I convince people to buy things, he said.

What sort of things? I said.

You gave up too easily, he said. Then he blushed, but his eyes met mine. A floater, opalescent and the size of a loonie, dropped onto his mouth. When I looked away it hung on the brick pillar of the bank. Kevin asked what was wrong and I said I had something funny going on with my eyes. He said I should get it checked out, that I was probably dehydrated.

He said, You look pale.

Your father did this, I said. I flung my arm out at the bank as if everything we had just experienced in there proved I was the injured party.

Please, he said. Really?

What should I do? I said. You tell me.

It's so easy, he said. He was rolling the skateboard back and forth under his green and blue suede sneaker.

My husband had given me the funds to refinance the convenience store and I celebrated by taking Kevin out for dinner at the Keg. Kevin said there had been a fight between my husband—my ex-husband—and his new girlfriend. She didn't think he should bail me out; hadn't things been squared up in the divorce? She said it wasn't his fault if I wanted to throw all that money away. They had both raised their voices. She'd started to cry, according to Kevin, and she'd asked if my husband really loved her.

What did he say? I asked. But Kevin, who was eating a steak, just looked at me with surprise and pity. He put down his fork and knife and with his elbows on the table, held his face in his hands. He stayed like that as he drew in two long, deep breaths and sighed. Then he picked up the knife and fork again and devoured the food on his plate and took the napkin off his lap and tossed it on the plate and said, I've had enough.

It had begun to rain that night, on the drive back to the cabin; the wind was so high I had to grip the steering wheel tight to keep the car from swerving across the line. Water shivered down the glass. A transport truck passed, covering my car in a hard wave of slush, and I could see absolutely nothing except the writhing tail of black rubber, still detached from the passenger wiper, squiggling so hard it looked as though it was trying to bore its way through the window to suction itself to my face.

Marion Sullivan wore linen in earth tones, drapey things. Not the gabardine navy suit jackets with brass buttons, the tight all-weather Reitmans skirts stretched across thighs gone to fat, worn by most of the real estate agents I'd encountered.

Marion didn't say anything about my husband's betrayal; there was nothing cloying in her approach to selling real estate.

She was offering a deal. Not a great deal, but a credible deal.

When I said that my husband was seeing someone else she touched my hand with her fingertips. My hand on the table and she'd stroked it; I felt her long false nails graze the skin on the back of my hand. An erotic charge that radiated from between my legs all through me.

She leaned in over the table, her high cheekbone resting on the heel of her other hand, and talked without drawing breath about the man she was seeing.

He's not much to look at but I'm telling you, the arms on him, the muscles he got, she said. Works in a camp outside

Fort Mac, up on that scaffold, and you have to haul things up with rope, a hundred feet sometimes. There's some that complain about the food, but you don't hear him complain, she told me. They has steak once a week, they has chicken. Six weeks on and two home, and I give it to him. I make it worth his while. What he lavishes me with. You see this pin. That's a diamond chip.

But you can't go walking in the woods up there, the wolves will get you. They can be aggressive. And the bears. Coyotes are shy, but they get together in packs on the periphery of what do you call society, they attack. The money is good but you're a hundred feet up and dangerous? If somebody up there gets word, or say somebody passes it around, that you used to have trouble with your back, that's it, you're gone. You're done. They don't invite you back. There was them that had to go further north and by the time they drove back they were two hours in the bus and starved then and missed supper. And some of them complained and they were let go, complaining does not go over.

Marion Sullivan touched me for the second time then. This time pressing one knee between mine under the table.

Do you hear me, she asked. I said I had heard her. Complaining gets you nowhere, she said. This is a man, we sleep together when he's in town. Not a looker, but the arms on him. She was gathering our napkins and the empty Styrofoam soup bowls, the plastic spoons. Squishing it all together.

You have to make people do what you want, Marion Sullivan said. People love to be guided. You're doing them a favour. The hardest thing is deciding. Decisions are exhausting. You ease them toward what you want. Jimmy, that's his name, he does what I want. She was standing up and she blew a breath up over her top lip to get a wisp of hair off her forehead. You decide for people they will follow you. Doesn't matter what you decide, they follow.

Let's go see this condo, she said. Two walls of glass. View of the harbour. I think you'll be excited.

You would not believe the money I make on a bucket of salt beef. They buy it by the piece. The stuff turns me; the brine watery, a dark-wine colour, smelling mineral. Thick clots of fat floating on the top, thick as candle wax, and the way the chunks of meat roil up from the bottom when people dig around with the ladle for a choice piece—so I make them do it themselves. There's a box of surgical gloves next to the tub. They are powdery inside, an invisible talc, and the tongs are attached by a string to the bucket.

Everybody coming into the store in August was talking about the fire in Bay de Verde. The fire meant the plant had shut down before everyone had earned enough stamps to get them through the year. They wouldn't be eligible for EI. There had been a promise; the plant owners were committed to providing work. But there was the question of how many hours. Everybody needed hours. They needed the overtime for their stamps if they wanted to get through the winter.

I went with her to view the condo. The two walls of glass were covered in plaster dust. The milky light. High ceilings, and noises reverberated without the furniture to absorb sounds. Plaster dust on the hardwood, floating in the air like smoke. A man on a ladder with a mask and goggles turned off the sander and twisted to look at us.

In the sudden quiet, without the sound of the sander, his breathing in the mask was loud, like a death rattle—a sound I knew because my mother had died earlier that summer and I had been present when it happened, a rasping, ragged breath, strangled and wilful. Even Marion Sullivan shut up for a minute or two as the dust whorled; cloudbursts of silt, billowing in the draft that had come in with us. The dust looked like two figures waltzing, twisting around each other. There was a white film on my jacket when I stepped outside again.

It turned out that Marion Sullivan—a lively, but not manic, former social worker—was borrowing from investors at eighty percent interest. She had borrowed from a city councillor. She had borrowed large sums from all the real estate agents in her office, who were devoted to her. She had not paid them anything in months.

Soon there were delays with the renovations. That happens. With renos there are always delays. Then one of the condo buyers wanted his down payment back. Next people were phoning the radio call-in shows. They were reporting that Ms. Sullivan was not returning their calls. I left a message on her cell. Then several messages.

At first, I will admit, I could not accept she had lied to anyone. I felt indignation on her behalf, a fierce but ultimately shallow loyalty. Then, though I understood she had lied to most of her customers, I could not believe she lied to me.

Finally I understood. Everything I had taken from the divorce was lost.

Jocelyn Strong, my neighbour in the back, Percy's daughter, has five children: the eldest, Libby, is seventeen, the first to move out, gone to live in St. John's. I'd heard, while I was working behind the counter at the store, that she had shacked up with an abusive boyfriend and I'd heard drugs and maybe sex work.

People will say anything. Then I saw her in town, while I was shopping at the Dollarama. I needed plastic platters to put out baked goods at a fundraiser we were having for the people who lost their homes in Bay de Verde. I knew they had silver-looking platters that weren't bad for what I needed. There was a woman in the line-up ahead of me with a dozen coffee mugs. Libby Strong was serving behind the counter, wrapping the mugs in individual sheets of paper. My sister, who was with me, had struck up a conversation with the woman about Lysol wipes.

You just keep them under the bathroom sink, my sister said. Toothpaste or whatever, you can just pull one out and wipe things down. It's very convenient. Everything is sterilized.

The woman stepped out of the line to pick up the Lysol wipes, and she was standing there, reading the instructions. My sister said she didn't know how she had got on without them.

You have three sons, you want something you can clean up after them with, she said.

When I got to the counter I said hello to Libby. She had the white, white skin of her mother, of all the Strongs along the shore, with the same freckles, the orange-blonde hair, pale eyebrows, blonde eyelashes. Three studs in her plump lower lip, a lot of concealer around her left eye.

Libby Strong's eyes like her grandfather's, pale blue with a black rim around the iris. The girl spent a long time with Percy when she was little. She has his composure. Wiry like him, stalky. Comfortable with prolonged silences in conversation. The kind of quiet talk that occurs in people who live in rural areas. The sense that insight forms long before the utterance. Not a need to drag things out, but no impatience. As if speaking were a minor sacrament or a cost.

Libby, I said. Look at you.

I like town, she said with instant defiance.

I suppose you got your high school?

I got all As, she said. She was checking in the woman's Lysol wipes, but the scan wouldn't read the bar code so she was passing it vigorously in front of the scanner, over and over, and each time it dinged to let her know it hadn't registered. Finally it went through.

All A-pluses, actually, she said. They told me I was going to win two prizes, and one of them was for perfect attendance, and the next day I told Mom, I'm staying home. I wasn't walking across no stage for perfect attendance. But the scholarship I got, that's what let me move to town.

Your mother was in, showing me the pictures from the prom, I said. I don't know where you got that dress. I know it wasn't from around here.

Online, and I'm after selling it on Kijiji and making fifty bucks off it.

I hope you never had a stranger come to your home, I said. We met at a Tim Hortons downtown, she never had a car, Libby said.

Your mother mustn't be very happy with you gone. Even up in Cowan Heights I can see Cabot Tower, she said. I can see all the way downtown because in Cowan Heights, you can see. You can see everything up there.

Are you going to university? I asked. All you Strongs are so smart. You could do anything you want.

No, I got this job, she said.

Your mother must miss you, I said. She was counting my plastic platters. I knew there was a rift between Libby and her mother. They weren't talking.

You got six here, she said.

Six, is it?

She held up a single platter to the pricing gun and the red laser flickered and the tone rang six times.

Mom is too controlling, Libby said.

My sister put the Lysol wipes on the counter. Ring them in, she said.

I'll pay for them, I said.

She'll pay for them, my sister said. I'm going to give them to her. Make a convert. She's a skeptical one, but I can break her spirit. I mean if you have them in easy reach. The toilet bowl. You live with men you have to be wiping the toilet all the time, they don't do it.

Libby Strong met my eyes when my sister said about living with men. So Libby knew that my husband and I had separated. Maybe she even knew the divorce had gone through. That meant the whole shore knew. Of course she did. Even out here in Cowan Heights, with a new life ahead of her. Even at the age of seventeen she would know everything. She had also figured out that my sister didn't know most of it. She had weighed my failure to communicate this against her leaving her mother's house. She had weighed my humiliation against what she was doing to her mother. She saw she had the upper hand. She wouldn't give me away, but I'd have to stop trying to make her feel guilty. I glanced at my sister and felt a shooting pain, brief, near my temple, and I could see the floaters again. I tried to determine if I felt weak, or if my heart was beating faster, or slower. If there were any accompanying symptoms. A splotch in my vision obliterated a row of BIC lighters in a cardboard display box near the cash. When I looked up at Libby one of the floaters trailed down her cheek and onto the nametag pinned over her chest.

Lysol's antibacterial, Libby Strong said.

That's no way to talk about your mother, I said. Saying she's hard to live with. Your mother is up there with four youngsters underfoot. She's on her own. She works like a dog.

I like it here, Libby said. She put the platters in a bag.

Looks like you got a shiner, I said.

Dad's living with somebody else now, she said. Had me over for Sunday dinner to meet her. Real nice lady.

It was meant to sting me, refer to my own situation. Jocelyn Strong's husband did a three-week rotation on the White Rose but they'd shut her down. Their house in Low Point was a two-bedroom and when all the men on the White Rose were laid off the marriage went sour and he'd moved into St. John's.

Listen, I said. I wrote my cellphone number on a scrap of paper. If you ever need to talk to somebody.

The door of the Dollarama swung open and a man came in and fought with one of the stacks of mesh-wire shopping baskets, trying to free the top one. But it was hitched to the others. The stack of baskets was up to his chest, and it swayed and shook as he struggled to free one. All the baskets lifted up and slumped and he was cursing. Then he got the basket free and kicked the stack and it fell over. He turned toward us and it was the man I had seen on Low Point beach. He didn't recognize me. But he knew Libby.

You have a break coming up? he asked her. She flushed.

I'm not getting no breaks for a while, she said.

I have something for you, he said. Out in the truck.

Go out there, and I'll come out, she said. I'll come out in a minute? Just as soon as the other girl comes in from her break. She just went out, she has a smoke. She's been gone long enough. She'll come back now the once. There's two of them gone on break, actually, smoke break? They'll come back together? They're gone this good while now.

Libby was scared of him, the way I had been scared at the beach. She was talking fast and soft, placating, the ends of her sentences rising in a question the way the kids in town talk, the girls Kevin hangs out with. She didn't sound like Libby. The man walked over to the counter and wedged himself in front of the line. Everyone else in the line-up had fallen quiet. My sister flicked the lid on Lysol wipes and pulled the first tissue out and the waft of ammonia mingled with the stink of the man made my eyes water.

I'm not sitting out there in the cab by myself, he said. Fuck that.

I'll get one of the girls to cover for me, Libby said. You go on, you're going to get me in trouble.

This is bullshit, he said. He put the basket down on the counter in front of me. I'll tell you what, he said. But he reached out a finger and touched the thin gold chain on her wrist. Libby had rested one hand on the counter in front of her. And the chain on her wrist was very thin and gold, and he moved his index finger over it, where it rested on the back of her hand. He stuck his finger under the chain, and turned it so the chain was very tight, twisted around the top of his finger, making it very red, and the rest of the chain bit into the skin of her wrist, and then it broke.

That was cheap, he said. That was no good. It's okay, Libby said. Look, the girls are back.

That was a cheap piece of jewellery, he said. That's from Walmart, is it? Piece of fucking garbage. You see how easy that broke? I hardly fucking touched it.

I'm coming out now, Libby said. The man turned and left the store, got into a truck in the parking lot and started it. Let it idle. Revved the engine.

Libby looked at the scrap of paper with my number on it. She had been holding it in her other fist. She knew what

I had been implying, when I gave it to her. That she wasn't okay. She should go home. And she was afraid I would tell her mother about the bruise around her eye. But she let the paper with my number on it drop in the garbage bucket behind her.

I have a place, she said, in Cowan Heights.

I hope it's not with him, I said. She turned to glance out at the parking lot, which was packed. Then she held out my bag of plastic platters and, taking the Lysol wipes back from my sister, dropped them in the bag too.

Thank you for shopping at Dollarama, she said. I have to go on my break.

When my sister and I got outside it was raining and the truck was gone.

One evening at the end of August, the man appeared at the foot of my bed. He was as solid and present as the bedpost. Though I was fully awake, or felt I was, my body was paralyzed. I could not move. He picked up the corner of the eiderdown from the foot of the bed and pulled it off my body. I was wearing my pyjamas with the panda bears, but my skin was covered in goose bumps. I was full of terror but my heart was beating very slowly, like a drum at a memorial service, a deep, hard muffled beat that may have been the ocean. Still, I could not move. The cellphone was on the bedside table and with tremendous effort I flung an arm out and slapped my hand around and got the cell, but there weren't any bars.

The kids who robbed the store abandoned the stolen van they were driving and took off into the bog and got so far and gave up. It had been November and the bog was partially frozen and they'd run over a long flat white surface and the ice cracked and they were up to their waists. Of course there are sinkholes and you can disappear; a few cows have been lost that way, all the community out with a rope around the cow's neck pulling with all their might and the eye rolled back, until they give up and shoot the terrified animal between the eyes before it sinks all the way under.

When the teenagers came out of the woods back onto the highway they were surrounded by five cop cars with the lights going. Both holding syringes in their raised fists, threatening to jab anyone who came near them. The cops drew out their tasers and the youngest cop, trigger happy, shot the girl. She was a long time before she could move. The boy dropped the syringe and was arrested peaceably. The army surplus bag of cigarette cartons, and whatever else was on the shelf he'd happened to clear out, had disappeared in the bog.

The whole town of Bay de Verde had been evacuated. Houses gone. Beverly O'Grady was staying with her sister in Low Point and she'd come in for a tin of Carnation.

They got everybody put up in the gym, she said. They're waiting for the ammonia tanks to blow.

A reporter from VOCM had stopped for gas and was eyeing the apple flips. There had been a new batch of them that morning and they were almost gone.

Elaine Barrett came after Beverly and she said, The calls are coming now, they're saying thirty-eight hours is all they can promise. Thirty-eight hours for everybody but you got to go to the two other plants.

That's a start, I say.

Thirty-eight hours is no good to anybody, she says. You can't get enough for stamps with thirty-eight hours. People are screwed unless they get overtime. People are saying the Thai workers should be sent back. If there's not enough work for people here. They should go on home.

I snapped the plastic bag for her bread and milk.

I knows they're sending money back to their families and that, she said. But people are put up in the gym down there. A lot of them homes got no insurance. Burnt to the ground. I'm lucky I got my sister up here. I'll have one of them apple flips and give me five Scratch'N Wins. Then she bit at a hangnail so her finger bled a little stream of thin bright blood, which she licked away. She was wearing plaid pyjama bottoms and a jean jacket with a rose on the back in plastic jewels and silver studs.

Thousands, hundreds of thousands, it had seemed. The cod throwing themselves in the air and diving back down. The ocean weirdly calm but for the plinks of the fish leaping up and sending out concentric rings from the dimple where they dove back under the surface. I wondered if there had been some shifting of tectonic plates out there. Was there a tidal wave coming? But we would have heard about that. I wasn't surprised to see a stranger at the beach, because of the fish. Because it was an unnatural occurrence and all kinds of people had stopped to look. He might have just been driving past, coming from the other side of the island. He might have just caught sight of it and pulled over.

I was trying the phone, the man said. But you got no reception here, do you?

You can't get a signal in some places, I said.

Where are you from? he asked. You don't belong here. He winced, a kind of slow spasm.

I grew up in St. John's, I said.

You want a drink? the man asked. He lifted a bottle to show me.

No, thank you, I say.

Too good for a drink? I looked back over the cliffs and saw that the cars were all starting up and heading home. There would be something about the fish on the news. It was almost dark and the wind was picking up.

I'm just out for a stroll, I said.

I'm Lorraine Cake's cousin, he said. Lorraine will vouch for me.

I don't care who you are, I said.

You got a husband or anything? he said. Fine woman like you don't want a drink?

I tried to walk away from him then. But he was following me, close enough he jostled into me when he slipped a bit on the beach rocks. He made a grab at my elbow. I was heading back up the dirt lane from the beach to the highway that leads to the store. At the top of the hill, near the church, I'd get a few bars of service.

Not going to answer me? he asked.

Yes, I am married, I said. The church was maybe five minutes away, lit with garish red floodlights the new minister had installed at Christmas last year. They lit up the building all through the summer and fall.

Percy's truck drove past then and I waved him down. Nice-looking woman, the man said, as I got in the passenger side of the truck. Percy swept Coke cans and crumpled bar wrappers off the seat.

Heading up to the store? he said. Yes, I said.

Who is that? Percy asked.

Some asshole, I said. The guy was in his own truck then and he tore out in front of Percy Strong and zoomed away, down the road toward the highway.

Bat out of hell, Percy said. He stopped at the store and he came in with me for smokes. He bought a few Scratch'N Wins and won twenty bucks and I opened the cash and handed it to him.

Have an apple flip on me, I said. I asked about the layoffs in the camps north of Fort Mac, where he had a year and a half to go before he got a pension.

The likes of which you've never seen, he said.

After he left, the grey monitor affixed to the ceiling showed me the empty aisles. The engines of the milk coolers buzzed hard. The store was empty. I felt clammy and chilled, a burst of intense fear. There was a dazzling floater hanging over the stand of chocolate bars across from the cash. I tried to get rid of it, focussing on the box of Turkish Delight bars at the end of the row. My armpits were sweating, my heart felt out of whack. Then the episode passed.

There was a rush around nine thirty, several cars at the pumps. Lorraine Cake came in and I asked about the man.

Said a cousin of yours, I told her. I described him and his truck.

Lorraine said she didn't know anyone who fit the description I gave of the man at the beach. She was certain she didn't know anybody like that. She questioned me on each detail. Then she asked me did I see the fish.

I never heard tell of anything like it, she said. They're saying the scientists will be down here tomorrow.

Scrabbling over the beach rocks, trying to get back up on the highway where I would be more visible to the passing traffic, and where I could get away from the man, the enveloping stink of him, I had suddenly remembered a dream I'd had the night before. In the dream, on my left breast four new nipples had grown overnight. They were raised and stiffened, raspberry-coloured, incredibly tender.

They were large nipples and threatened, it seemed to me, to spurt milk. They really hurt, the way nipples hurt when a milk duct gets blocked and the skin cracks but is constantly damp with seeping milk or blood. I was thrown back twenty-five years to when I'd given birth to Kevin. The gentian violet I'd used when I got thrush. The word *thrush*, something a barn animal would be afflicted with. The shock of it, because we were encouraged to continue breastfeeding, despite the pain, so sharp it brought instant tears, and the baby's mouth also painted that indigo purple, an ugly stain so everybody knew what was going on.

The new nipples in the dream made my breast porcine, and in the swollen follicles around each nipple, stiff, silver hairs were sprouting.

I filled with a shame so intense my main preoccupation in the dream was to hide the extra nipples, until terror made me show them to my husband. When I took off my T-shirt the nipples were gone. The skin was inflamed and there was a mark and swelling where each new nipple had been, like a mosquito bite.

At midnight I shut the store and walked back down the road to the cabin. The ocean was calm then. No sign of the fish. In the kitchen I made myself some tea and I thought I saw a movement in the garden, in the bushes. Jocelyn's light came on at once, and there I was in the glass with my cup pressed to my chest with both hands.

That night in the cabin, I woke because of the smell. It was like the smell of capelin when they use it as fertilizer, mixed with the dirt on a hot day. The man was at the foot of my bed. I could not move at all. I was paralyzed. Everything felt heavy, even my eyelids. Two floaters hung above the man's left shoulder for a moment, then they were moving slowly across the wall toward the window. After straining very hard, I managed to fling my arm over my body to the bedside table and I had the cellphone in my fist. But my fingers were like pieces of wood, tingling with pins and needles. I could barely hold the phone. I was afraid it would slip out of my hand. He got on his hands and knees at the foot of the bed and straddled me until he had worked his knees into my armpit and held my wrists down and then dug both his knees into my chest. I couldn't breathe. And then he put his hands around my throat. He was wearing latex gloves. He was wearing the gloves I had near the salt beef bucket at the store.

He lowered his mouth onto mine and began to suck what little breath I had from me. When he pulled away from the kiss his face was gone. There was just a featureless, black clot of darkness surrounded by a burning aureole of light from the bare bulb hanging on a wire from the ceiling behind him. With one hand he was working at his belt.

I felt the phone in my hand change shape, transmogrify. The man shimmied forward on his knees, thrust his hips out, waggling his penis near my face so it hit my cheek; then the whole room filled with a sweet stink it took me a moment to recognize: vanilla. He must have bathed in it.

I knew rather than felt that the cellphone had turned into a syringe, and with more effort than I have ever exerted in my life, as though I were lifting a hundred pounds, I forced my arm off the bed and drove the needle into his side. I felt it sink deep and hard; I felt the long needle crack as it drove against a bone. I gasped raggedly, drawing deep breaths, soaked now in sweat, sitting up on the bed. He was gone. My phone lit up. It was a text from Kevin. He asked me to buy a frozen pizza on the way home. I saw it was a text from more than a year ago.

It was then I heard the screen door at the back of the cabin wheeze open, the door off the kitchen, and a key in the lock of the back door and then the back door swinging open and the stamp of two feet on the rug. Someone was getting the dirt off his shoes. The clatter of an animal in the hall; it sniffled and trotted to my room. The dog. It was my husband's dog. He found me, dug his snout into my lap, pawed me, moaned. Then he turned and barked, twice. Sharp high-pitched barks at the wall. I hauled him out of the room by the collar.

My husband switched on the kitchen light and his reflection in the black window appeared to be suspended above the garden; the branches of a maple tree in the field beyond shot through his back. He turned to face me and there were floaters on his face, two coins of shimmering light over his eyes; I blinked and blinked until they faded.

I thought we could talk, he said.

Please, I said. Really?

What do you want from me? Tell me what you want, he said.

Okay, I said. But you will do what I say.

I saw his shoulders slump with relief.

You're willing to talk? he asked.

I said: I'm going to decide.

INCHES

KATHY PAGE

THE BUILDING was the colour of dried blood, and the door slammed heavily behind them. Inside, it stank of cigarettes. Several benches were bolted to the black-and-white tiled floor. The office was to the left; a pink-faced young police officer with very short hair slid open a much-smeared window.

'Yes, Madam?' he said. Earlier, Louise had thought of jumping out of the car, and now she thought of pulling free of her mother's grip and running, but where? She was wearing flip-flops and had no money on her; also, part of her wanted to know if this could possibly be real, and if so what would happen next. Her mother's fingers dug into her arm.

'Constable Ryan? Mrs Miles. I called earlier. I've brought my daughter in because she's beyond my control,' she said. The officer switched his gaze to Louise, standing there in her jeans and T-shirt, and she stared back at him, noting a fold of neck fat that bulged above his collar. 'I'd like to make a formal complaint,' her mother said, and the officer picked up his phone. Her mother's grip loosened and Louise tugged her arm free.

'Constable Ryan. A mother with a teenage girl beyond parental control,' the officer said. 'Yes. Mrs Miles. Please sit down and wait,' he told them, gesturing at the benches behind them, and obediently, they both did.

'Look what you've brought me to,' Louise's mother said, clutching her bag on her lap.

'I didn't ask you to read my mail.'

'Mail that you were having sent to your friend's house!'

'I wonder why.'

'Don't you take that high tone with me—'

The door next to the sliding glass window opened abruptly, and the short-haired officer motioned them to come in. They followed him to a small but very high, cell-like room where a much larger, older and completely bald officer sat behind a metal desk. The door closed behind them with a loud metallic clang.

'Sergeant Whitney,' he told them. 'What is the problem, madam?'

'I believe my daughter has been having underage relations.'

Call it instinct. She was vacuuming. It was a Friday afternoon and she was doing the stairs and landings and main bedroom. Monday and Tuesday were for the washing and then the kitchen and bathrooms and Wednesday and Thursday were for the living and dining rooms. The house was finally under control and things were much better since she'd spoken with Harry about the accumulation of books and the fussy, old-fashioned effect it gave a room, especially since his book jackets did not match. He had eventually agreed to limit himself to three shelves on the unit to his side of the living-room fireplace. After all, she had pointed out when he chafed at this, he was not actively reading most of them, and was there not plenty of storage in the attic, as well as a huge, free public library in town?

On the matching shelves to her side, she kept her du Maurier collection and a few other good-looking hardbacks, along with framed photographs and ornaments, so the look was not really symmetrical, but the chaos had been contained, and the two landscapes that hung above each of the sets of shelves, Cornwall and Box Hill, were the same size and framing and so had a soothing, balancing effect. And as for Louise's dreadful room, the rule was that she had to pick everything up and vacuum on Sunday mornings, or else forfeit her pocket money, and that worked fairly well, too. Valerie had been untidy as a child, but grew out of it, so there was hope! Lily, of course, had always loved to have things nicely put away.

She had finished vacuuming the upstairs landings and for some reason opened the door to Louise's room. There was that ghastly smell of incense. She noted the curtains still half closed, the plant on the windowsill dropping its leaves. The new carpet covered in papers, a stapler, staples, Sellotape, used cotton balls. The mirror and a clutch of cheap cosmetics beneath it, coated in dust. The bed made, but only just, books scattered and piled beside it, the bedside table stacked with cups and water glasses. The wastepaper bin empty, but maddeningly surrounded with balled-up paper … Her eyes settled on the desk, the surface of which was invisible beneath he accumulation of notebooks and yet more books. The titles, *Being and Nothingness, The Doors of Perception, Self and Others,* were enough to make your eyes roll out of your head. Was that what they studied at school now? Or was it something Harry was encouraging? And then she saw it, in a half-open drawer, a blue envelope.

'You seem to be getting a lot of letters from someone,' she had said when those envelopes had started appearing.

'Yes.'

'Who is it?'

'A penfriend,' Louise had told her, flicking her hair out of her eyes and frowning as if a mother did not have a right to know who her children were in contact with. Boy or girl? Boy. David. Living in Lancashire. What were they writing to each other about? Art, books and music, ideas, things of that sort. It sounded plausible.

How did they get each other's addresses? Louise had looked up at her then and said, 'At school, Mum, it's a scheme,' and despite knowing Louise to be the worst—and also the best—liar of all three girls, she had believed her. Weeks passed before she realized that the letters had stopped coming to the house. She meant to ask Louise why, but forgot. And now this: the letter was addressed, in that small, very regular hand to *Louise Miles, c/o Miss Andrea Marsden*. The thing had gone underground. She took the letter downstairs and sat at the dining room table to read it.

Dear Louise,

Thanks for your letter. I'm sorry to hear that you have been feeling depressed. It sounds like breaking up with Andy last year was unavoidable, and probably even a good thing, because of the difference in your ages and him wanting to go travelling before university and all that. It would be far worse if he went off and then came back six months later only to tell you he had met someone in Peru or wherever, or lied about it and then dumped you when he went off again in September. Or even if he didn't, but expected you to just wait around for him to come back at Christmas and then who knows.

He sounds like an OK bloke. And at least you have had a relationship of some kind! I'd be happy to say the same, but even though I do go out and socialize more these days as you suggested, I still find it v. hard to approach girls.

I was very interested in what you said about the physical side of things between the two of you. I've never thought how it might be for a girl the first time she sees an erect penis! We are very used to seeing them ourselves but I can see that it might be a shock, even if you have felt it through cloth before. So how big would you say his was? From what I've read in magazines and agony columns and so on I know there's a lot of variation, but most are about six inches long when erect but they can be much less and a fair bit more. The width can vary too. Do you think girls might even prefer them not to be too big? Mine is fairly standard …

Sergeant Whitney leaned towards them over his grey metal desk, the pen dwarfed in his in huge hand. He frowned and looked from her mother to Louise and then back again, giving each of them several seconds of his attention.

'I see. Just to be clear, ma'am, it's the boyfriend your daughter used to have that you are complaining about, not the one who wrote the letter?'

'Yes. That boy—young man—Andrew Smiley, betrayed our trust. He sat in our living room having tea while this was going on. He is nineteen now. At the time, he was eighteen and she would have been under age, so yes, I certainly want to report it.'

'I don't!' Louise said, the clarity of her voice, its almost steadiness, startling all three of them. Sergeant Whitney returned his attention to her. 'No one did anything wrong,' she continued, 'and anyway it was months ago, and it's *all over*.'

'You could be pregnant!'

'No, Mum—'

'Of course you could. Would you stop interrupting me!'

Whitney ran his hand over his bald pate, then placed both hands heavily on his desk.

'Let's all calm down now. Do you have that letter with you, Ma'am.'

'Yes!' she said. But when she looked in her bag, it wasn't there.

'I think I left it on the kitchen counter,' she said. That was where she must have put it, on her way to the low chair by the phone, where she sat to call the police and then to wait for Louise to get home from school.

'Please get into the car,' she'd said to her as soon as she came in through the front door, careful not to say why, in case Louise refused.

'Why?'

'You'll know soon enough … I've read that letter from David Armstrong,' she told her once they were on the main road.

'What letter?'

'The one in your desk.'

'Oh,' Louise had said, staring out of the car window and smiling, as if it were nothing, *nothing*. Goading her: 'What was it about?'

Whitney drummed his fingers on the metal desktop, studied the pair of them some more.

'Well, we'd certainly need to see the letter,' he said. 'Meantime, I'd like to have a word with the young lady.' He picked up the phone and called for someone to escort Evelyn back to the waiting area.

Louise sat very still. Whitney was a big man and part of her wished her mother was still there, though another part was glad she had gone.

'Your mother's very concerned about your behaviour,' Whitney began. *Stop staring at me*, she wanted to say. 'She's worried that she can't keep you under control so that you stay safe. If I was your parents, I'd feel exactly the same. And if you go on like this, you'll end up on the streets… Believe me, we see girls from nice homes in that line of work and it's not a pretty sight.' The whites of his grey eyes gleamed in the fluorescent light.

'I haven't done anything wrong!' Louise told him, in the same, almost steady voice. 'And I have no intention of ending up on the streets.' Her hands had balled into fists. She willed them to relax.

'Let me tell you, life is not about what you think you intend,' Whitney said. He pushed his chair back, half stood and, propped by his arms on the desk, leaned towards her, breathing heavily. 'No. Life is about *consequences—*' he jabbed his index finger at her '—how one thing leads to another.'

Despite her efforts, Louise's eyes welled up. She wiped the tears away with her sleeve, stared back at the lowering face, the grey irises floating in their bluish whites. She knew it was very important not to look away or down. 'Now, tell me, did you have—' he lowered his voice, 'did you have *sexual intercourse* with—' he studied his notes 'Andrew Smiley?'

'No!'

'What *did* you do, then?'

'I don't want to talk about it.' Her hands were shaking now, so she sat on them.

'Well my advice to you, young lady, is that it's best not to do things you don't want to talk about.' Whitney let out a gust of stale breath and sat back heavily in his chair. 'Now,' he said, 'listen carefully to what I'm going to say…' He paused. She stared back at him. 'What we need in any investigation is proof. In this case that would have to include a physical examination of you by a police doctor, in order to establish whether intercourse has taken place—'

'What?' She didn't decide to stand, or to knock the chair over as she did so.

'Pick that chair up and sit back down, please!'

She picked up the chair, didn't sit, but took a step back and stood behind the chair, holding the back of it. He glared at her, she stared back, ready—whether to fight or to flee she had no idea. She was pretty sure the door was not locked, but what about the one at the end of the corridor? She noticed, behind him, a yellowing poster of a car crash.

'Your mother,' he continued 'says you were *fifteen* at the time of the sexual activity, but you are *sixteen*, now?' She gave a small nod. Beneath her shirt, sweat ran down her spine.

'So in that case, we'd need your authorization for the physical examination. We can only proceed if you are in agreement.'

She was crying properly now, face in hands. Whitney walked around to her side of the desk and sat on it, his navy blue pants stretched tight over his thighs. He seemed far too close. She could hear his breath.

'Well I'm not,' she said.

'Then it's very unlikely that we can proceed, and I'll tell your mother that when I talk to her ... You should bear in mind what I've said to you.'

It was dusk when they emerged from the police station. Her mother's eyes seemed larger than before, very shiny. She gripped the steering wheel as if to throttle it.

So what *did* you do?

Silence.

Did this happen under our roof?

No.

Where?

Silence.

In his house?

Silence. She would not be saying, in his room above the kitchen, with the books and paintings and the single bed. His long bony body. The rough stubble. How they took off her blue top, but, by agreement, not her jeans. How his face flushed as he struggled with his zip, pushed his jeans and underpants down. And then, the way his penis sprang out from the confines of the clothes, livid, taut, huge-seeming—though probably, in retrospect, about sixish inches—and how he had asked her to touch it, and then, the instant the skin of her fingers met the skin of his penis, which he called his cock, and maybe she would too, the sperm-stuff blurted out. *Sorry,* he said then, grinning. They'd both laughed.

'Believe me, the police may be spineless, but I'm not leaving it there. There are going to be consequences for you, and I'm going to take this up with Andrew's parents.'

'It's nothing to do with them! Or any of you.'

Louise, crying again, was thinking about how Andrew had ended it, walking in the woods near his home on a damp day, beads of water on the spiders' webs, and both of them had cried, and then hugged at the bus stop before she climbed on; how she had been pleased with herself for not pestering him when she felt low in the aftermath, never once calling or sending him a note. None of which her mother would ever know. All of which would be ruined if—

There was a near miss when the vehicle in front stopped to let out a passenger. Another at the roundabout.

'Mum!'

Evelyn struggled with the gear stick.

'You're making me ill. I can feel my heart banging in my chest.'

Evelyn, her bladder at bursting point, left the car on the drive to avoid parking it in the too-narrow garage, and rushed inside to use the bathroom; so Louise found the letter on the kitchen counter and, to the sound of her mother peeing in the next room, stuffed it into the boiler, saw it catch fire before slamming the door closed, then ran up to her room and locked the door.

Harry arrived, with the steak and kidney not even started. They had to settle for poached eggs on toast … It was hard for Harry to make sense of what had happened. An incriminating letter about penises that had disappeared. Andrew, who had come to the house a couple of times and talked about physics and modern art, and then another boy, this David, in Lancashire, to whom Louise was secretly writing about things that should never have happened, but in any case should be private. But then, the police! Utterly ineffective and spineless, she told him, to think we pay their wages! Surely not the best place to start, he thought … What was she thinking? And now, this idea that they should call Andrew Smiley's parents, people they had only occasionally glimpsed in a car and twice chatted to on the doorstep, and make some kind of accusation.

'I'm not at all sure that's a good thing to do,' he said, pushing aside his plate with its smears of egg.

'Are you telling me I'm wrong? That we should let our daughter do whatever she pleases?'

'No—'

'Are you afraid to deal with them? Because I'm not.'

'But what would be the point of it? I think we should try not to blunder about and I'd rather think it all over.' The phone rang and Evelyn took the call: Valerie. Louise had called her from upstairs.

'The thing is, Mum, times have changed. These are the kind of things teenagers do. It's all fairly normal. And from what she says, they were pretty responsible. Though I do think the letter-writing thing is rather strange.'

'Did we ask for your opinion? And does being a trainee vet qualify you to pronounce on this?'

'No, I'm just offering it, Mum, for you to consider. Of course you're right to be concerned in case something's amiss or she's pregnant, but I don't think that's the case. She's quite upset and—'

'Do you think *I'm* not upset?' Evelyn hung up and, even though it was after midnight over there, called her oldest, Lillian, in Perth, who after all had studied Law.

'What do you think?' she asked.

There was a long pause.

'I'm out of touch on the British legislation on the age of consent, but I do expect the police officer knew what he was talking about,' Lily eventually said. 'I can see both sides, of course. It must be worrying for you, but on balance, I think it's best not to aggravate things. And no, I really wouldn't call the boy's parents.'

'I expect you'll feel differently when your two are teenagers,' Evelyn told her, and again, hung up.

Neither she nor Harry slept very much.

He got up as soon as it was light.

'Are you going to speak to her or not?' she asked him when he came in from the garage where he had been sanding an occasional table that she wanted refinished.

'In due course.'

'When would that be?'

'Please stop hectoring me,' he said, and knew as the words left his lips that it was a mistake.

'So somehow, I have become the one in the wrong here?'

'No. Please, Evelyn, let's not talk like this.'

'Like what? All I am asking is for you to do your part … And remember, please, not to leave that book on the table. It goes on the shelf.' *For heaven's sake*, Harry did not say, *this is ridiculous!*

'I do sometimes think you're doing it to spite me,' Evelyn said.

'Doing what? Reading?'

'You know full well what I mean. Leaving your things all over the house.'

'I left that book and my notebook on the dining room table, so far as I remember. I was reading it with my coffee before I went out to revarnish that side table for you, and I intended to return to it. Why shouldn't I leave a book on the table? Where else do you want me to put it?'

'Away. On the shelf, or is that too much to ask?'

'I intended to return to it.'

'How many times do I have to say—'

'Evelyn, you're being unreasonable.'

'Don't patronize me!'

Unreasonable, he felt, put things mildly—truth was, there was a line between strong minded and outrageous that Evelyn now crossed with increasing frequency. Though sometimes it was his fault, for goading her. Or, according to his daughters, for letting her get away with murder. Or even, as he admitted to himself, because there were still times when he found Evelyn's anger arousing, and enjoyed making up afterwards …

'I am reading it,' he told her, sitting down and reaching for the book. 'Or will, when I have a chance.'

Hadn't he already read at least one biography of Edward Thomas? she had asked him when he brought the book back from the library last weekend. Didn't she send one to him during the war? Why read another?

Fair enough, he thought, searching now for the page where he had left off in the early hours, but the war was a very long time ago and this was not a biography but a pair of memoirs, written by the poet's wife. And he couldn't really say why he was so drawn to it, though one thing was that you began to see where the man's poems came from, how much of his life went into them, and how much reading, too. He was being given an intimate glimpse of a man by turns depressed, desperate, brilliant, and also a picture of an unequal marriage: how the two of them struggled, how impossible the whole thing was, even though Helen put a good face on it. He sometimes wished he could speak to the pair of them—make Edward see what luck he had to be so thoroughly loved, or else commiserate with him for his inability to accept her gifts; he wished he could warn Helen that she would never get back the measure of what she gave, and yet at the same time encourage her to continue … For what else could she do, being who she was? Some people could not help but love, and most people were the prisoners of their own natures. He identified with both players in the Thomas marriage, but especially with Helen because she was forever fitting herself around someone driven and intransigent. And it was oddly gripping, he had tried to explain to Evelyn, though also strange, to learn about the intimacies of another couple's married life.

'When are you going to fix that side table?' she had asked. And now the question was: When would he talk to Louise? *Talk to.* He stared down at the page, but the words would not open themselves to him, stayed sealed, like some sort of hieroglyphics.

She appeared at about noon, white faced, dressed in jeans and a grey granddad vest that Evelyn particularly hated. In silence, she filled and plugged in the new electric kettle, reached for the jar of Nescafé, spooned, poured, stirred.

'Your father wants to talk to you,' Evelyn announced. Louise did not reply, or offer to make a cup for anyone else. Now, it seemed, he had both of them against him.

'Let's go outside, just the two of us,' he suggested. Evelyn would not like it, but it was the only way; she would hover otherwise, and interrupt. It was hard enough without that.

They sat at the slatted garden table, out of earshot of the house, she with her back to it, shivering in the breeze.

'Do you want the rug?' She shook her head, but he went to the shed and fetched it. 'You have upset your mother,' he began, and paused, waiting for her to point out that she, too, was upset. She did not, so he cleared his throat, began: 'The main thing is that we're concerned for your well-being. Even if there is the pill and a different approach to sex now, that doesn't mean it's wise to rush into things … You still need to think carefully about what you do with your boyfriends.'

'Actually, I do,' she told him, staring into her black coffee, hair like a curtain, shutting him out.

'How did you feel about Andrew?' he asked.

'I liked him a lot.' She glanced quickly up at him then, gulped a mouthful of coffee.

'Were you—in love with him?' Excruciating, he felt, to pry like this—yet oddly, she did not seem to mind.

'I'm not really sure what it was,' she replied.

'Then why go so far?' he asked. She shrugged, leaned back, cup in hand. The sun was on her hair and face now and she looked more like herself again.

'I liked him, and I was curious,' she said. 'And Dad, it's just a part of the human body.' Well yes, he thought, but also, no. No just about it.

'Don't reduce sex to the physical,' he said. 'Your mother and I were very much in love, when we … '

Her gaze landed squarely on his face.

'How has that worked out, then?' she asked, the pure cheek of it catching him off guard and rendering him speechless. 'You really should stand up to her more,' she continued. 'Hold your ground. Don't give in so much.'

In their different ways, all three of his daughters seemed keen to tell him that he was too accommodating with Evelyn. And he could see why. Of course he should be able to leave a book on the table! It was not as if he lacked backbone. He had withstood schoolyard bullies, the Germans, and countless liars and fools at work. Evelyn, though, was a different matter. Part of the problem was that he didn't see it just as *giving in*. It was doing what he could to make things work. He could bend, she could not.

'The thing is, that makes for a pretty miserable atmosphere,' he told Louise. Again, the shrug, the stretching of her neck to the side, up, to the other side, down again. Her blonde hair all over the place, the fringe obscuring her eyes. She, the last child, was the one who most resembled him. Same eyes, everyone said. She flicked the hair away, stared right back at him, 'Have you ever thought about giving up on it? I mean, sometimes I do wonder what's keeping you two together. It can't be me.'

Harry took a deep breath.

'I love your mother,' he told Louise, his throat suddenly raw.

'Dad,' she said, just sixteen and sitting in the sun with her feet propped on the garden chair he had made when she was two, 'Dad, these days, lots of people get divorced, you know. You two might be happier apart.'

Was he unhappy? At this moment, yes, but in general? Marriages were not equal or fair: Look at his own parents, look at Evelyn's mother's senseless devotion to a man who did nothing for her. It was stupid to pretend otherwise.

'I can't imagine being without Evelyn,' he told Louise, unaware that she would, within a year abscond to France with yet another boyfriend, causing further months of worry and argument. 'People aren't perfect. But neither are you, and you love them even so, and even though you know it won't ever change—'

'It'll probably get worse, in fact,' Louise said.

A step too far.

'I didn't ask for an opinion and we're supposed to be talking about you,' he told her, speaking more loudly than before, as if to a larger audience. 'Whatever you think, we are your parents, and we need to know who you are seeing and what is going on. This is our house and you are only sixteen and we don't want—that kind of thing—happening in it, in our house I mean, is that clear? And I think this correspondence with the boy in Lancashire has to stop. And it would be very helpful if you apologized to your mother for all the worry you have caused.'

There was a long silence.

'I'll do that if you stop her from calling Andy's parents,' she said.

'I'm not sure I can do that,' he said. 'I will try.' Louise shrugged, stood, stretched.

'I'm going to stay at Sandra's,' she said, and walked back to the house, leaving her mug on the path.

Evelyn was glaring at them from the kitchen window and he did not feel like going in. He just wanted the whole thing to be over. To enjoy the damn weekend! But best to get it over with.

'Well?' she asked as he braced himself on the doorframe and eased off his garden shoes.

'I think she is sorry to have upset you … ' Evelyn said nothing. She was wearing her apron and her hands were wet from the sink. 'And I expect she'll apologize. I did stress that she can't just do whatever she wants in this respect.' The kitchen tap, he noted, needed a new washer. It was drip-dripping into the stainless sink making a dull enervating plopping sound. He tried not to hear it, put his arm around Evelyn's shoulders. She stood unyielding, her eyes on his face. 'It's been difficult and I think we should just see how things go from now on... As for calling the Smileys, let's not. Not now. I really don't think it will help.'

'You are all the same,' she said, pulling suddenly away.

'What on earth do you mean?'

'All four of you, ganging up against me. No, don't try and touch me!' He stood in the kitchen, stunned, heard her rush upstairs and slam the bathroom door.

'Don't be so bloody stupid!' he shouted, then flung the back door open and strode outside.

Most of the vegetable bed was sown or planted but he still had some double digging to do at the far end. He yanked the spade out of the earth, shoved his sleeves up and set to work on the next row. It was about fifteen feet across the width of the plot. He kicked the blade in hard with his heel, levered up the heavy spadeful, tipped the earth down next to the trench. A house full of bloody women! What the hell was he supposed to do now?

He dug on. It was dense soil, with patches of two kinds of sticky clay, one grey, another yellowish: remediable, and already far better than it used to be, but still hard work. Fat pink earthworms slithered through the clods of earth. Occasionally you found an old bit of pottery or a clay pipe. He pushed on, worked up a sweat. As the end of the row he switched to the fork and roughed up the compacted ground at the bottom of the trench. He threw in some compost, then began again, turned the new spadeful into the waiting trench. He worked steadily now and began to feel more like himself.

She could not help it. That was the thing. It was best to keep right and wrong out of the equation.

He finished the digging, hunted down a pair of secateurs and set off around the rest of the garden. He found some late daffodils, narcissi, tulips, cherry blossoms, and, in the circular bed at the back, roses about to open. He added some asparagus fern and some early peonies, which not only smelled wonderful, but were one of the consolations proposed in Keats' *Ode on Melancholy*.

The flowers in one arm, he again pried off his boots at the kitchen door. Both it and the front door were locked, and the key under the brick was gone.

He'd worked on mines in the war, so it only took him half an hour with some strong wire and pliers. Even so.

The house, filled with a thick, unnatural silence, seemed to resist him as he arranged the flowers in a vase found under the sink, then set it on a tablemat on the dining room table. The house responded: So what? Upstairs, he tapped on the bedroom door, and hearing nothing, cracked it open. The curtains were closed. Evelyn was either asleep, or pretending to sleep; he wanted to lie beside her but he was filthy and it was in any case a bad idea.

In the ensuing week, he slept in Lily and Valerie's old room with the geometric print wallpaper, slipped into the bedroom for fresh shirts and underwear while Evelyn was not occupying it, made his own toast for breakfast, and ate dinner before he caught the train home.

Downstairs, they were never in the same space unless passing through. He spoke to Evelyn whenever she appeared: he was very sorry for his part in the misunderstanding; could they sit down together and talk it over?

Was there something he could do? She did not reply; acted, indeed, as if she neither saw nor heard him. It was, he felt, both magnificent and pathetic at the same time. Infuriating, too. Evelyn left him notes: *Kindly wash your teacup. The gas bill has come. I am not doing your washing.*

On the train to and from work he wrestled with a letter to her, struggling to move it beyond the stock phrases that first came to mind: *I hate it when we are estranged. We should not let small differences come between us. No one could mean more to me than you do. I love you still as I always have …*

On Friday, he left work early, stopping on the way to the station to buy a card to write it in. At home, he sat in his shirtsleeves in the dining room (the flowers had been moved from the table to the sideboard, and were all but dead), trying to read Winston Graham's *The Black Moon*, when he heard Evelyn emerge from the living room to answer the phone.

'Evelyn Miles speaking. Yes, I did, thank you for calling. Thank you. Yes I am still—' He found it strange to hear her interrupted, but when she spoke again, her voice rang out proudly: 'The grammar school. Including French. Shorthand and typing. Two years at a city legal firm, Willis and Smythe, and then over twenty years' experience of running a household … ' Again, she fell silent, and Harry sat at the table, motionless, listening with his entire body. 'There have been some changes here, so I think it is time for me to move. Yes, a live-in position is exactly what I am looking for …' Again, she fell silent. 'It's a fairly small household,' she continued, her voice a little less confident. 'Four … No experience of supervising staff, not as such, but it's certainly something I could do—'

He understood immediately how on Monday she must have waited until the two of them had left the house before getting up. Still sick with rage, she had put on her sunglasses, walked to the newsagents and bought the copy of *The Lady* that he'd noticed on the phone table that night, and, next door at the baker's, a croissant, something she never could resist. At home, she'd have searched the classifieds at the back. There were advertisements for housekeepers under 'Help Wanted.' She'd have chosen which vacancies to apply for on the basis of how soon they wanted someone and how much she liked the name of the house: Hartcourt Place, Withinden Manor, Somerset Court, then typed the letters of application on the portable she kept zipped up in its vinyl case in the spare room, signed them with her full name, Evelyn Anne Miles, and carried them to the postbox at the end of the road before making early dinner for herself.

'I understand,' he heard Evelyn say now. 'Thank you.' She could not bear to be slighted and he knew how her pulse must be thudding through her, that she could hear it when she closed her eyes. He heard the faint *ping* and the dull clunk of the hand set as she hung up. There was a new kind of silence, and then an awful moaning sound. He made his way to the hall where she sat on the low chair by the phone, her hands fisted, weeping. It was the most terrible thing. He knelt on the parquet and took her in his arms.

'What idiot was that?' he said, 'And why would you go away when I want you so much?'

And there, hanging on the wall behind her was the still life they had bought years ago in the local art sale. And on the phone table, the 'Sunflowers' notepad she used, open, blank, the pen ready next to it.

He knew she would not answer, and that they would never speak of this humiliation or of what had led to it. But he felt her relax just a little and let him take her weight.

A DAY WITH CYRUS MAIR

ALEX PUGSLEY

LL MY life I've been thinking about Halifax—generally as it is expressed by its families, somewhat specifically by the Mair family of Tower Road, and super-specifically by Cyrus Mair, a friend and rival whom I met one afternoon when I was exactly five years and two days old. Of course the old Mair house on Tower Road is no longer there. The remains were demolished long ago to make way for two apartment buildings. But the final ruination of the family was set in motion years before, on the day I met Cyrus Mair, when his father's body was found floating in Halifax Harbour, on this side of McNabs Island, the first in a series of bizarre events that would conclude with a house fire on the snowiest night in a century. But what of Cyrus Mair—whiz kid, scamp, mutant, contrarian pipsqueak, philosopher prince, pretender fink, boy vertiginous, koan incarnate—where was his matter and how was he formed? Cyrus Mair came into my life on the afternoon of my sister's ninth birthday, on a day of gifts and escapes and inventions, the drama beginning with me ringing and

261

ringing at my own front door, waiting to be let in, idly probing with my tongue a front tooth newly loosened. Inside,
my sister Bonnie came to the door in her sparkle dress—I
could see her distorted through the stained glass of the
door's windowpanes—to ask what I wanted. Now Bonnie
was smart. She knew how many seconds there were in a
year, that blue and yellow made green, and she could count
up to forty in French. Once we'd been happy allies, the two
of us venturing nude and hatless into our parents' cocktail
parties, but in the past months a coolness had prevailed between us, and now that she was nine she assumed an offi-
cious attitude toward younger kids, acting as their de facto
guardian, and in these moments she became the Big Sister
who wiped your nose and reminded you to use the basement door—which is what she was doing now, her eyes
scolding, her finger circling. By parental decree, children
were supposed to use the back or basement door unless
there were special circumstances—but I *was* special circumstances. I understood we could use the front door on our
birthdays, and a mere two days earlier, when it had *been* my
birthday, I'd proposed the idea of moving my front-door
privileges from my birthday to any other day in the year—
and I was choosing today. Bonnie, I saw, had conveniently
forgotten this amendment. But I was used to being misunderstood. I was something of an exceptional child, to tell
the truth, and from the age of four and a half on I had the
uncanny and somewhat underappreciated ability to repeat
the "Witch Doctor" song for hours at a time without stopping. My performances didn't win over all my audiences,
true, but nonetheless I persevered—just as I persevered now
in ringing the front doorbell. Bonnie appeared again, this
time with my oldest sister, Carolyn, both holding helium
birthday balloons, and in a burst of tandem head-shaking

and hand-waving, they conveyed the instruction to go around to the basement door. I stood on the porch, furious, knowing that many of the world's mysteries eluded me but starting to understand better and better that my older sisters wanted to destroy everything I held to be important. Slamming my fist against the glass of the door, and perhaps not really knowing exactly what I wanted, I left off ringing the doorbell and ran in madness to the end of the block, where, contrary to family rules, I ran across Victoria Road. Farther up the street, past the crazy Pigeon Lady's house, and safely away from all birthday festivities, my shoulders relaxed and I shifted into another of my personas, which was Aubrey McKee, Boy Detective. I started memorizing passing license plates for possible future reference and attempted what was known in my trade as a forward tail. This was a sidewalk surveillance technique that involved tracking a subject who was actually *behind* the operative. I'd noticed, for example, on the other side of the street an unknown, fair-haired kid, and as he went about his way, following a single sheet of coloured paper down Tower Road, absorbed in the little world a child has, I was giving him enough time to draw alongside me. But looking across the street now, the boy in question was gone, the sidewalk empty save for a few recent puddles, so I simply proceeded toward South Street and the Halifax School for the Blind. This was an enormous stone building, a remnant from another century, and setting foot in this territory was always iffy because it meant one might encounter, as my sister Bonnie described them, "a bunch of blind albino kids from P.E.I." I'd sometimes seen sightless children waiting on the school's front steps, and one winter afternoon I'd heard floating out of open windows the sound of piano lessons, but I'd never seen a blind albino kid—not even from any province. All the same, as I snuck toward the school's playground, I was mindful of Bonnie's cautions and, panicked that I would be randomly chased by creatures with pink gogs of bloodied flesh where their eyes should be, I slinked myself under the black wrought-iron fence and into the green and sun of the playground. Once inside, I resumed my maneuvers. Some weeks before, I'd lost a Hot Wheels Batmobile in this playground and since then I tended to line-search under the swings, kick at dirt clumps in the sandbox, and scowl at any happy kids playing on the teeter-totter. The playground's perimeter I investigated with the mindset still of a Boy Detective, planning to work my way into the center as I went, but this idea I promptly abandoned in favour of the monkey bars, from the top of which I was soon hanging by my knees—my head low-drooping—and noting the traces of sun on the nearby Victoria General hospital, the wrinkle pattern of the crumbling black asphalt at the edge of its parking lot, and a deep puddle directly below the monkey bars superb in its facility to reflect the upside-down sky. Turning the other way, I noticed a yellow-and-green seed pod, from a maple tree, spinning in the wind, and I was staring at it some moments before I saw, out of focus in the distance, the fair-haired boy I'd seen earlier. He was waving from a softly rotating merry-go-round. I'd not seen him come into the playground, and it was as if he'd somehow sprung out of the blue or teleported from coordinates elsewhere in the galaxy. He looked about five years old, his hair was corn-silk blond, and he was costumed miscellaneously. He wore a silk pajama top—pale blue with navy trim on the collar and cuffs—and over this was an adult's black dress belt, so big it went round him three times, cinched very tight, causing the pajama top to flare out like a skirt below the waist. Completing the ensemble were grey jodhpurs and Oxford shoes, untied with no socks. All this he sported without a trace of self-consciousness, not for a moment considering that his clothes were anything but regulation. He was shy, forward, joyously alert, and within his blue eyes—a blue so bright as to seem slightly radioactive—shimmered a quick originality. He was an inquisitive sort, happily idiosyncratic, blinking and thinking and holding his breath at three minutes after four o'clock on a September afternoon. I'd never seen the kid before—and I knew a *lot* of people from nursery school, the bookmobile library, and even the Public Gardens—and asked where he was from. He made no answer, still holding his breath, his head tilted philosophically—and I was wondering if he were one of those semi-autistic kids who stare for hours at a green eraser—when he finally exhaled to say, "I'm not even here!" His eyebrows, I noticed, were sun-bleached to whiteness. "I'm supposed to be somewhere else but I'm not there either because—" His voice rose. "Because I'm an escape artist!" He was English. Or at least spoke with an English accent. In later years, when I remembered this moment, I would think of him as one of those hyper-articulate British schoolchildren, one of those blond choirboys whose accent is so fluty, and whose syllables are so precisely enunciated, you want to thump them in the head with a rubber fish. I ran to the merry-go-round and grabbed the handrail closest to me. Giving it an almighty heave, I spun the boy as fast as I could. The contraption revolved twice and I timed my next push for maximum acceleration. After a few unstable rotations, the boy jumped off, woozying a few steps and bringing his fingertips to his eyes. "Oh my lumbago," he said, falling to the grass. An eyedropper bottle tumbled out of his pajama pocket. The boy picked it up, wiped away some grime, and showed it to me. "This is my newest invention," he said. "A potion of many ingredients!" He gave me the bottle. I held it to the sun. Inside its blue glass were a few types of liquid, a small key of some kind—as if from a lady's jewelry box—as well as some shifting blobs of oil. "All I need to complete it," said the boy, taking back the bottle and looking at me wildly, "is a drop of human blood."

I asked why he needed the potion.

"I'm making it," he said, shaking the bottle, "in case a sea pirate comes home to find that I've been abducted by a goliath. This is the potion that can bring you back to life. This is the potion that can grant you one wish!" He looked at me, conspiratorial. "I've also invented a word—shropter."

I asked what it meant.

"I don't know yet." He searched for something in the front pocket of his jodhpurs. "My very first invention was a treasure map of many escape routes." He brought out the sheet of coloured paper I'd seen him chase along the sidewalk. It was marked up with scribbles of all kinds. I liked it straight away and immediately wished it were mine. "Probably it will fall to me to escape. But it may do for my father as well. Do you have a father? I have a father. I've only met him twice. But I'm going to see him again, I should expect. That's why I've become interested in inventions. And you?"

I had four sisters, I told him, and made a shrugging reference to Bonnie's birthday party, adding that I didn't much want to go.

"Why? Is she a biter? I've known some biters. She's younger?"

My sister was older, I said, and wasn't much of a biter. Then, on impulse, I opened my mouth to display my wobbly front tooth.

"Ooh," said the boy. "May I?" He touched at my tooth

with a fingertip. "Yes, that will come out directly." He made a strange sort of smile, exposing his own front teeth. "I still have mine. See? But yours will grow back. They do grow back." He glanced down, as if searching for something he seemed to find missing in the grass, then looked at me to confide, "There's a skeleton inside you, you know. A complete and utter skeleton. Beneath your skin."

This news I received with some confusion for I connected skeletons with ghouls and graveyards and scary cartoons—and I couldn't be sure if this kid was telling the truth or if he was merely, and this impression had been building over the past few minutes, indulging in some form of slap-dash free association. What kind of person would tell you there was a *skeleton* inside you?

Giving the merry-go-round a last shove, I said I was going back to my sister's birthday party but he could come if he wanted.

"A party?" He winced. "Maybe. But I don't like ice cubes. I don't want to taste them and I don't like the sound they make in my teeth. One second—" He put a hand on my elbow, conspiratorial again, and evaluated me. "You know, you could grow a moustache if you wanted. And no one would recognize you. Except French people. There's a seagull!"

I looked up—only to realize he was pointing at the shadow of a fleeting bird, a shape that was presently ribboning across the grass and puddles of the playground, gliding past the curb, and unfolding into South Street ... And so this boy, this unexpected child, this curious young party, this was Cyrus Mair. There was something incomprehensible and quivery and completely recognizable about him. He reminded me of the imaginary kid, a character in my own private mythology, who ran along the side of the highway, keeping pace with my family's car on road trips—a fantastically swift boy who hurdled over cement culverts, ducked under fallen trees, never tripping, never tiring—and as I watched Cyrus Mair in the playground of the Halifax School for the Blind chasing a seagull's shadow, on the way to the rest of his life, pushing his fingers along the posts of the wrought-iron fence, trying to touch every one, now going back to tap the post he missed, I thought him reckless and exuberant and smart. He was fabulously weird. I wanted to know what he knew. I couldn't really guess what he was dreaming up in his mind, nor what games and inventions occurred there, but I liked him. His world was in a constant state of becoming, and this Friday afternoon was the beginning of a fascination that would last a sort of lifetime for me because, even if I didn't know what I wanted, like everyone else I would not be able to stop paying attention to the creature known as Cyrus Mair.

"Do you like jokes? I like jokes. Did you hear about Napoleon?" Cyrus turned to me. "Josephine sucked his bone apart!" It was probably the single worst joke I'd ever heard. His jokes made no sense at all. I didn't get them. I didn't get them the *third* time he told them. But each joke went over huge with Cyrus Mair, his giggles bursting into the air like birdsong. I did not share his high spirits at first. But, at a later juncture, around the time we were sneaking into my backyard and towards my family's basement door, the phrase "Coat-Cheese" arose in our conversation, an example of the usage for which might be "Coat-Cheese, Coat-Cheese, you're a fat Coat-Cheese," or "Coat-Cheese, Coat-Cheese sitting in a pie," or even "Coat-Cheese, Coat-Cheese stuck inside a toilet seat, Coat-Cheese, Coat-Cheese pooping in your eye," all of which formulations

seemed astonishingly relevant to our developing understanding of the afternoon, and by the time we entered my
house to tiptoe up the basement stairs—Cyrus bending
over with laughter and slapping his thigh to keep himself
from falling—we were sweaty and gleeful and manic with
intrigue. The birthday party was in full fling: a dozen teenybopper girls hopped up on peppermint cupcakes and
cream soda. Cyrus was happily assimilating all the details
of the party—the table of wrapped gifts, helium balloons
bouncing against the ceiling, the girls in their swishy party
dresses—assimilating these details but perhaps not pro-
cessing them. "There's a lot going on in this house," he
said. "I think we need a drink." He moved instinctively to
the living room and my parents' liquor cabinet where he
fetched out a bottle of Rose's Lime Juice Cordial. "Ah."
He twisted off the cap. "The good stuff." He brought the
bottle to his lips and glugged off several swallows. "That's
the spot," he said, tightly shutting his eyes. "I feel a bit
drunk already."

I asked what he was going to do when he had the last
ingredient for the potion, the drop of human blood.

"Good question," he said, passing me the lime cordial.
"My plan is—wait. Before we go further, I need to know
something." He took a step back and put his hands on my
shoulders, much in the manner of a captain steadying the
nerves of a young recruit. "Are you a Crab or an Anti-Crab?"

I asked what he meant.

"Well," said Cyrus, puzzled. "It's quite simple, really.
I'm an officer in the Anti-Crab Army. Like my father. And
the world is either Crab or Anti-Crab. Which are you?" He
peered into my eyes. "I think you're Anti-Crab."

Swigging from the bottle of lime cordial, I made a few
nods to show I was inclined to agree.

"Good. That's all you have to tell them. That and your serial number. Remember that when you're being tortured."

"When I'm being *tortured*?"

"Exactly!" said Cyrus, making a move to race into the party, his pajama top coming loose from his belt and billowing like a sail.

The cake was being served—a special in-house recipe my oldest sister, Carolyn, made for each of us on our birthdays—a vanilla sponge cake embedded with store-bought candies and coated with milk chocolate icing. Carolyn was handing out plates of this delicacy to the last guests when, seeing Cyrus and me, she sliced off two more pieces.

"Ah," said Cyrus. "Chocolate Thermidor." He swiveled to me. "But maybe you shouldn't."

"Why not?"

"You know—" He tapped at his own front tooth. "The wiggler."

I said I would use the other side of my mouth to chew.

This seemed to reassure him and he focused his attention on his own piece of cake. He took a large bite and chomped the cake experimentally—before spitting a mouthful to the linoleum floor. "Just as I suspected!" He made an odd smile. "Raisins." He kicked at the offending gob with one of his Oxford shoes—which was loose on his foot now, the laces free from the top eyelets. My sister Carolyn assured him there were no raisins in the cake, and Cyrus, seeing his blunder, for he had mistaken a red jujube for a raisin, bent to the floor to pick up the candy. He was popping this in his mouth, to the fascinated horror of at least three of the girls present, when my sister Bonnie returned from a bathroom break. "Who the hell is this kid?" She pointed at him. "And who invited him to my party?"

I was explaining I'd invited him, that he was my guest, when, rather as if he'd been waiting for the appropriate moment, Cyrus stepped to the center of the room to say, "I'm the world's best escape artist!"

Bonnie regarded him, skeptical. "Um," she said. "No, you're not."

"Oh, yes I am," said Cyrus, swallowing the red jujube. "I can escape from any ropes or shackles or booby traps you devise for me. And—" He flung his hand above his head to point at the ceiling. "I throw down the gimlet!" He was beaming at the girls, daring to be contradicted. "You could tie me up and I shall escape anything."

A small girl in a turtleneck dress—her name was Alice Gruber—produced a pink skipping rope and Bonnie took it and thrust it at Cyrus. "Prove it."

Taking the skipping rope, Cyrus wrapped it around his left wrist three times. "I wrap it like this and you—" He offered his hands to Alice Gruber, who seemed shyly delighted to be participating. "You tie it nice and tight on my other hand."

Alice Gruber tied a simple bow knot firmly around his right wrist. He offered his tied wrists for us to inspect. "See? So I shall go behind these drapes." He walked to the windows, where my mother, because of our too-close proximity to the next-door house, had installed floor-to-ceiling curtains. "And I shall escape and disappear by a count of ten. Ready? On your marks—Go!"

Cyrus's small outline, and especially the heels of his shoes, showed in contours in the fabric of the curtain. The girls looked at one another, uncertain, so Carolyn started loudly counting, the rest of us joining in and finishing—noting, of course, that Cyrus's shoes were exactly where they had been when this started. Bonnie jerked the curtains open, revealing the skipping rope fallen into Cyrus's empty shoes. For two or three seconds we were fully amazed, as if the laws of the universe had shifted without us understanding why, until Bonnie pulled the curtains all the way open, revealing Cyrus giggling, barefoot and triumphant, at the end of the window. "Yes!" His face flushed red as he took back his shoes from Alice Gruber—who had picked them up in her new capacity as magician's assistant. "My second greatest escape today! I told you. I can escape from torture chambers or wire cages or anything at all."

The birthday guests were certainly amused and so was I. But not so the birthday girl. My sister with narrowing eyes was rethinking the wrapping and tying of the skipping rope, deducing correctly that Cyrus had made sure the skipping rope crossed on the underside of his left wrist, allowing for a quick release when he twisted his hands *away* from the crisscrossed rope. Once free of the rope, he slipped out of his shoes and snaked along the window to hide flattened within the curtains.

Bonnie brought a chair from the dining room, keen to continue the challenge, and asked if Cyrus could escape if he were tied to the chair and blindfolded and locked in the hall closet.

Cyrus studied the door to the hall closet. It was an antique-looking door with a skeleton key resting in its lock. "It would be my third great escape today," he said, considering. After procuring a newspaper, which he positioned on the floor beneath the lock, and making us promise we wouldn't tinker with its placement, he raised his hand to point again at the ceiling. "I accept the gimlet!" Bonnie then went to work, securing him to the chair, tying his hands behind his back with the pink skipping rope, binding his ankles to the chair legs with kitchen twine, and using the sash from her sparkle dress as a blindfold. All through this preparation, Cyrus held his breath, flexing and swelling his shoulders to make himself bigger. With Carolyn's help, Bonnie bumped Cyrus and the chair over to the hall closet, dumped him in, and turned the key in the lock—just as my parents came through the front door. They were confused to see the birthday party gathered around the hall closet, and more than this, I could tell from their posture and solemnity that Something Complicated had happened in the outside world. It was only now I realized how irregular it was that neither of my parents had been home to direct the events of Bonnie's birthday party—it was a tribute to Carolyn's wherewithal the party's proceedings had gone so smoothly. So we dispersed, innocently returning to loot bags and balloons in the kitchen, and leaving five-year-old Cyrus Mair chair-tied and blindfolded on the hardwood floor of the hall closet.

A note of civic history—Howland Poole Mair, K.C., known popularly in the province as H.P. Mair, served as the fourteenth premier of Nova Scotia many years before Cyrus and I were born. Most of the Mairs were given to highly variable and eccentric vanishing acts but the disappearance of H.P. Mair was bold even for them. On the day he vanished, H.P. Mair was senior counsel to one of the city's oldest law firms, Merton Mair McNab, and the circumstances surrounding his disappearance, and the convergence of inward meaning and outward implication these circumstances implied, would generate speculation for many years. I saw him only twice, the first time when I was four and he was eighty-one, outside St. Matthew's United Church one winter morning, when my father made a point of introducing his children to a passing older man, elegantly dressed, sharply stern.

Tall and bald, to me H.P. Mair most resembled a stretched-out version of the Banker in the board game Monopoly. I remember singing for him the first verse of my newly-composed "Extravagant Yogurt" song, a routine to which he gave a quick and single roar of laughter, and I remember my father treating him with uncharacteristic deference—a consequence, I would later learn, of my father having articled with H.P. Mair when he first graduated law school. My father would accept a position with a different law firm, but his debt and connection to H. P. Mair he always respected. Not so my mother. "The Old Grey Mair," she said. "He ain't what he used to be. *Such* a peculiar fellow. We'd be at some party. He'd walk in, speak to no one, watching from the corner. You try to talk to him, he'd just shake his head and walk away. If you ask me, he needed help. But your father loved H.P. Mair. Thought he was brilliant. Sure, if brilliant means drunk. If brilliant means stumbling home drunk from The Halifax Club, then he was a genius. He used to show up sozzled at our back door. I'd give him the vacuum cleaner and tell him to start in the living room. The man was just gassed. Juiced to the gills. Alcohol ruins so many families, Aubrey. At the end he didn't know where he was. At the end he sort of knew he was yesterday's man. The last year of his life, he was calling your father at all hours. In the morning. The middle of the night. The man was over-billing, double-billing, he needed money something terrible. Had a wife with expensive tastes, for one, plus this other woman, and drinking all the time. That once-brilliant mind, all that booze. The month he disappeared, he came to see if your father would represent him because he was about to be disbarred and God knows what else." My father was president of the Nova Scotia Barristers' Society at the time, a member of the same disciplinary committee that was investigating

H.P. Mair, and so was obliged to recuse himself from acting for him. H.P. Mair went missing three weeks later. He
had lunch at The Halifax Club near noon and was later
seen purchasing a bottle of Mumm's champagne at the
Clyde Street liquor store, the cashier giving a statement
to the police that, the last she saw of him, H.P. Mair was
walking in the sun down South Park Street. Officers found
his house with its doors open, his purple Mercedes-Benz
in the driveway. His vanishing would become the talk of
the province. There were theories he'd been abducted or
murdered, that he'd run off to Bermuda to avoid prosecu-
tion, that he'd committed suicide in Maine. For a while he
was the missingest man in Canada and seemed destined to
become one of those figures, like Judge Crater or Captain
Slocum or Ambrose Bierce, who simply evaporates from
the twentieth century. But twenty-one days later, on the
morning of Bonnie's ninth birthday, a body was glimpsed in
the ocean off Black Rock Beach by two Waegwoltic kids in
a Sunfish sailboat. The authorities recovered the drowned
man, finding on the fully clothed corpse no identification
except for, in a soaking suit pocket, my father's business
card. My father was asked in for questioning later that day.
This was the reason my parents had been absent from their
daughter's birthday party. After identifying the body as the
remains of H.P. Mair, my parents went along to relay the
news to the widow—a peripheral family friend. Vida Mair,
who had been estranged from her husband for six years,
lived alone and alcoholically on the seventh floor of the
Hotel Nova Scotian. Not only was she vexed to learn of
her husband's death, but she was also out of her mind with
worry that one of her extended family, her husband's son
with another woman, a five-year-old who had been placed
provisionally in her sister-in-law's care, had gone missing the

night before. Phone calls were made, a search party rallied, and a Missing Persons file opened. It was with somber and serious worry for this errant child that my parents walked in the front door of our house on Tower Road, somewhat surprised to find the very object of their concern tied to a dining room chair on the floor of their hall closet, thrashing like an animal in a trap.

"What in God's name is that noise?" asked my mother.

Speeding to ground zero, I spun the key in the closet door, yanked the door open, and bent down beside Cyrus Mair. I pushed away the blindfold. Although he was on the verge of liberation, his expression did not change. His eyebrows were tense with concentration, and now that I was this close to him, I could see that three of his eyelashes had gone white—or had started white—and I noticed, too, a spiral of absolutely white, de-pigmented hair splotching out of the top of his head. He was silent, sullen even, as if he realized he'd misjudged the situation—or the situation had misjudged him. "If you help me escape," he whispered, struggling against Alice Gruber's pink skipping rope. "If you help me out of this booby trap, I'll help you escape from anywhere. And I will remember. Will you?"

"Remember what?"

"Everything!"

I said I would help him if he showed me all of his escape routes. "You promise?"

"I promise," said Cyrus Mair, his blue eyes very wide. "I do."

Twenty minutes later and the party was in the breakfast nook among second helpings of cake, some softening-but-still-airborne balloons, and Bonnie's plunder of unopened birthday gifts. Cyrus had very easily integrated

himself into the gathering and babbled intimately with anyone—as if he'd known each of us all his life. Bonnie, feeling
contrite over his imprisonment, and sensing my parents'
distant but frank interest in this child's welfare, tolerated
his presence. The other girls accepted and approved of him,
especially Alice Gruber, who, in a tizzy of overexcitement,
had begun applying chocolate icing to the tip of his nose.
"That's dis*gus*ting!" Cyrus said to Alice Gruber, straining to
make the word as emphatic as possible and wiping at his
nose. He turned to Bonnie, who was reading a gift card.
"I think you should always keep a present that you don't
open," said Cyrus, moving his own piece of cake away
from the groping fingers of Alice Gruber. "That way you
can always go back and open something you don't have."
Alice Gruber let out a squeal of laughter at this remark—
then right away covered her mouth with both hands, shutting down any further noises. Bonnie opened the beautifully wrapped present anyway, displaying to the table a
page-a-day pocket diary. I thought it very splendid with its
gilded pages and royal blue binding, as well I should, for I
remembered it was my gift to Bonnie. My mother and I
had charged it at Mahon's Stationery the week before, my
mother deciding that the gift of a diary would encourage
Bonnie to read more. Bonnie remarked casually that she
already had three diaries, that I could keep this new one,
and flipped the gift back to me. She went on to the next
present and so did everyone else. Everyone except Cyrus
Mair, who stared at the diary as if mesmerized, as if he'd
never imagined such an invention could exist.

Finishing my own piece of cake, I became aware of
my parents talking in the kitchen. I was not really sure of
the topic of conversation, but sifting into my vicinity was
the sense that Something Complicated was ongoing, and

overheard in my mother's side of the conversation were phrases such as "heart flutter" and "shock of the water" and "the whole thing is unthinkable." This last phrase was delivered as she stared out the window at a favourite tree, a Japanese maple always first to turn in autumn, and the phrase acted on Cyrus's imagination with great force and meaning. The boy, even as kids go, was tremendously suggestible and in another moment he'd wandered out of the breakfast nook. "The whole thing is unthinkable," repeated Cyrus, touching at his pajama pocket and his potion of many ingredients. "But if you can't think it—how can you say it? How do you even *know* it?" My mother came over to warmly smile at Cyrus, explaining that she was glad he'd had some birthday cake, he was welcome to another piece, perhaps some ice cream, and he shouldn't worry because arrangements had been made to get him safely away. She sent a look to me to show she was happy with my own performance and then joined my father—who in quiet tones was speaking into the black rotary telephone in the dining room.

"There really *is* a lot going on in your house," said Cyrus, following my mother into the hallway. There seemed to be too many ideas fizzing at the brim of the moment, mostly beyond a kid's immediate ability to sort or commit to understanding, and Cyrus, standing now in front of the telephone desk in the hall, was choosing simply to register the details of the desk's sundry contents—a white wooden golf tee, the Halifax-Dartmouth Yellow Pages, a school stapler, a hardcover copy of *Tom Swift and The Visitor from Planet X*, as well as a box of envelopes provided by St. Matthew's Church for the Sunday offering. He studied the cover of the Tom Swift book and said, to no one in particular, "Every book is the same book. That's why you read them. Unless it's a mystery book. And then it's eponymous." Holding the eyedropper bottle as if it were a wand, Cyrus passed it over the desk's paraphernalia. "This could be a church," he said. "And these bits its candles. But you have to be careful because people will turn you into a bob." He looked at me with real purpose. "People will turn you into a *fact*."

The front doorbell rang. After a furtive look into the hallway, Cyrus turned to me. "I'm getting curious again. I can feel it. And when I get curious, I'm supposed to breathe and count to twelve. But I can't because I'm feeling—shroptered." The word seemed to make perfect sense to him now and I nodded to show I understood. The doorbell rang again and I stepped into the hallway to see what kind of oddity would be ringing and ringing at a front doorbell. There on the porch, framed through the doorway, was a giant of a man. He wore a heavy black raincoat and a brimmed, flat-topped hat. He was, I would learn later, a driver from Regal Taxi. But in form and demeanour he reminded me terrifyingly of Bill Sikes from the movie *Oliver!* seen by me a few weeks before. So frightened was I of Bill Sikes, and so scared to see this fellow staring into our house, that a cold shiver spread across my shoulders. I felt as if I were in the presence of something perfidious and to know such men were in the world was to consider possibilities far beyond sponge cake and birthday presents. While I was perturbed to see this man, Cyrus was absolutely horror-struck. Whether he recognized him as an actual enemy or simply guessed at worsening possibilities, I wasn't sure, but Cyrus's nervousness quickened toward an almost epileptic intensity. As he backed against the wall, scanning the rooms for alternate exits, I felt something weird was happening to the ground floor of the house. Cyrus's jumpiness was making me triply aware of my surroundings and items within his awareness began to resonate with newfound, probable energies, and so the stapler on the telephone desk seemed to vibrate, the wicker chair at the telephone desk, a few seconds before so upright and static, seemed to teeter and slide to one side, and my very thoughts seemed to variously spin, as if the merry-go-round of my mind had been pushed in new directions. "Just after my best greatest escape," whispered Cyrus, his eyes leaky with anxiety. *"That's* when he starts staring all over me?" He tucked his pajama top into his jodhpurs and readied himself for a getaway. But I could tell he was worried. He had that skeleton-inside-you sort of look again. "But if I'm not even here," he said. "And if it's unthinkable, how could anyone find me?" His questions were frightening for me to consider and as I thought over the scenes of the afternoon I felt I couldn't be sure if I hadn't dreamt all the days before this, the small world where I had *my* own life and times, my Boy Detective games and Batman figurines. The moment was oddly emotional for me. For some reason, I picked up and pressed into his hand the gift of the page-a-day pocket diary, explaining that my sister Bonnie had three other diaries, she preferred pink diaries anyway, and he should take this diary for his own inventions.

Cyrus turned to me, touched to be given such a souvenir. There was a glisten of perspiration on his forehead and he blotted this moisture with a swath of pajama sleeve. "But I don't have anything in return because—wait a minute." He gazed at me. "Say! I don't know your name."

I told him.

"Aubrey McKee," he repeated. "I don't have anything. Except perhaps—" From his pajama pocket he took out his potion of many ingredients. "Except this." He leaned closer. "There's enough for one sip. Would you like to make a trade?"

The progression of events that follow, I still have trouble sequencing. I remember opening the eyedropper bottle, squeezing the bulb pipette, and stealing a swallow of the potion—and tasting the ferrous bitterness of the key through the liquid—just as the late-afternoon light was streaming through the stained glass of our front door, creating a gleam of rainbow on the hardwood floor, and the Regal Taxi driver moving inside our house, my mother turning to greet him with perfect charm when little Alice Gruber, kicking at a sagging scarlet balloon, ran to my mother to ask, if Cyrus Mair had to escape again, could she at least keep his shoes? Whether it was my mother's murmur or Cyrus's shriek that came next, I'm not sure, but I recall Cyrus sprinting barefoot into the front hallway, clutching the blue diary, aiming for the still-opened front door but in his panic running smack into the newel post of the staircase. Then I was in the hallway, watching him bounce backwards through the air and rear-end my sister Carolyn, and Cyrus was sprawling on the floor, his right leg twitching, only to spring up straightaway and dash under the sweeping arms of the taxi driver and outside toward the puddles of the sidewalk. I was appalled. Shouldn't this kid have *told* me when he was going, how he was going, where he was going? It seemed to me then that everyone was deliberately betraying their promises to me, and with a sense of berserk purpose, I put my head down and made for the front door, planning to catch up with Cyrus Mair. The door was swinging shut, and I saw I would soon crash

into its stained-glass window, but I chose to persevere—
my upper lip hitting first, my nose squishing, the door-
glass shattering, my loose front tooth detonating out of
my mouth, and as my tongue touched at the gap in my
mouth where once my tooth had been, a trickle of warm
blood mixed with the residue of the potion's bitterness
and I saw through the smithereening glass Cyrus Mair
escaping down the sidewalk, blue pajama top blousing
out of his jodhpurs, and I closed my eyes, swallowing a
drop of the completed potion, but finally knowing what
I wanted—for I wanted to *be* Cyrus Mair.

Shashi Bhat's stories have appeared in *The Malahat Review*, *PRISM international*, *The New Quarterly*, *Grain*, The *Dalhousie Review*, and other journals. She was a 2018 National Magazine Finalist for fiction, has twice been longlisted for the Journey Prize, and was a finalist for the RBC Bronwen Wallace Award. Her debut novel, *The Family Took Shape* (Cormorant, 2013), was a finalist for the Thomas Raddall Atlantic Fiction Award. She is Editor in Chief of *EVENT Magazine* and teaches creative writing at Douglas College.

Tom Thor Buchanan is from Dryden, Ontario, and now lives in Toronto. His work has previously appeared in *Cosmonaut Avenue*, *Metatron*, and *Joyland*. He was also an artist-in-residence at the Robert Street Social Centre in Halifax, NS.

Lynn Coady is an award-winning novelist who has published six books of fiction, including the short story collection *Hellgoing*, which won the 2013 Scotiabank Giller Prize, and *The Antagonist*, which was shortlisted for the Giller in 2011. She lives in Toronto where she writes for television.

Originally from New York, **Deirdre Simon Dore** received a BA in Boston, an MFA in Vancouver and currently lives with her husband, dogs, and livestock on a small farm near a large lake in British Columbia. A former woodlot owner, she is a writer, a painter, and a volunteer with hospice, homeless shelters, and theatre. *The Malahat Review*, *Geist* and *The Fiddlehead* have published her fiction. Awards include: Western Magazines Award for fiction and The Journey Prize. She is currently compiling collections of short fiction and poetry for publication.

Alicia Elliott is a Tuscarora writer from Six Nations of the Grand River living in Brantford, Ontario. Her writing has been published by *The Malahat Review*, *Grain*, *The New Quarterly*, *CBC*, *Globe and Mail*, and *Hazlitt*, among others. She won a National Magazine Awards in 2017 and was chosen by Tanya Talaga to receive the RBC Taylor Emerging Writer Prize in 2018. Her short story "Unearth" has been selected by Roxane Gay to appear in *Best American Short Stories* 2018. *A Mind Spread Out on the Ground*, her debut book of essays, is forthcoming from Doubleday Canada in March 2019.

Bill Gaston's stories have appeared in *Granta*, *Tin House*, and numerous times in *Best Canadian Stories*. His fiction collections have been nominated for the Giller Prize and twice for the Governor General's Award. "Kiint" appears in his seventh and most recent collection, *A Mariner's Guide to Self Sabotage*. He lives on Gabriola Island, B.C.

Liz Harmer was born and raised in Hamilton, Ontario, and currently lives in Southern California. Her essays and stories have appeared in *The New Quarterly*, *The Malahat Review*, *Hazlitt*, *Literary Hub*, *Grain*, *PRISM*, *This Magazine*, and elsewhere. Her essay "Blip" won the Constance Rooke Creative Nonfiction Award in 2013 and a National Magazine Award for Personal Journalism in 2014; her unpublished story collection was a finalist for the Flannery O'Connor Short Fiction Award in 2014. Her first novel, *The Amateurs*,was published with Knopf Canada in 2018.

Brad Hartle's fiction has appeared in *The Malahat Review*, *The Fiddlehead*, *The Dalhousie Review*, and *The Windsor Review*. Originally from Winnipeg, he lives in Edmonton where he works as a speechwriter for the Premier of Alberta.

David Huebert's fiction has won the CBC Short Story Prize, the Sheldon Currie Fiction Prize, and *The Dalhousie Review*'s short story contest. His work has been published in magazines such as *The New Quarterly*, *The Fiddlehead*, *enRoute*, and *Canadian Notes & Queries*. David's short fiction debut, *Peninsula Sinking*, won the Jim Connors Dartmouth Book Award, was shortlisted for the Alistair MacLeod Prize for Short Fiction, and was a runner-up for the Danuta Gleed Literary Award.

Reg Johanson is a writer, teacher, and editor living in Vancouver on Coast Salish territory. He is the editor of a collection of Annharte's critical prose, *AKA Inendagosekwe* (CUE 2013), and the author of *Courage, My Love* (LINEbooks 2006), *N 49 19. 47–W 123 8. 11* (Pacific Institute of Language and Literacy Studies, 2008, with Roger Farr and Aaron Vidaver), *Escraches* (Lefthand Press, 2010), *Band of Gypsies* (Heavy Industries, 2011), and *Mortify* (Standard Ink and Copy Press, 2012). His writing has appeared in *The Capilano Review*, *Fifth Estate*, *West Coast Line*, the *Open Text* anthology series (CUE Books), and elsewhere.

Amy Jones is the author of the short fiction collection *What Boys Like* (Bibiloasis, 2009), which won the Metcalf-Rooke Award and was shortlisted for the ReLit Award, and the novel *We're All in This Together* (M&S 2016), which won the Northern Lit Award and was a finalist for the 2017 Leacock Award. She is a past winner of the CBC Short Story Prize and finalist for the Bronwen Wallace Award, and her short fiction has been anthologized in *Best Canadian Stories* and *The Journey Prize Stories*.

Michael LaPointe is a writer in Toronto. He has written for *The Atlantic*, *The New Yorker*, and *The Paris Review*.

Stephen Marche is a Toronto writer. His most recent book is *The Unmade Bed: The Truth About Men and Women in the Twenty-First Century*.

Lisa Moore has written three novels, *Alligator*, *February*, and *Caught*, as well as a stage play, based on her novel *February*. Her young adult novel is called *Flannery*. She is also the author of three collections of short stories, *Degrees of Nakedness*, *Open*, and *Something for Everyone*. Lisa teaches creative writing at Memorial University.

Kathy Page's fabulist short fiction collection, *Paradise & Elsewhere* (2014), and her subsequent collection, *The Two of Us* (2016), were both nominated for the Scotiabank Giller Prize. She is also the author of eight novels, including *The Story of My Face*, nominated for the Women's Prize; *The Find*, a ReLit finalist, and *Alphabet*, a Governor General's Award finalist in 2005, reissued in 2014 to become a Shelf Awareness Pick, an Indie Next Great Read, and a Kirkus Best Book. "Inches" is from *Dear Evelyn*, 2018, a novel in stories. Visit www.kathypage.info.

Alex Pugsley is a writer and filmmaker originally from Nova Scotia. He won the 2012 Writers' Trust McClelland & Stewart Journey Prize. His story, "Shimmer," was included in *Best Canadian Stories* in 2017. "A Day with Cyrus Mair" is taken from the third chapter of the novel, *Aubrey McKee*.

Russell Smith was born in Johannesburg, South Africa, and grew up in Halifax, Canada. His most recent book is the short story collection *Confidence*. He writes a weekly column on the arts in the *Globe and Mail* and teaches fiction in the MFA in Creative Writing program at the University of Guelph. He lives in Toronto.

"Food for Nought" by Sashi Bhat first appeared in *The Malahat Review*

"A Dozen Stomachs" by Tom Thor Buchanan first appeared in *Joyland*

"Someone Is Recording" by Lynn Coady first appeared in *Electric Literature*

"Your Own Lucky Stars" by Deirdre Simon Dore first appeared in
The Fiddlehead

"Tracks" by Alicia Elliott first appeared in *The New Quarterly*

"Kiint" by Bill Gaston first appeared in *The New Quarterly*

"Never Prosper" by Liz Harmer first appeared in *The New Quarterly*

"For What You Are About To Do" by Brad Hartle first appeared in
The Malahat Review

"a titan bearing many a legitimate grievance" by Reg Johanson first
appeared in *The Capilano Review*

"The Candidate" by Michael Lapointe first appeared in *The Walrus*

"Twinkle Twinkle" by Stephen Marche first appeared in *Wired*

"Visions" by Lisa Moore first appeared in *Taddle Creek*

The following magazines were consulted: *The Antigonish Review,
Canadian Notes & Queries, Capellano Review, Electric Literature, Event,
Exile, The Fiddlehead, Geist, Grain, Joyland, The Malahat Review, Matrix,
The New Quarterly, Numéro Cinq, Prarie Fire, PRISM international, The
Puritan, SubTerrain, Taddle Creek, The Walrus,* and *Wired.*